ACKNO~

I had the idea of writing a book for some time but never thought I would ever get round to doing it, until COVID hit our shores. I worked all through 'lockdown' but found myself getting very bored whilst isolating. Its ok having an idea, putting it on paper is a different story, literally. I soon realised that the main character in the book would need parents, relatives, friends, school friends, teammates and players in his football team. I really didn't realise the amount of work I was about to undertake.

My first acknowledgement is to all the characters who are in this book, most of them are named after people I have worked with, played football with or are just friends and family. Their names have been changed slightly, but to you all my thanks for having your names in my head at the time of writing.

They say that most writers get 'writers block'. I was no exception. To my beloved wife Tre, thanks for giving me the space when I needed it and the encouragement when I felt like giving up. You are my rock. Tre was also the very first person to read my first draft. She gave me some great feedback and genuinely loved it.

My family are very important to me and having their full support has been very important to me throughout my life. My parents always let me make my own decisions, but I knew that they were always there if I ever needed them. I owe them an awful lot and could not have asked for better parents. My late father loved to read and could write short stories and poems with consummate ease. He was my hero and I hope this book is a credit to him.

My sister is a special woman, and she has always put me on a pedestal. I really hope she knows how much I love her and how wonderful she is.

My daughters are my angels, I love them with all my heart. They are both upset that their names weren't used in the book. To rectify that, Sophie and Kath, I love you both.

Finally, to all those lovely people whom I gave a draft manuscript to, thank you. I received lots of feedback, most of it I'm pleased to say was extremely positive. You all gave me that drive I needed to follow this through to the end and if it wasn't for you, I probably wouldn't be writing this now. You all know who you are X.

SCHOOL

OF

FOOTBALL

Contents

CHAPTER 1

'Welling get changed, you're going on.'

Greg Welling had been standing on the touchline of Audley Grove Secondary Modern football pitch for the past eighty minutes getting wetter, colder and very frustrated. He was stood there watching his team mates get a severe hiding and football lesson by their biggest rivals and closest neighbouring school, Westfield.

'Ref,' Mr Rogers shouted, 'ref substitution.'

Welling's' team mates looked over to where he was standing and in a silent gesture of disdain gave an almighty sigh. They knew as well as he did that he was only getting on the pitch because the game was up, and it didn't matter if he came on or not. They were going to lose anyway.

'Owens you're off son' barked Mr Rogers.

'You're having a fucking laugh, aren't you?' he shouted back as reality set in that he was getting replaced by Greg friggin' Welling, the small skinny kid whose dad was a Police Inspector and more importantly on the Board of Governors.

'That's enough of your bad language Sonny Jim,' he reprimanded Owens, 'any more of that and you'll find yourself in detention.'

'But he's crap sir, we all know it, even he bleeding knows it' came the reply and said loud enough for Greg to hear.

It was true and Greg Welling knew it but ever since he could remember all he had ever wanted to do was play football. He lived, breathed and ate football, it was his life.

Back in the changing rooms everyone sat through the normal after match bollocks speech given by Mr Rogers. He had no real interest in kid's football and was only managing the Year 1 and 2 teams out of peer pressure rather than desire. The same was said of Mr Savage who managed the Years 3 to 5. In all, the school's football teams were in poor hands.

'Welling, why are you here?' muttered Pokey.

John Poke was the best player in the team and had plenty of football scouts watching him play regularly. He was also regarded as one of the tough kids of the year and detested kids like Greg. Pokey lived in a poorer area of the town and believed that Greg was handed everything on a plate.

'Why don't you just piss off and join the chess club or something you soft shit. We don't want you in our team, you are crap.'

'Leave him alone Pokey' piped up Mark Jenkins, the Goalkeeper.

He was an excellent keeper and also had plenty of football scouts watching him. His only problem was an unstable home life that really affected his attendance levels at school. He was also a big lad for his age, nearly six-foot-tall and thick set with it. He was not considered a tough nut of the year, but no-one messed with him either, they all probably knew what the outcome would be.

'We need as many players as we can get Pokey and Greg comes to every training session and every match, that's more than most of the tossers in this team.'

'Who you calling a tosser?' mumbled Lee Pier the right winger.

'Well mate if the cap fits' smirked Jenkins.

'Fuck you' was the reply.

Team harmony was not one of Audley Groves strong points.

Walking home that afternoon after the 4-0 loss all Greg could think of was one thing, listening to his most beloved football team on the radio, West Ham. Coming from Torquay, one of the largest towns in Devon, Greg was the only West Ham fan in the school. Many of the other kids supported Liverpool as they were winning most of the Domestic trophies and were conquering Europe. They were all glory hunters. There were a few Arsenal fans as they were also fairly successful. Most of the other kids supported either Leeds or Man Utd as they were just following the teams that their Dads supported. Greg couldn't see a problem with that; there was nothing wrong with being brainwashed.

Greg also admired the football manager Terry Venables. He enjoyed watching 'Mr Venables teams play football. Crystal Palace (Terry Venables) former club played entertaining, free flowing football not normally witnessed on the shores of UK. They didn't play the humdrum 4-4-2 formation that existed within most clubs in the football league but a refreshing new style. It hadn't completely worked though, and Crystal Palace departed company with his services. He then took charge of QPR who embraced his continental ideas.

It was only a twenty-minute walk from the school to his home. He lived in what was classed as a 'very nice' area of the town, although at his age he knew very little of that. Home was a modern four-bedroom detached house, where he lived with his parents and sister Alison. Alison was nearly three years older than him and as far as sisters went, she was OK. They didn't see eye to eye on certain things but that's because he was very immature, so she said. He did love her though and always looked out for her when he could.

Most sons love spending time with their dads, but Greg was different. He loved his dad, but he adored his mum, she was the reason he loved football. Carol Dicks was raised in East London with her four brothers who were mad on football and West Ham in particular. Whilst growing up his four uncles would have been found hanging out around the streets near their beloved Boleyn Ground every other

Saturday looking for some unsuspecting fans to have a fight with. It was the 70's after all.

Carol had tried her hardest to be the sweet little girl her mum had wanted her to be, but her brother's persuasive powers eventually broke her down. She was initiated into 'their gang' mainly because she had some hot friends who her brothers wanted to get better acquainted. So, who better to introduce them? Carol was also someone who could look after herself and although she was the youngest sibling none of her brothers dared mess with her. They were all very protective of her so God help anyone that messed her about. When Carol brought home Dave for the first-time alarm bells rang around the Dicks family. Harry, Paul, Tom and Mike Dicks were all in agreement that Carol dating a 'copper' was not a good thing. David Welling was from a very nice area in South London and was also in agreement that dating a member of the well-known Dicks family was not a smart move, but he was madly in love with Carol. It brought great joy to the brothers when they heard that David was getting a promotion and moving to Exeter until the news broke that he had indeed proposed to his beloved Carol and she was to follow him to Devon.

David Welling had no desire for football but was indeed a rugby fanatic, a game played by thugs and watched by gentlemen. A true mans' sport. David would have loved nothing more than to see Greg scrummaging in the middle of the pack like his idol Bill Beaumont but alas this was not going to happen. He had taken Greg to a few matches, but

Greg struggled to understand the rules or be enthralled by the games. Greg had his mum's genes and was never going to be a rugby player. Carol on the other hand still loved football. She had followed her love of West Ham with her brothers and throughout her teens had a massive crush on Bobby Moore, the Worlds' Greatest defender, in her eyes anyway. She had always wanted a son and Greg had grown up loving football just like her. She loved nothing more than telling Greg of her youthful tales and how West Ham had won the World Cup in 1966, they did after-all have the Captain, and the two goal-scorers. Did Greg love that?

CHAPTER 2

Greg plugged his headphones into his radio and with a bit of fine tuning found the radio station he was looking for. West Ham were playing away to Roma in the second leg of the UEFA Cup quarter finals, after a 1-1 draw at Upton Park. It was a big night for Greg as this was the first year West Ham had played in Europe that he could remember. He had a pen and paper in front of him to write down his notes; he loved the strategy of the game. He also had a copy of the Daily Telegraph open at the football pages and most importantly his Subbuteo Table laid out. He was also aware of all the other newspaper talk, as he had managed to read most of the back pages after his paper round. Greg had lied to his local Newsagents the year before about his age as he wasn't quite 13, the prescribed minimum age for paper rounds. As they knew his father, he had been given the next available round, most lads didn't last long on the rounds due to the poor pay and the early starts. Greg's mum had given permission for him to do the round and so Greg was now in full time employment. One hour a day, 7 days a week 363 days a year earning £4.00 per week. There were no papers on Easter Sunday and Christmas Day, well-earned days off. His boss Mr Rankin, or Pete as he was allowed to call him allowed him days off if they were booked well in advance. Greg's parents presumed he had taken on the paper round to get some extra money, but Greg had other ideas. In the mornings, he would be the first paperboy at the shop and would gather his papers and arrange his round in record time. He had a new bike that he had been given at Christmas which had ten gears, (five more than his previous bike) and on a good day could be back to the shop within 45 minutes. This was when his day really started. Pete Rankin had a soft spot for Greg as he was never late for his round and was polite to his customers, unlike many of the other lads. He knew Greg loved his football and was more than happy to allow Greg to borrow a copy of all the newspapers on his return from his round. Greg would then sit in the little room at the back of the shop and read through all the back pages for the next half an hour or so. By the time he returned the papers and left he was overloaded with football knowledge.

It was 19.30 hours and the teams and positions were announced. Greg wrote them down in his notebook. He then arranged the football figures on his Subbuteo table to familiarise himself with the teams playing that night. This gave him the best insight as to how the teams would play and the strengths and weaknesses of both teams. He listened intently to the radio commentary and was enthralled by how a commentator could get so much information over to the listener. If Greg couldn't be a Football Manager when he was older then a job in football commentary would be the next best thing, think of how many games he would get to watch.

GOAL. 1-0 to Roma. To be fair it had been coming. Listening to the commentary it was going as Greg had feared, Roma were one of the top teams in Italy and West Ham were struggling in the English First Division. Greg perused his notes and looked at his positioning of the players on the Subbuteo pitch. He knew that Roma were causing West Ham problems down the right side of the pitch, and they had to man mark Roma's best player Paolo Zola. Why won't they do something about it before it's too late Greg thought? Another goal to Roma and it's all over.

Half time arrived and Greg's dad entered his bedroom as Greg was getting into his pyjamas. 'How's the game going?' he asked although none too bothered.

'Were losing dad and they aren't playing very well.'

'Never mind son' it's only a game, eh.'

It wasn't only a game to Greg; this was his life and he wanted to shout out to his dad, but he couldn't. Greg smiled at his dad and just replied 'yeh.'

David Welling looked around Greg's room, it was tidy for a teenage lad and he was proud of the way his son had grown up.

'Your mum will be up in five minutes, OK. Good night son, love you.'

'Love you too dad.'

Carol appeared a few minutes after. 'I hear we're losing then!'

'Yeah, second half is about to kick off' replied Greg.

'Where is all your football stuff?' she asked.

'Under the bed mum'.

Carol was torn. She and David were united in their discipline of the children and didn't let either child play themselves off against the other, but she also knew this was a big night for Greg.

'Right young man, its deal time. I will let you sit up and listen to the second half, but you must leave your light off and all your stuff stays under the bed. If dad finds out he will go mad, deal?'

'Deal mum, I love you.'

'I love you too'.

Carol gave Greg a kiss goodnight and turned to walk towards the door. She turned back towards Greg, crossed her arms to make a cross and said 'C'mon you Irons'.

Greg gave a great big smile and shouted' 'Appy Ammers'. The lights were turned out.

Greg awoke a little later than normal, tired after his later than normal night. He got dressed and cycled to the Newsagents getting there just after Pete had opened. He half smiled at Pete but never said a word. Arranging his paper round, he quickly filled his bag and left the shop. Pete knew that last night's 2-0 defeat had hit Greg hard. Greg returned nearly an hour later leaving him only 15 minutes to read his papers.

'Leaving it a bit late today aren't we Greg'.

'Don't think I'll bother today Pete' came a sorrowful reply.

'What do you think Harry Parker will do this morning then, not bother' was Pete's reply.

Harry Parker was West Hams Manager and someone Greg admired greatly.

'I'll tell you what he will do today Greg. He will re-run that game in his head and speak to his whole backroom team. They will analyse their tactics from before and during the game and try their hardest to work out what they could have done better. They certainly will be bothering today'.

Greg was the most determined young man he had ever met and knew of his desires to be a Football Manager one day.

'You never stop learning Greg. You must lose to learn how to win. Now you only have 10 minutes to analyse them back pages and to work out what you would have done differently.'

Greg grabbed a copy of the Sun, Daily Star, Daily Mirror and Daily Express leaving behind the Daily Mail and The Times as he wouldn't have time for them. He would read his dads Telegraph this afternoon as it was always full of information!

'Thanks Pete, I can't stand losing.'

'You should be used to that supporting West Ham' laughed Pete, but Greg didn't laugh, his head was in a mound of Newspapers.

CHAPTER 3

Saturday morning came around very slowly for Greg. He had endured two days of football banter, or abuse depending on how you looked at it with regards to West Hams loss on Wednesday evening. It was made even worse as Liverpool had won another European tie, again. He couldn't quite understand other fans; Greg always supported any English team in Europe. Why would you want a foreign team to beat an English team?

Saturdays were great. Greg would complete his paper round in as quickly as possible so he could spend extra time reading all the back pages of the papers. It was pay day as well and he always enjoyed collecting his £4.00 from Pete. A small slice of Greg's pay went on a few packets of Panini football stickers. Panini are a publishing company that produced sticker books and the stickers to go inside them. The books were free but the cards came in packets of five. The football books had all the teams in Division 1 in them. The club emblem, Manager and playing squad all had spaces where the stickers would be placed. Unfortunately no one knew what cards were in each pack and eventually you would end up with duplicate cards which would be used to swap with other collectors. At 10p a packet Greg could afford to buy a good few packets but his swaps collection was getting bigger and his sticker book wasn't particularly getting any fuller.

Pete always dropped a chocolate bar into Greg's pocket as he was leaving the shop. It was his way of showing his appreciation of Greg for being so reliable and honest, especially for a schoolboy.

'Thanks for this week Greg, see you tomorrow.'

Pete knew that a paper round was a very non-glamorous job. He had seen many boys and girls come and go and endured many parents calling him in the early hours reporting their child sick for the day. Greg Welling was different, he never took time off and he was never late. That kid had great work ethics; he would go places.

Greg's best mate was Mike and he lived on the other side of town. He was a wacky kid who was totally individualistic.

They were complete opposites but got on like a house on fire. Mike lived in a small house with his parents and older brother. Mike loved his family but often found himself an outsider in his own house so he would spend as much time as possible around Greg's. He really liked Dave and Carol, they treated him like another son. He also really liked Alison and would have liked nothing more than her to like him. Unfortunately, she viewed Mike like she viewed Greg. An annoying little irk.

Mike would usually arrive at the Welling's' house for about 9 am. He knew that Carol always made bacon and egg rolls for the family at around that time. Mike made sure that he only had a small breakfast before leaving his house. After their little feast, Greg and Mike would go out on their bikes. They didn't really care where they went, it was the freedom they so yearned for. Mike also had a paper round in a different shop so they always went out with a little cash in their pockets. They loved the fact that the money they had was hard earned.

For three hours or so they lived and played like two normal young teenagers. They giggled and messed about and pretended to be people that they could never be. Greg liked to be home for about 1pm. Carol always had some form of lunch ready for him. As soon as lunch was over Greg would run up to his room and get changed, he was off to the Match. He wished it was West Ham that he was off to watch but he would have to make do with Torquay United. They were in the bottom tier of the football league and had an average attendance of 2500 fans. Every other Saturday Greg would walk up to the ground, roughly a 30-minute walk and pay through the turn-styles. Carol always paid for his entrance, it was her treat to him, and after all she was always giving Alison money to go out.

Plainmoor was a good old-fashioned football ground. Three sides of the ground were standing only with seating on the popular side. The ground capacity had greatly reduced over the years and now had a capacity of just over 7500. Greg entered the ground at the Mini Stand end and quickly found his Saturday afternoon buddies, Steve, Graham and Danny. They all attended Westfield School which was the rival school to Audley Grove. Like him, they loved football and were true football geeks. The four of them stood and talked until both teams ran onto the pitch. Steve always brought his small wireless radio with him. It was poorly tuned in to the BBC radio sport channel and gave the boys immediate news on the latest scores from all the other divisions.

Steve and Danny were both Liverpool fans and Graham an Aston Villa fan. Grahams family had moved to Torquay from the Midlands with his parents 5 years ago to open a small hotel. The first half was a boring affair and ended 0-0. The four boys analysed the first half and agreed what course of action they believed Bruce Richo the Torquay Manager should take for the second half. The teams re-appeared and lined up exactly as they did for the first half. The boys were not surprised as they were aware of Richo's reluctance to change things. The second half carried on in the same vain as the first. Substitutions were eventually made with the minimal of strategies. It was another poor half but ended with Torquay United beating Rochdale by a goal to nil. After the final whistle the four boys hung around the ground for ten minutes or so after the game catching up on all the football results. They all left happy with all their respective teams winning. Greg even more so as West Ham had thrashed Wolves 5-0. They said their goodbyes and went their separate ways, agreeing to meet up in two weeks' time.

Greg's Saturday nights were always quite boring, he didn't really like Saturday night TV so he would sit in his room reading his Shoot magazine or any other football book that he hadn't had the joy of reading yet. His birthday and Christmas presents normally consisted of football literature that would last Greg most of the year. Greg had a great agreement with his mum, which his dad had reluctantly agreed to, Greg had to be in bed by 9 pm every night of the week except Saturday when he was allowed to sit up and watch Match of the Day. It usually started between 9:45 and 10 pm and normally lasted for an hour. This arrangement was great news for Greg as it was his only chance to watch Division 1 football on televison. He also didn't need to get up as early on a Saturday or Sunday as the papers didn't arrive at the shop until an hour later than in the week. Pete was relaxed about when the weekend papers should be delivered and if all the rounds were completed by 9am he was happy. Greg hoped that as West Ham had won by such a big score, they would be one of the first matches on. The highest scoring games or big derbies were always on first with the 0-0 draws the last. Greg loved MOTD but as hard as he tried, he always struggled to stay awake for the last few matches. Saturdays were always such a busy day. Luck would have it that West Ham were the second match on, and Greg went to bed a happy lad, looking forward to Sunday and another day of football.

Sundays were another day when Greg could enjoy watching football to his heart's content. He completed his paper round in the normal time and read most of the Sunday papers in Pete's back room. The Sunday papers were always full of football reports and news so Greg had to be very picky in the papers and reports he read otherwise he would have been in the shop all day. Greg had just said his goodbyes to Mandy, (she ran the shop every Sunday for Pete to allow him a day off) when he noticed a box of Panini Football stickers had fallen onto the floor. He picked them up and turned to tell Mandy, but she had disappeared into the back area, the shop was empty. Greg did something he had never done in his young life before, he stole. He didn't know why, he just did. Twenty packets of stickers were stuffed into his jacket pocket and the rest he placed back onto the counter. Greg left the shop and immediately felt a sense of wrongdoing. The adrenalin rush he had originally felt was very quickly replaced by an immense guilt. He was halfway home when the guilt got the better of him and he decided to return to the shop. How would he be able to explain to Mandy about why he had 20 packets of stickers on him, could he put them back before she noticed? He got to within 100 meters of the shop and 'bottled' it. He couldn't go back in, anyway no-one would know, it was a one off and he would never do it again. He got home had some breakfast and unwrapped his stickers. He managed to add a few to his sticker book but the rest just became 'swaps', the guilt he felt definitely didn't do his haul justice. He disposed of the wrappers into his little West Ham rubbish bin and got changed ready for his next adventure.

The Twent Fields were a 15-minute cycle ride from Greg's house and had six football pitches situated in the open fields. Every Sunday they were occupied by an array of different aged teams of all standards. This Sunday consisted of an over 40's League Match, two local Sunday League matches and four schoolboy Sunday League games with ages from 8 – 15. Greg loved cycling between the pitches watching each game for ten minutes before picking the game he wanted to watch for the second half. Nearly all the matches kicked off at eleven, so he was spoilt for choice. Greg picked one of the local league games, Heale Athletic vs Gallumpton Rovers as it was already 2-2 and had attracted a larger crowd than the other matches. The standard of football was also so much better. Greg positioned himself near to the Heale Athletic Manager as he liked to listen to what the Managers were saying. His dad would have been appalled by the bad language dished out on the sidelines but to be fair Greg heard a lot worse at school. Within 10 minutes Gallumpton had scored and were pressing for a fourth goal. The Heale Manager was going mad at his team. They were getting ripped apart by the opposing number 10, he was running the game. Greg was stood next to an old gentleman called Ray whom he regularly saw on Sunday mornings. They had become good friends because of their love of football.

'I would man-mark their number 10 with Heale's number 7, he's their fittest player and a good tackler. Take him out of the game and then they have nothing' Greg said.

'What the fuck do you know?' came a scathing remark from the Heale Manager.

Greg didn't realise that his comment to Ray had been over heard by the now extremely cross Heale Manager.

'Leave him alone,' shouted Ray, 'he's right though, he may be a kid, but he knows his stuff'.

'I've been managing teams longer than he's been alive' was the comment back.

Greg was very embarrassed. For one he hadn't realised his comment would have been heard and taken to heart. Secondly, he hadn't realised how high a regard Ray had for him. Goal, Gallumpton had scored again, with their number 10 at the heart of the move. Ray looked at the Heale Manager who shot him a discernible look.

'Woody, Wilko, get here now.'

The Heale Manager had called over his Captain and his number 7.

'Wilko, I want you to man-mark their number 10. From now on he doesn't touch the ball, wherever he goes, you go. If he leaves the pitch for a piss, you go with him. Have you got that?'

'Yes boss, loud and clear.'

'Woody, let's get hold of the ball and try and get something out of this match eh?' was the rallying cry from his Manager.

'Right gaffer, but what's with the man-marking? We've never done that'.

'Well we fucking do now so get out there and get something out of this game.'

The game changed dramatically over the next 30 minutes. Wilko did his job to the letter and stopped the No10 playing and getting booked in the process. Gallumpton lost control of the game and Heale scored two late goals to earn a very credible 4-4 draw. Ray and Greg said their farewells and agreed to meet the following week. Greg got on his bike to leave.

'Hey sunshine' a loud shout came from the Heale Manager. 'What's your name?'

'Greg'.

'Well Greg, we're playing here next Sunday if you want to come over to give me a few more tips.'

'Ok,' shouted Greg, 'you might want to think about playing a 4-3-3 formation rather than a 4-4-2' shouted Greg as he got further away. The Heale manager stood aghast, a 4-3-3, he didn't know whether to laugh or cry. That may well work. Who was this kid?

CHAPTER 4

The start of the week went by as normal. It was just a normal mundane week until Greg returned to his house on Wednesday afternoon. He was usually met by his wonderfully happy mother, but this day was different. As Greg entered the house he was beckoned to his room by his mum. She was stood in the middle of his room holding 20 empty packets of football stickers.

'I thought I could trust you to spend your money wisely young man, and you spend nearly half your paper round money on these,' waving torn empty packets close to his face. 'Wait till I speak to Pete; he should know better than to sell you all these stickers.'

'I didn't buy them from Pete, I found them', lied Greg.

'Where did you find 20 packets of stickers Greg?'

'They were near the shop, so I picked them up and brought them home.'

'Why didn't you return them to the shop?' asked his mum.

'I don't know, I just brought them home, I didn't think it would hurt.'

Carol gave Greg a look of dis-belief and left his bedroom. Greg breathed a huge sigh of relief, that was lucky.

Thursday afternoons after school were football practice. Most of the team usually turned up apart from those whose mouths or poor actions got them into detention. Mr Rogers was in the changing rooms when the boys started turning up.

'Right lads, get changed as quickly as you can; I'm on a tight schedule.'

Football practice consisted of a two-mile run around the school cross-country circuit for warm up. The strikers and forward players practised dribbling with the ball and shooting whilst the defenders practised defending corners and heading. The midfield players basically got to do what they wanted as they all thought they were prima-donnas and too good to practise anything. Greg really couldn't believe how poor the training was. Why did they never train together as a team!

Saturday arrived in good time and Greg was looking forward to spending the day with Mike as Torquay United were playing away that weekend. Mike was having difficulties with his bike. He had also b purchased a 10-gear mechanism to replace his old 5 gear but now needed a new chain as his old one had stretched to its limit. The weather was awful, so Carol volunteered to drive Greg round to Mike's straight after she had popped into Pete's to pick up a birthday card. They managed to get a parking space directly outside of

Pete's shop and Greg and Carol both entered. Carol saw Pete behind the counter and gave him a welcoming smile. He was attractive for his forty years and she really couldn't understand why he was a bachelor. Pete caught sight of Greg and gave him a huge smile.

'Alright champ' greeted Pete, as if he hadn't seen Greg for weeks when in fact, he had only seen him in the shop a few hours earlier.

Greg smiled back in his cheeky way and felt a sense of pride that Pete held him in such high esteem. Carol found the birthday card that she was after and gave Pete a one-pound note. After handing back her change Carol and Pete exchanged small talk for a few minutes when, the subject got onto the shops latest stock-take. Pete ushered Greg over next to Carol and started to explain that he thought one of the paperboys was stealing from him. It was at this time when Pete asked Greg a question that was to rip his heart in two. Could he keep an eye on all the paper boys as he believed one of them was stealing football stickers from the shop! Carol shot Greg a look that he had never seen before and he reluctantly agreed to keep an eye on all the boys for Pete. The drive to Mikes' house was in total silence until they arrived.

'I will pick you up at 5 young man, make sure you're ready as I am going out tonight.'

'Yes mum, love you.' There was no reply.

Greg and Mike enjoyed a quiet afternoon, they quickly managed to fix the gear cogs on Mike's bike and fit a new chain. After, they sat in Mikes' bedroom listening to the new Madness Album that he had bought with his pocket money. They had both recently started listening to music and the new Nutty Boys sound that was SKA music appealed to them both. This was the start of their musical adventure and they were both very excited about their journey into pop music. Greg had decided that he would 'tape' a copy just as soon as Mike would lend him the LP record.

Carol arrived five minutes early and Greg was ready, he didn't know the extent of his mums' anger and he certainly didn't want to make it any worse. He got into the car but said nothing; he didn't know what to say. It didn't take long for Carol to speak.

'I don't think I have ever had such a bad day as I have today Greg' she said.

'First I find out my son is a thief and then I find out he is a liar. I never expected to ever have to say those words about my son'.

'But I'm not a thief or a liar mum' pleaded Greg.

'Oh, and how do you explain everything?'

Greg was now close to tears and knew that his mum was in the same fragile state. Greg explained what had happened on Sunday morning and that he had regretted what he had done as soon as it had happened. He also explained that he had returned to the shop to replace the stickers only to "bottle it" at the last second as he didn't know how to explain himself to Mandy or how to return the stickers. He then went on to explain how he panicked when his mum had asked him about the empty packets as he couldn't have told her the truth. Carol calmly drove the final mile to their home and parked the car outside the house as she was indeed going out later that night.

She then turned to Greg and said, 'You have got to make this right Greg. You must tell Pete the truth and face whatever he decides. You know that this is going to break his heart, don't you? He looks to you as the son he has never had.'

'I know,' cried Greg, 'I will tell him tomorrow, will you come with me?'

'Certainly not,' replied Carol, 'this is all down to you.'

'What about Dad, are you going to tell him?' Greg asked.

In a funny way he was more worried about telling Pete than he was of telling his dad. He knew that he would be grounded and that his dad would lecture him on morals and what was right and wrong but Pete! Greg started to cry again.

Greg ate his tea with Carol and Alison in almost silence, his Dad was working late. Alison picked up on the atmosphere and tried her hardest to find out what was going on, Greg and Carol were always so close, but not today. Greg was excused and spent the next few hours in his room reading his books. Alison was 'baby- sitting' Greg until their dad arrived home from work and he really didn't want her knowing what was going on. At around 9pm David Welling returned home after an exhausting 14-hour shift. He loved his job and the authority that came with it, but he hated the long days and nights and sometimes wished he had found himself a more mundane career. He ate his tea in almost silence with only the background noise of the television in the lounge as company. Alison was watching an episode of Cagney and Lacey (an American police series where the two main characters were female) which in Alison's' eyes was a very refreshing change to all the male dominated programmes. David knocked on Greg's bedroom door and entered without waiting for a response.

'Hi dad, you're home late.'

'Yeah, busy catching lots of crooks,' smiled David.' 'have you had a good day son?'

'I've had better Dad.'

'Do you want to talk about it or is it a teenager thing?'

'Something like that dad'.

'Anyway, if you want to get washed and put your pyjamas on you can sit up and watch Match of the Day with me.'

'I'm not going to watch it tonight dad, West Hams game was cancelled and I'm feeling tired, so I think I'll just go to bed in a minute.'

'OK then, have a good night sleep. Love you pal' was David's last response as he walked down the stairs. He knew Greg really must have had a bad day if he didn't want to watch MOTD.

CHAPTER 5

Greg woke up earlier than normal and arrived at the shop a few minutes before Mandy. He loaded his papers into his bag and completed his round in good time, his mind all over the place and not wanting to think about his future conversation with Pete. He returned to the shop and found Mandy out the back making herself a cup of tea.

'Hi Greg, you back to read the papers?' she asked in her always pleasant manner. 'Do you know if Pete is up yet, I really need to speak to him' hoping that Pete was still in bed or better still, out.

'He just came down to grab a paper, I'll go get him, keep an eye on the shop for one minute for me.'

Mandy disappeared up the stairs to Pete's flat, above the shop. Mandy re-appeared about 30 seconds later and made a joke about missing out on the hundreds of customers she must have missed while she was away. Greg smiled but only in a polite way. Pete came down the stairs looking the worse for wear having been out on his regular Saturday snooker night.

'What can I do for you Greg on this lovely Sunday morning?'

'Can we speak somewhere in private please?' Greg almost begged.

'We could go up to the flat, but we can't go up there on our own. Your mum and dad wouldn't be happy if they found out'.

Pete almost sounded embarrassed explaining his reasons why.

'It's ok, mum knows I'm here'.

'Well in that case, after you' Pete pointed up the stairs.

Within ten minutes, Greg had run down the stairs and left the shop without stopping to say goodbye to Mandy. He got on his bike and cycled as fast as he could with floods of tears streaming down his face. He wished he had never set eyes on a bloody Panini sticker. His whole life was in ruins and he was only 13 years old. Everyone was going to find out that he was a thief, the kids at school would bully him even more and his dad would have to live with smarmy remarks from his work colleagues. Carol would have to endure endless conversations from her mobile hair dressing clients. Even the thought of his sister having a hard time at school upset him. He arrived home and ran directly to his bedroom where he fell onto his bed in despair. He swore to himself that he would never steal again and that he would try his hardest to rectify his mistakes. He fell asleep on his bed, lying in his own self-pity.

A slight knock on his door woke him. The sight of his mother was normally a pleasure to behold but this time he felt apprehensive.

'Have you spoken to Pete this morning?' her voice was calm and re-assuring.

'Yes mum, he was really upset. He told me that he couldn't trust me anymore and that I wasn't allowed to enter the shop again unless with you or dad. Pete was horrible to me'.

Carol walked over to Greg, sat down and gave him a big hug. He burst into tears and apologised to his mum for everything. 'It's going to be ok Greg. Just promise me you will never do anything like this again'.

'I promise mum'.

CHAPTER 6

Greg knew the only way he could cheer himself up was to cycle over to the Twent Fields and watch a few games of football. That would take his mind off things. He got his bike out of the garage and cycled over to the fields. There were lots of games going on simultaneously and there were spectators everywhere. Greg knew it was getting near to the end of the season and lots of the games being played were very competitive for one reason or another. He cycled around until he caught sight of Ray who was stood to the side of some goalposts of pitch number 2.

'Hiya Ray, fancy seeing you here.' Greg gave Ray a welcoming smile.

'Alright kidda, how's the Brian Clough of Torquay getting on'?

Greg was very fond of Ray and looked upon him as a grandfather figure. Ray had four grandchildren whom he hardly saw. His two daughters lived only an hour away, just outside of Bristol but only visited on rare occasions. They had their own lives now and struggled to include Ray into theirs. Ray was very proud of his daughters and grandchildren and would always have a story about them to tell Greg. Greg was duty bound to listen and knew that Ray appreciated his toleration, despite his young age.

Greg spent the next five minutes telling Ray about his misdemeanours trying not to burst into tears, (there were kids from his school playing in a few of the matches and he didn't want to get spotted sobbing on the touchline). Ray stood in silence for a minute or two and Greg wondered whether he had made another bad move telling him. He didn't want to lose Ray as a friend as well.

'Sometimes we do things in life that we are not proud of and that we regret immediately. You sometimes must make them mistakes to make yourself a better person. I believe that you are a good person Greg Welling. If that is the worse you will ever do in your life then you will grow up to be a great person'.

Greg felt himself grow about a foot in size. 'Thanks Ray.'

'You're welcome son.'

'What's the score Ray'? Greg asked after a few seconds.

'No score yet Greg. The game has just kicked off and both teams are still working each other out. Bit of a grudge match this one, both teams are hoping to get promoted this year. The last time they played four players were sent off so we could be in for a bit of fun'.

Greg stood and watched and heard the dulcet tones of one of the team's Managers, it was coming from Heale Athletic. Heale were playing Brixham United and had just gone a goal down to a Brixham penalty. Ross Rush, (his parents hadn't really thought about his name that much) had been the manager of Heale Athletic for the past five years. Ross had played for Heale 17 years in different standard leagues with Heale and in his day was always regarded as a good solid player. After deciding at the age of 36 that his knees could no longer tolerate the pot-holed pitches of Devon he retired and was quickly asked to replace the ageing and not so confident Heale Manager. It was the logical next step and he duly accepted the role. Ross missed the cut and thrust of playing and struggled with the man-management of the modern players. They were always making excuses for missing training and were all prima-donnas these days; everyone thought they were Johan Cruyff. He also had a full-time job at a local garage, so he sometimes struggled to juggle his home life with football pittfalls.

With about five minutes to go till half-time Greg was approached by a man in a tracksuit who was probably in his late twenties and slightly overweight.

'You Greg.' he said looking straight at Greg.

'Yeh.' Greg replied slightly worried as to why and how he knew his name.

'Ross has asked if you will join him for a chat' explained the man.

'I don't know a Ross.' was the worried reply by Greg.

Pointing to the other side of the pitch the track-suited man pointed out Ross who was motioning for Greg to join him.

'Oh, is that his name?' Greg replied. 'Are you coming over Ray?', Greg asked. 'Sure, will you cycle over, and I'll wander over in a minute. Sounds like they need your football brain son'.

Greg smiled and quickly cycled over to where Ross was standing.

'What do you think Greg? we are pretty bad today eh?'

Ross was not enjoying the match and was downbeat.

'No worse than last week'. Greg couldn't resist a little dig.

'So, son, you've about five minutes to explain why a 4-3-3 formation would work and why it would suit our game'.

Greg couldn't believe that he was being asked for advice but duly obliged. He quickly explained that with a solid back four, holding midfielder, (Ross didn't quite get that position) two midfielders, two wingers and one striker they would be a much more potent threat in attack and more solid in defence.

Ross looked at him and said, 'no offence kid but where the fuck did you get to know all this shit?'

Greg shrugged and just said 'Dunno really, I just love football.'

They looked at each other for a few uneasy seconds until the blast of a whistle broke their silence. Ross turned to face the pitch and ushered his players over to where he was standing.

'Right lads over here, get some oranges down you, grab some water or juice and huddle around, were gonna change things around this half'.

Ross started trying to explain the formation and how he wanted the team to play but started to get tongue tied. The players were looking disinterested and started to question Ross.

'Right you lot, shut the fuck up. Greg get over here and explain to these muppets how this 4-3-3 works.'

Greg stood in dis-belief; he froze to the spot.

'Well come on then, were back out in 5 minutes, it will take this lot 5 hours to get it, so you best get a move on'.

Greg could feel 16 sets of adult eyes burning into him and wanted to run away but to his surprise found himself walking towards them.

'Right,' he said, 'listen up'. He then gave his first ever team talk.

The team listened intently not quite knowing what was happening but intrigued by this little kid in front of them. After 5 minutes or so Greg had finished and one of the players asked, 'What's your name kid?'

But before he could reply an old voice from behind him shouted, 'Meet the next Brian Clough lads, you can all call him Cloughie'. Greg turned around blushing as he shot Ray an embarrassed smile.

The first five minutes of the second half was a total shamble and if it wasn't for Heale's goalkeeper having a game to remember they would have been three or four goals behind.

'I don't think this is going to work Cloughie, it was worth a try but I'm going to go back to a 4-4-2'.

'No please don't,' begged Greg. 'they'll get it right in a minute, I'm sure of it', Greg said, although watching the past few minutes he wasn't so sure anymore.

'Five more minutes and that's it. We really need to win this game Cloughie and we definitely can't afford to lose.'

Heale had a better few minutes and were applying a bit of pressure. From a corner they equalised 1-1.

Ross looked over at Greg, 'I'm still not convinced Cloughie but I'll keep it the same for now.'

Greg smiled more through relief than anything but was still sure the game could be won. Heales players got more comfortable in the formation and passed the ball around with much more confidence. At the end of the game Brixham had scored another goal but that wasn't enough against the four goals from Heale. The Heale players left the pitch feeling triumphant. They had not played so well against such a good team for months and they were also in touching distance of a promotion place. Ross gathered his team around and gave a quick team talk. They all agreed that they had played well, and that the new formation was the way forward, but little did they know, Greg had other ideas.

Ross began packing the spare balls and kit away whilst the players put on their tracksuits and re-hydrated. He would then take down the goal nets and gather in the corner flags. He was approached by Jim Lines, the Manager of Brixham.

'Hey Ross, great win for you today. We really couldn't cope with you in the second half, you played like a different team'.

'I've got a secret weapon Jim; would you like to see it?' Ross replied, his smile covering his entire face. He then pointed to a small young boy who was stood next to an elderly gentleman and proudly exclaimed 'Jim, meet Cloughie'.

Greg looked up and smiled his embarrassed smile not sure what Jim and Ross were talking about.

'Yeh right,' sighed Jim, 'whatever you say.' and walked off none too sure what Ross was actually on about.

Ross finished tidying up and wandered over to where Greg and Ray were stood. They were catching the final few minutes of a youth cup semi-final that had gone into extra time.

'Greg, we are playing away to Newton Abbot Albion next week in the Cup, fancy joining us?'

I won't be able to get to Newton Abbot Ross; my dad won't let me cycle that far'.

'I could pick you up and take you over in my car if you want?'

'I don't think I will be allowed but I'll ask my mum.'

'I will be here at ten next Sunday, if you want to come, meet me here ok'? Greg was chuffed that he had been invited along and really hoped that he would be allowed to go. He continued to watch the game when he heard a unified shout of 'Cloughie' from across the pitch behind him. It was most of the players from Heale. They all shouted their goodbyes with a few thumbs up thrown in for good measure.

CHAPTER 7

Luckily for Greg, he rarely saw his dad in the mornings as he was either at work or in bed after finishing late. Greg still hadn't worked out what he was going to tell him about why he was no longer doing his paper-round but the thought of telling the truth really pained him.

His day in school was uneventful. Every lesson came and went without the anticipated nod from a teacher telling him to report to the Head of Year or worse, Headmaster. Why was it taking so long for them to summon him? Surely the school had been informed by Pete of his stealing escapade, were they still trying to work out their best course of action? Would he be suspended or even expelled? The last lesson passed by without any issues and Greg was relieved that school was finished for the day.

School football practise had been planned for Monday afternoon as their next match had been re-arranged for the coming Wednesday afternoon. Once again, the training was mundane with a lack of effort by all the players, especially Mr Rogers who was obviously in a hurry to get away, (probably going out with his boyfriend Greg thought) having a chuckle to himself. Training finished ten minutes early with some team news at the end. Greg was starting at left back as Steve Owens was unavailable due to his recent suspension from school. He had decided that he would make "Chinese Stars" in a metal work lesson instead of the normal objects the curriculum required. This wouldn't have been too bad, but he had decided to try them out and threw one at one of the kids in his class. Unfortunately, he had done such a good job in making them that the "star" lodged itself in the lad's leg resulting in an ambulance being called and three stitches. Greg was happy that he had been picked but knew he was never first choice. Mr Rogers also remarked to the team the news that Torquay United would be using the schools new all-weather 5 A-side sports pitch to train on. They would be using the facilities on Monday nights. (The school had recently had the pitch installed using the benefit of a local council grant). Greg was more excited at this news than he was about being selected for the team. He would have to sweet talk his mum into letting him cycle down to the school on Monday nights. He would be able to watch some proper training sessions rather than the rubbish the school served up. He had read many magazines and football books about training techniques but had never watched a professional team train, it may only be Torquay United, but it was a start.

Greg arrived home from school and heard his mum laughing in the lounge. It wasn't with his dad as he was still at work or Alison who was at hockey lessons. Intrigued he entered the room and saw Pete sat on the sofa with a cup of coffee in his hand. Greg stood in an awkward silence, he never expected Pete to be in his house and especially not now. Carol looked over to where Greg was standing 'Greg, come and sit down, Pete has something to tell you'.

Greg reluctantly sat down on a chair opposite Pete and tried not to look him in the eye, still feeling bad for letting him down. 'I had a visit from one of your friends today Greg.' said Pete.

Greg thought for a while about who he could mean. All his friends were at school all day and why would any of them visit him anyway?

'I can see you are a little confused Greg, it was Ray'.

Greg had never thought of Ray as a friend, just a friendly old man who he talked to on Sunday mornings. Greg allowed himself a small smile.

Pete continued to talk to Greg, 'So Ray visited the shop early this morning. He told me that you had admitted to him what you had done and how sorry you are. He holds you in very high regard and looks upon you as a grandson. You should feel very proud that he wanted to speak up for you. I also hold you in high esteem but feel totally let down by your poor choice of actions.'

Greg felt himself welling up and couldn't help his eyes watering.

'I can see that you are still upset about it Greg and I hope that you have learnt from your mistake.'

Greg could only look and nod at Pete as he knew if he tried to speak, he would break down in tears. 'I am willing to overlook your mis-demeanour on one condition'.

'Anything you want.' Greg managed to squeeze out of his larynx.

'Right now, I am one paper boy short and this morning I had to do a paper round myself. I would need you to resume your paper round first thing tomorrow morning, no way can I do that round again.'

Pete and Greg both smiled at the same time.

'Thank you' said Greg appreciatively. 'Thank you very much'.

Greg didn't quite know what to say or do next. Luckily, Carol intervened asking Pete if he would like another cup of coffee. Pete politely refused and made his excuses explaining that he was due back to the shop. He said goodbye to Carol and told Greg not to be late in the morning, although he knew he would be the first of the paper boys to appear. Greg said goodbye to Pete and closed the front door. He turned around and saw his mum standing in the hallway looking at him. She smiled and held out her arms to him. Greg could no longer control himself and ran into his mother's arms, sobbing uncontrollably.

Greg had a good game on Wednesday afternoon. They had played a local team in the Devon Cup and won 4-1. Greg unfortunately scored an own goal but was solid at the back and contributed well to the win. The atmosphere in the changing room after the game was full of banter in which Greg was included. He felt part of the team for once. The team were through to the quarter finals and were confident of progressing; they were as good as anyone else just clueless in tactics or team spirit.

CHAPTER 8

Greg spent the rest of the week convincing his mum to let him go to Newton Abbot on the Sunday. She eventually 'cracked' and agreed to let him go once she had met Ross. She had agreed to drive Greg to the fields on Sunday morning and meet Ross before giving her final decision. Greg wasn't sure what that would achieve; did she think he would abduct him or something? Anyway, that was her decision and it wasn't an all-out 'no' so all was not lost.

Greg had a great Saturday. Mike came around straight after he had finished his paper-round, as Carol had promised them a 'fry-up' for breakfast. Mike bought over his 'Madness LP' and they managed to record it onto a tape cassette using David's new stereo system. Greg had used an old cassette that had some of his dad's classical music on it but he never listened to it so he wouldn't miss it. Luckily his dad hadn't written on the cassette sleeve, so Greg wrote down all the song titles. After it had recorded Greg borrowed Alison's cassette player and they spent the next thirty minutes in Greg's room singing and jumping about pretending they were 'The Nutty Boys'. After their music theatre they decided to walk into town. They had some money in their pockets which they were desperate to spend. Mike had been saving his money for weeks and had seen a pair of second-hand German Parachute boots in the market in town. He really wanted a pair of Dr Marten boots (Docs) but they were far too expensive. Greg had seen a red Harrington jacket and had just enough money to afford it. Harrington jackets were all the rage, black was the most popular, but they also came in beige (not very common) and red (normally associated with 'skinheads'). Greg didn't really know why he liked the red one but didn't want to be associated as a skin head. They usually wore high legged Doc's, tight bleached jeans, white t-shirts, braces a red Harrington and of course had their head shaved. Greg really wanted a beige one, but they were hard to come by, so he chose the red one. He didn't want to be like everyone else and wear a black one. He could imagine that his uncles would have dressed as 'skinheads' in their day and he wasn't sure if he liked that idea or not.

Both boys got what they wanted in town and headed back to Greg's for a bite of lunch. Carol had gone out with Alison for the afternoon so Greg cooked his favourite gourmet meal and the only one he could, beans on toast. Mike left after his feast and Greg got ready for his trip to Plainmoor. Greg's dad was at home and had joined the boys for lunch. He volunteered to drop Greg up to the football as he was off to play a round of golf. On the way to the football David Welling turned off the radio and pulled the car over to the side of the road.

Looking directly at Greg he announced, 'I know about the shop and Pete. You must understand that although you and your mum are thick as thieves, your mum and I are a partnership and we don't keep secrets. I know there are certain things that she keeps from me but nothing of importance'.

Greg looked at his dad and replied, 'why didn't you say anything earlier?'

'Greg, in my job I come across a lot of people who make mistakes, many of them big mistakes. Most of them don't learn from them but a few do, make sure that you're one of the few that do. None of us were angels growing up, look at your uncles for gods' sake, but even they have turned out OK. No lectures or bollockings from me and no more bad choices from you son, OK?'

'Got it dad, sorry for everything.'

David drove the last mile in almost silence and dropped Greg outside the ground. 'Enjoy the game Greg, and up the Gulls'. Greg wasn't used to his dad being all football orientated and smiled to himself. As Greg got out of the car his dad shouted, 'up the Ammers'. Wow Greg couldn't quite believe his ears.

'Have a good round of golf dad.'

'I will Greg, I will.'

Greg quickly met up with Steve, and Danny. Graham had gone back to the Midlands for the weekend with his parents. He was going to watch Aston Villa play West Ham today. Greg was jealous but also wasn't overly confident of West Ham's chances. Torquay were playing Bristol Rovers and if they won today, they had a chance of promotion to the Third Division. Bristol Rovers were only three points behind them, so they were also in with a shout. With only two points for a win things were very tight at the top of the Division. There was a good crowd in the ground as Rovers had brought a strong contingent. The atmosphere was good and there was a real buzz in the ground. The hardened Torquay fans were trying to keep up with the well-tuned and very vocal Rovers fans, which made the ground sound fuller than it really was. Greg thought it would be one of the highest attendances of the season and was really looking forward to a good game.

What a difference ninety minutes make. Torquay were absolutely embarrassed by a great passing team who thrashed them 4-0. By the end of the game almost half of the home fans had made their way home leaving an even more vocal Bristol support to out-sing and nearly outnumber their hosts. Greg, Steve and Danny always stayed until the end of the game; after all they had paid for it. They were huddled around Steve's radio; Steve and Danny were happy as Liverpool were beating Man City 3-0 and going back to the top of Division 1. West ham and Aston Villa were involved in a thrilling (not) 0-0 draw. Greg knew that was bound to be the last game on MOTD, it was going to be a long night.

Greg tried his hardest to stay awake until the end of MOTD but woke up to a film playing in black and white. West Ham were indeed the last team on and as much as he loved watching them, he wasn't bothered about missing them tonight. The following morning, he completed his paper round and ate another fried breakfast courtesy of his mum and headed down to the football pitches with Carol. Ross was waiting in the car park when they arrived. He was in a deep conversation with Ray and never noticed Greg arrive. Carol introduced herself to both Ross and Ray and Greg left them to it. He grabbed a ball and went for a quick kick-about. He didn't want to know what they were talking about. After about five minutes Ross shouted over to Greg for him to join them. It was agreed that Greg could travel to Newton Abbott, but only if he stayed with Ross at all times and that Ross was to drop him home after the game. Greg was nervous; feeling apprehensive but excited at the same time. Ross led Ray and Greg over to his car. It was a big Ford Escort estate. In the boot were footballs, football nets, and two bags of football strips (Ross's wife cleaned the strip every week). Ross and Ray got in the front and Greg into the back. As Greg opened the back door, he noticed that someone else was sitting in the back seat. Getting into the car Greg recognised who it was. Daryl (Rushy) Rush was in the same year at school as Greg and was also in the football team. He usually played on the right of midfield as a winger and was a very good player. Greg always thought that Rushy should play in centre midfield as he wasn't quick enough to play as a winger. He was a strong tackler and was one of the fittest players in the team.

'Alright Greg?' good to see you,' said Rushy in a chirpy voice.

Greg never could work out Rushy, he was fairly quiet and although he got on with everyone never hung out with anyone either.

'Yes, thanks Rushy,' replied Greg, 'what are you doing here'?

Rushy let out a big laugh, 'you don't know, do you? Ross is my dad. He has come home the last two Sundays telling the family over Sunday dinner about this child genius that he had met at the pitches. I didn't for one moment think it would be you Greg.'

Once again Greg felt embarrassed; he didn't know if he could cope with all the banter at school if this got out.

'Dad reckons you have a talent for monitoring games and changing tactics for the better. I thought I would come along and see for myself.'

Greg was quite nervous. What had turned out to be some fun had somehow got quite serious. These Sunday league teams took their football very seriously as most of them had at one time or another hopes of making it into the profession. Why then would any of them listen to anything he would say!

They arrived at the Newton Abbot pitches with about 30 minutes to spare. Being an away fixture, they got to watch the home team manager put up the 'nets' and place the corner flags. Ross approached Greg and gave him the low-down on Newton Abbot Albion. They, like all the other teams in the league played a very basic 4-4-2 system. They had two very good strikers who had scored 50 goals between them this season and were the reason they were situated so high in the league. Albion had already beaten Heale twice this season winning 3-0 in the league and 5-0 in a pre-season friendly. Ross was struggling to find a way of stopping them scoring let alone beating them. Greg recommended using a sweeper who would play just in front of the back four. He explained to Ross that if the two strikers were that good the defence needed protection. Ross liked the idea but wanted to know where the team would lose a player. Ross had also explained that although Albion's defence was very good the two central defenders were getting on and slowing down. Greg then suggested playing a 4-1-3-1-1 formation. Ross was totally bemused. He had never ever heard of any formation like that before and thought Greg had made it up. Greg explained that the three in midfield would stay tight and stop Albion getting the ball. The player in front of them and the lone striker had to be super fit as they would have to cover the winger's role plus striker role. Albion's' two central defenders wouldn't know how to mark just one striker and hopefully cause confusion in their defence. Greg was full of passion in his explanation of team tactics and Ross was full of admiration for him. It all seemed to make sense, but Ross was really struggling to get his head around all the tactics. Ross finished his chat with Greg and wandered over to the other side to consider his options. Did he go with his normal 4-4-2 knowing that Albion would combat that or go with Greg's crazy 4-1-3-1-1.? He was the Manager of the team and yet he didn't know what to do. He spotted his players turning up in their cars and crossed the pitch to meet them. He hurried to his bags and pulled out 17 strips which he let the lads pick out, some of the shirts were bigger than others and as there was a mix of sizes amongst the team the shirts had to be distributed properly.

In reality though, it was a free for all. During the melee of kit gathering Ross announced that he needed all outstanding 'subs' to be paid immediately. He was annoyed that the same culprits had once again neglected to pay and was again overdue. ('Subs' were paid for the washing of the kit, upkeep of footballs, nets, training kit and basically anything that cost money to keep the team going. Lots of teams had sponsors which helped dramatically with the upkeep of running the team. A referee had to also be paid by the home team which also ate into the club coffers. Ross was working on finding a sponsor but with work and family commitments he struggled to find the time). The cost of subs was only £5.00 per month and was usually paid at the beginning of the month.

'I ain't got no money on me gaffa,' came from the cockney twang of John (Wilko) Wilkinson. He was 25 years old and was the teams' star player. He had been on the books of Leyton Orient as a teenager and had shown great promise. Like many kids he had got in with the wrong crowd and at the age of sixteen spent six months at a young offender's institute. During that time, Orient had let him go and he left education and became a plumber's apprentice. He loved the plumbing trade and settled into a normal life saving money to get himself a flat of his own. At eighteen he was playing for Dagenham and Redbridge as a semi-professional and had hopes they would be promoted into the Football League. His life changed dramatically on a night out with his younger brother Matt. Matt had got into an argument with a group of lads inside a nightclub and had taken a bit of a beating. The group of lads had been thrown out and after John had cleaned Matt up, they decided to get a cab and go home. The taxi rank was only a few minutes' walk from the club and approaching the rank Matt spotted the group of lads that had attacked him. John had not witnessed the fight as he had been trying out his best chat-up lines on an unsuspecting young lady in a different area of the club. He was upset that he wasn't there for his brother when he needed him. John approached the five lads who had no idea who he was. He looked around the floor for anything that he could use as a tool and saw half a broken brick on the other side of the road. He knew how to look after himself but the odds of five to one wasn't greatly in his favour. He crossed the road and picked up the brick. The five lads paid him no attention until he spoke to them, one hand hidden behind his back.

'Alright lads, you guys been in the Mayfair Club tonight.'

They all laughed together, and the biggest lad of the group said 'Yeh pal, we had to leave early though, had a bit of trouble with some gobshite.'

John laughed with them then announced 'that gobshite is my brother' and without hesitation threw his head toward the biggest lad landing it on the bridge of his nose.

John felt bone and cartilage shatter and knew that the head-butt would put the biggest lad out of the fight. The four other lads were caught unaware and before they knew it John was upon them. John swung his arm and the brick made contact with the second lad, sending him sprawling onto the floor with blood pouring from his head. John was just about to attack the three other lads when he was grabbed from behind. He couldn't believe he had got the numbers wrong and now he was in trouble. It was with relief (at the time) that the two people who grabbed him were Police Officers. They had been in a nearby 'chippy' grabbing some well-earned food before kick out time in the pubs and clubs. They had spotted John pick up the brick and had realised he was about to commit an offense although not sure what.

John was initially charged with attempted manslaughter which was eventually reduced to a lesser charge. His barrister had tried her best to defer a custodial sentence, but John was sent to prison for two years. This was due to the injuries sustained by the two lads. The lad that was head-butted needed surgery to repair his nose and had also suffered a fractured cheekbone. The lad hit with the brick spent a week in hospital. He lost a lot of blood at the scene and required surgery on his head that night. He had suffered severe concussion and required twenty stitches in his head. He was also scarred for life. John spent eighteen months inside before being released for good behaviour. Whilst inside his brother had moved to Torquay to be with his girlfriend, he had met her whilst on a lad's weekend in

Devon. Matt invited John down to Torquay after his release for a break and apart from going back to collect some belongings had been there ever since. John now lived with his fiancé and one-year old daughter in Newton Abbot. He was now a self-employed plumber and his life was pretty much complete.

'If you haven't got your 'subs' today Wilko you're off the team.'

'You're joking ain't you gaffer. I'll pay you next week I promise.'

'Sorry son, but I'm pissed off with you lot not paying up on time. If you can't be bothered to pay you won't play.'

Wilko wandered off to find his bag. He dug through it hoping to come across a loose note or some coins, but he already knew that he wouldn't find anything. Greg put his hand in his pocket and realised that he still had his pocket money on him. He walked over to Wilko who was still desperately looking in his bag.

'Wilko,' Greg whispered. Wilko looked up and saw Greg stood over him holding a five-pound note. 'Is that enough to cover your subs?' he whispered again.

He knew that if Ross saw he would be angry with them both. Wilko looked at Greg in dis-belief. This kid called Cloughie who could read a football game was going to lend him five pounds. He didn't want to accept but also knew that unless he coughed up some cash to Ross, he wasn't getting on the pitch today.

Wilko took the money and winked at Greg. 'I'll pay you back next week Cloughie, I promise. Oh, and thanks kid, I owe you one'.

'Gaffer, I've found a fiver in me bag,' shouted Wilko. 'Does that mean I can play now?' he asked as he grabbed what kit was left.

Ross ordered the team to get changed as quickly as possible and go for a warm-up before announcing the team and tactics. The warmup was to be taken by Paul 'Woody' Woodall the club Captain and loyal servant to the club. He had known Ross for most of his life and they had become good friends. With ten minutes to kick off Ross called the team over.

'Right guys, I don't need to remind you that these 'muppets' have done us twice this season. Their strikers are the best in the league and if they get a chance, they will take it. We need to stay super tight on them and don't give them a chance, got it?'

'Yes boss.' came a unanimous reply.

Ross named the starting eleven and announced the formation as a solid 4-4-2. The players all looked at each other and then at 'Cloughie'. They all knew that this was Ross's idea and could see the upset in 'Cloughie's eyes. They were also very aware of who the boss was and after a quick

Captains talk wandered on to the pitch. Greg had decided to join Ray on the other side of the pitch leaving Ross and Rushy together with the subs. The game panned out as it had in the two previous games and even after a quick re-shuffle at half time, Heale were totally outplayed losing 4-1 with both Albion strikers netting two goals apiece. Greg reluctantly joined the team for an after-match team-talk which had been started by Woody the Captain. After he had finished Ross took over.

'I'm sorry lads but I have let you all down today.'

'Cloughie had come up with a game plan to beat Albion today but I bottled it and decided to play our normal way knowing that the chances of winning would be slim. I'm not saying that if we had played 'Cloughie's way we would have won but we would have probably had more of a chance.'

The Heale players looked at each other not knowing what to say.

'We are playing these guys again next week in the League. I want every one of you at training on Tuesday night. We are gonna spend 30 minutes doing normal training and then 30 minutes talking tactics because next week we are going to play a 4-1-3-1-1 formation.'

The players looked at Ross then at Greg. 'I know,' said Ross, 'I don't even know what that is myself, but I do know one thing, I really want to wipe that smug smile off Albions faces'.

'Right lads get yourselves away and I'll see you all on Tuesday'.

'Cloughie, you and I are going to spend every second of our drive home talking about tactics cos right now I really haven't got a clue what you're on about and I've got a team to beat next week'.

CHAPTER 9

Greg kept himself to himself at school and had a select group of friends that he enjoyed spending time with. No one bothered him as he didn't threaten the egos of any of the "tough nuts" and he wasn't one for causing mischief. Many of the girls thought that he was good looking, but he wasn't recognised as a 'good catch'. There was one lad however who had taken a dislike to Greg and always tried his hardest to wind him up. His name was Paul Barnes. He came from a large family that were well known in the town for mainly the wrong reasons. Paul was the youngest of six children and all but two of his siblings went to Audley. This gave Paul great leverage in the hierarchical school pecking order. It was always a bonus knowing that you had four older siblings to help you out of any little scrapes that came your way. Paul used this to his advantage all the time.

Greg was sitting at his desk waiting for the form teacher to arrive and take the register. It was just before 9 am and Miss Howard was always late for Monday morning register. Greg had the dis-pleasure of sitting at the desk directly in front of Paul. 'Oi Welling, I was talking to Rushy last night. He says you're gonna be a football manager. What a fucking laugh. You couldn't manage to get up in time'.

This really tickled Paul and he let out a great roar of laughter. A few of the other kids had picked up on this story and had joined in with the laughter. No one really liked Paul Barnes but it was definitely better to be on his side than against.

Greg felt embarrassed and without thought turned around and shouted at Paul, 'shut the fuck-up or I'll lamp you'. Greg immediately regretted what he had just said.

Silence spread around the room and all eyes zoomed in on Paul. Greg prayed that Miss Howard would walk into the room and let him off the hook but as always, she was late again. Paul stood up not knowing what to do but knowing that he had to do something to save face and the family name.

'If you want to lamp me, 'Welling' then you can try it after school at Chappell Woods', (this was the place where all the kids went after school for a pre-arranged fight). Eyes now appeared on Greg. He had never been in this position before and didn't know whether to back down or accept the challenge. The classroom door flung open and in strolled Miss Howard, full of the joys of Monday morning. 'Morning class' she announced excitedly. A few mumbled replies came back her way as everybody was still enthralled by the Paul, Greg stand-off.

'I'll be there Barnes, just make sure you are' came the answer from Greg. At that moment he felt like somebody, for once. His nerves were shot to pieces with the thought of having a 'scrap' after school.

Greg spent the rest of the day keeping out of the way of most people which is very difficult when you are the talk of the school. Well, probably not the whole school but most definitely the Second-Year kids. News travels fast though. Any hint of an after-school fight, no matter who it was between always brought great joy to many of the school 'nutters'. Mike heard the news early in the day and although he had no lessons with Greg that day, he ensured that he found him as soon as he could. Mike knew that Greg couldn't pull out of the fight and was worried for him. Even though Greg was his best friend he had no idea if Greg could fight or if he even knew how to fight. It wouldn't be long before he would find out.

The last lesson at school normally dragged on for an eternity. Not this one. As soon as the lesson began it was pretty much over. Greg spent most of it in a blur. He couldn't believe how stupid he was and how easy it was for Paul Barnes to have wound him up. If the situation were to occur again, he would need to re-evaluate his position before answering.

Greg grabbed his coat and bag and made the short trek towards Chappell Woods. He half hoped that one or some of the teachers had got wind of the fight and would be at the woods to call a halt to proceedings, (which sometimes happened if the interest got out of hand and news made its way to the staff room). He met up with Mike and a few other loyal friends: Steve, Daz and Ty. They were waiting at the school gates. Greg knew that most of the kids who would be watching the fight would be cheering on Paul. This was Paul's territory and the local kids were quite loyal to each other. The four lads made their way to a small opening in the woods and were surprised to see a very large gathering of very excited school kids. Paul Barnes had spent most of the day gathering up support and with the help of his siblings. They had engineered a large crowd. Paul Barnes was obviously very confident of beating Greg and achieving some more important brownie points with the local girls. Paul was already at the clearing and stood with two of his brothers and sister. They were seemingly giving him some last-minute advice from some of their previous scuffles. Greg was unsure of what he was going to do; all he knew was that he was 'bricking it'.

In December Greg's uncles had paid Carol a surprise visit to help her celebrate her 40th birthday. They had stayed for the entire weekend and Greg had spent as much time as possible in their company. To be totally honest, he was in awe of them. He loved listening to their stories and when his dad wasn't around, he loved listening about their boyhood scuffles. It was like listening to tales in a different world.

They always had some advice to give in every story they told. It was now time for Greg to act on some of that advice.

Greg handed his bag to Mike. Mike had never seen Greg so focused. He hadn't spoken to him or the other two since they met up at the school gates and he had a look of steel about him. The group of kids that had amassed for the fight saw Greg arrive and gave a loud cheer as there hadn't been an organised fight at the woods for weeks. It wasn't a great billing, but in the scheme of things a fight is still a fight. Greg took off his coat and threw it on the floor next to his schoolbag. He made his way towards Paul Barnes. The usual format for a scrap was the two combaters, many fights at the school involved girls, faced up to each other and the fight would commence. It was only over when one of the scrappers gave up.

Greg carried on walking towards Paul. Paul saw Greg making his way towards him but never noticed his steely eyes until it was too late. Greg launched himself at Paul with everything he had. Before Paul could move, he landed a clubbing left-handed punch into the nose of Paul Barnes. Paul never stood a chance to move out of the way and he hit the deck banging his head on a log on the way down. He was unconscious. Greg stood in a state of shock not knowing what to do. His aggression quickly left him, and he soon realised that everyone in the woods was stood staring at him in almost total silence. What seemed like an eternity of silence was shattered by the shouting of Wally Barnes,

Paul's oldest brother at the scene and third oldest altogether.

'You've fucking killed him and I'm gonna fucking kill you.'

Wally picked up a very large lump of wood lying at his feet and lunged at Greg. Luckily, Greg had returned to 'planet earth' and before Wally had even finished his life-threatening promise, he had turned and was on the run. Greg ran like he had never run before. He made his way out of the woods and onto a main road. He knew he lived in the opposite direction of the Barnes tribe and hoped that was enough to put them off the chase. He ran without looking behind for what seemed like a marathon but in truth was only just under a mile. He had lost his pursuers. He was so pleased the Barnes family all smoked and were unfit.

Back at the woods, confusion, anger and shock were the emotions amongst the local kids. Most were confused because, although there wasn't a fight, someone was lying 'dead' on the floor. The Barnes' kids were angry that they had lost face in this ridiculous scrap and were in shock at the loss of their younger brother.

'Someone call for a fucking ambulance!' came a shout from the crowd.

In the days before mobile phones this meant someone having to find a telephone box or going home to make the call.

'I don't need a fucking ambulance. Someone give me a fag'.

Paul was alive! There was relief amongst the gathering as news of Paul's recovery spread. 'What happened bruv,' Paul asked his brother Lance.

'You got knocked out you soft shit. Don't worry though, Wally is after him.'

Paul raised his hand to his head, it was sore. He had a huge lump where he had banged his head and the pain coming from his nose was agony, he knew it was broken. After a minute or two he stood up and sulkily made his way out of the woods and towards home. The large crowd had thinned out at the news of his recovery, some of them quite upset as there had never been a death at the woods before. Over-all it had been a pretty poor showing from the Barnes family.

Mike, Steve and Daz had left the woods pretty much straight after Greg's almighty punch. They wanted to stand and cheer but were far too sensible and liked their good looks to be so reckless and stay. Mike picked up Greg's abandoned jacket and bag and they left as quietly as they came. They made small talk on the way home until they all had to go their separate ways. Paul had not recovered before they left, and all knew the dire consequences for Greg if Paul was indeed dead. They certainly weren't celebrating Greg's victory.

Greg got home at the normal time; he had run most of it after all. He went straight up to his room and burst into tears. The adrenalin drop was immense, and he had a headache like never before. Today was the first fight of his life and although he had won, he wasn't particularly proud of himself. He was more upset that Paul Barnes had got underneath his skin and caused him to rise to the challenge. He wanted to use the house phone and call his uncle Harry and let him know what had happened at the woods. It was Harry that had given him some worldly advice on the art of fighting.

'If you're in a corner Greg and there is no way out there's only one thing to do. Make sure you surprise your enemy by throwing the first punch. You throw that punch with everything you have; it may well get you out of as much trouble as you may be in.'

Up to now, that advice had worked out well. Harry hadn't given him any advice about the aftermath of a fight though.

Tuesday's morning walk to school was surreal. The closer Greg got to school the more he could see people nodding in his direction and fingers being pointed at him. He realised that he was today's centre of attention and although a part of him liked it, another part of him detested it. He met up with Mike on the corner of Cricket Field Road, about quarter of a mile from school.

'How you feeling, Rocky?' Mike asked with a large smile spread across his face.

'Yeh, I'm good mate. I was knackered when I got home so I had my tea and told mum I had a headache. She went totally overboard as usual, made a fuss then packed me off to bed.

I must admit I slept like a baby and had to be woken by my alarm clock. I think I had thirteen hours sleep.'

Mike replied in his quick humour, 'If you slept like a baby, were you sick and did you shit yourself?'

They both laughed out loud.

'I take it Wally Barnes never got hold of you. You left the woods as quick as you landed that punch on Paul.'

'I wasn't hanging around Mike. I didn't even want to fight one of the Barnes' family let alone all of them. I'm just happy Wally smokes a lot. I didn't even look behind me for about a mile and when I did, he wasn't there. If I ran as quickly as that on the school cross-country circuit, I'd win it every time.'

They both laughed together. Greg was very happy that Mike was his best friend. He knew that he would need him in the next day or two. The two of them hung around by the science block until the bell had gone. It was a quiet area and only a few kids were hanging around. Greg said his goodbyes to Mike and headed towards his form class. Everyone was already in the room and to his surprise so was Miss Howard.

'Good morning, Master Welling, it's so nice of you to join us' came her sarcastic greeting.

Greg sat down at his desk trying not to look at anyone in particular but feeling thirty sets of eyes on him. Miss

Howard began to take the register. She called out the names in alphabetical order and the first name called was Barnes. 'Here' came a muffled reply. Miss Howard looked up and acknowledged Paul Barnes. She looked back down at the register and then looked back up in the direction of Paul Barnes. He had two black eyes and had obviously been in a fight. It was not unusual for one of the Barnes family to have been in a fight, but they never usually lost, it was normally the poor kid they had been in a fight with that looked the worse for wear.

'Anything you want to tell me Paul?' she asked.

'No Miss.'

Greg sat for the fifteen minutes of tutor time in silence. He sat next to a pretty girl called Hazel who never really had much to say to him. He thought he was invisible in her eyes. She hung around with a very popular group of girls who were fancied by nearly all the boys in their year and a few years above as well.

Near the end of the lesson she leaned over and said 'Barnes had it coming to him. I'm pleased you're OK. We were all worried for you yesterday.'

Greg smiled and blushed at the same time. It was nice to know that he had more friends than he thought.

'Thanks Hazel.'

She carried on looking at Greg, but her expression changed to a worried look.

'Some of the girls are friendly with Tanya Barnes. She has told them that you are going to get severely beaten up today. You need to keep your head down Greg. We can't have the Barnes' family ruining your good looks, can we?'

Greg smiled again but didn't answer this time. He already knew that a world of pain was heading his way, he just didn't know when or where.

Greg got to lunch with very little hassle. Even John Poke had given him the nod of approval whilst on the way to a maths lesson. Greg had seen 'Pokey' at the woods and knew that he didn't like the Barnes' family. Evidently there was a family feud between the Barnes' and Pokes going back generations. It felt nice to have the Pokey on his side for once. Greg made his way to the lower playground. The playgrounds were split into four sections on two levels. The higher playgrounds were separated in the middle by two stand-alone prefabricated classrooms, (these had been constructed a few years before due to the excess number of pupils at the school and were used to teach History lessons). The lower playgrounds were separated by a small knee length wall with hedging on top. Most of the hedges had been destroyed by kids jumping between the two playgrounds.

Greg could always be found in the bottom playground where he would eat his lunch and meet up with his mates.

This playground was also used by the footballers of the school to have a kick about. Two large pillars expanded across a flight of steps and quite conveniently were nearly the same length as a goalmouth, post to post. Football matches and knock out football competitions would be played throughout the lunch break with Greg joining in as much as possible. Many of the kids from the older years played and Greg was well known amongst this fraternity. Greg had decided to sit out the first game, FA Cup knockout. This game consisted of one goalkeeper and a large group of kids. Playing as individuals, once you scored you automatically went through to the next round. The last player to score was eliminated. This carried on until only one was left and was duly awarded the winner. Greg would normally have played but there were an awful lot of kids from the fourth and fifth year playing, and he knew he was out of his depth. Mark Jenkins was sat next to him; he would normally be playing goalkeeper but one of the older kids had taken his place.

The Cup competition was advancing well and there was a good atmosphere amongst the boys, with lots of banter. Greg had been on the end of a lot of it, but he didn't mind as it was all in good fun. He was in a conversation with Mark when he noticed the football match had stopped. He then noticed everyone was staring at him. From his right-hand side, he saw a group of kids walking towards him. At the front of the group was Paul Barnes getting 'frog marched' along by his older brother Wally.

'Greg, you had better run pal, get the fuck out of here.'

One of the kids had tried to warn Greg but it was too late. Greg had already decided that he was going to face his fate and that running would only delay the inevitable.

'Welling, I want a fuckin' word with you' came the screech from Wally's mouth.

Greg stood up and faced the oncoming gang, there must have been at least forty kids following Wally. Greg didn't really recognise any of them; all he knew was they were all a lot older and bigger than him. Greg could see the hate in Wally's eyes. He was obviously in a fit of rage and had been embarrassed by yesterday's fight. The gang of boys stopped in front of Greg. Paul Barnes was pushed to the front, facing Greg.

'You and Paul are gonna have a proper fight now Welling, none of your cheating shit.'

Paul Barnes threw a punch that landed to the right-hand side of Greg's cheek. It hurt like crazy, but Greg just stood there. Paul threw a second punch, this time landing on the opposite cheek. It hurt again but there was not enough power to knock Greg over. He could feel tears well in his eyes, but no way was he going to cry. Wally pushed Paul out of the way and threw two punches in quick succession that knocked Greg to the ground. Now that really hurt. Greg lay on the floor dazed. Without thought he staggered to his feet and faced the gang amassed in front of him. Another two punches knocked him to the floor again. One of them connected above his left eye, cutting him. Greg could feel blood pouring out of the cut. He tried to stand up but fell and tumbled back.

'You best stay on your arse Welling.'

Greg looked up at Wally and tried to stand up. He managed to get onto one knee when one of Wally's boots landed directly into his face, causing his nose to erupt in a stream of blood. He wasn't getting up after that.

Mark Jenkins stepped in front of Wally, 'he's had a fucking nough, alright' he bravely announced.

'I'll say when he's had enough' spat Wally.

Mark looked worried. He didn't fancy the 'slapping' that Greg had just been given. Just then, the group of lads that had been playing football appeared behind and to the side of Mark. One of the fifth formers reiterated Mark's words, 'he's had enough Wally.' Wally weighed up the opposition. The thought of a mass brawl thrilled him, but he wasn't sure if he had the backing of all the kids behind him, he knew that many of them were 'hangers-on'. The distinct sound of Mr Rogers voice could be heard in the distance. Wally looked around at the lads surrounding Mark and smiled. His job was done. He turned and left in the same direction in which he had came.

Mr Rogers appeared on the scene within a minute or two of Wally and his gang departing. He knew there was something untoward going on but if he turned up in the middle of it, he would have a lot more to deal with than if he turned up at the conclusion. He barged his way through the crowd and found a group of lads crowding around one particular pupil. Once again, he pushed past them to find Greg sat on some steps covered in blood.

'What on earth has been happening here?' he shouted.

There was silence, no one wanted to say anything, and they certainly didn't want their name getting back to Wally and his crew.

'Am I talking to myself here?' he shouted again.

'I fell over Sir and banged my head.'

'You fell over Welling?'

'Yes Sir.'

'It looks to me that you were in a fight.'

'Not me Sir, I just fell over playing football and banged my head.'

'Well in that case, you better come with me. You will need to see the school nurse.'

Greg was immediately taken to the nurse who took one look at him and called his mum. Carol was soon at the school and on her way to Torbay hospital with Greg in tow. Greg was given four stitches to the cut just above his eyebrow. Greg knew that he would have to tell his mum and dad the truth, he wouldn't dare lie to them again. He just hoped they would see things his way.

Carol was upset to see Greg in such a state. She had told him that there wouldn't be any questions until his Dad returned from work later that day. Greg didn't return to school for his last few lessons and went home with his mum. Carol made him put his blood-stained uniform in the wash and Greg gingerly showered, trying to keep the water out of his cut, it was still extremely sore. He then retired to his room to catch up with his magazines.

David Welling returned home from work just before 6pm and in time for dinner. The family sat down together in an unusual eerie silence. Alison was the first to speak. She had been given a very accurate account of Monday and Tuesday's proceedings by her friends at school. She felt quite proud of her brother for standing up for himself on Monday and for also facing Wally and his mob. David and Carol listened intently at Alison whilst looking at Greg. Alison recorded a good account but managed to leave out a few important details. Evidently Greg's fight in the woods was a scrappy affair with Greg just getting the better of Paul. She didn't think her dad would be over impressed if he knew Greg had taken some fighting advice from one of their uncles. Alison finished her story by saying that the Barnes' family were horrible people and that even though she didn't condone fighting she was proud of her little brother. It wasn't very often Greg liked having a sister but today was one of them times. David and Carol sat in silence eating their dinner. Carol was the first to speak, 'So Greg, what now? Am I likely to be taking you to hospital again or is this feud over?'

'It never was a feud mum. I didn't want to fight in the first place. I just got myself into a corner and couldn't back out. I'm sorry for fighting and you having to leave work early. I think it is all over now. The Barnes' kids will probably find someone else to pick on now.'

David looked up and calmly stated, 'Any more trouble from anyone of that family and I want to know. I'm sure that as a Governor I can have a say in their attitude of discipline in school.'

Greg looked at his dad in a pleading way 'Please, don't say anything dad, you will only make matters worse. I promise if they touch me again, I will let you know.'

'So will I,' piped up Alison, 'so will I.'

CHAPTER 10

Miss Howard arrived in class five minutes early. This was a first for her but she had a message to pass on from the headmaster and he wasn't the person to upset. She took the register on time and then informed Greg that he was to report to Mr Frances, the Headmaster. Greg had never had any dealings with Mr Frances and only knew him through what he had heard. All he knew was that Mr Frances was someone that you never wanted to upset or get sent to and right now he was on his way to his office.

Greg entered the top corridor of the main school building and stood outside the door with a large imposing sign reading 'HEADMASTER'. He drew a deep breath and knocked. There was no reply, so Greg knocked again. A loud and harsh 'Wait' echoed through the door and took him by surprise. He stood in fear for what seemed like an eternity but what was only a minute or two. 'Enter' came the next loud roar.

Greg opened the door and entered the room. He wasn't sure what he was expecting from a headmaster's office, but it wasn't this. It was a quite large imposing room. Mr Frances sat behind a grand bureau with two chairs sitting in front of it. There was an un-watered house plant in one corner and a hat and coat stand in another. There were some fishing pictures scattered on two of the walls and certificates and military regalia on the other two. Behind Mr Frances was a bucket in which stood three canes, they had all seen plenty of action. Greg hoped one of them wasn't going to be used on him today.

Mr Frances was nearing the end of an illustrious and colourful career. He had spent twenty-two years in the military working in the Intelligence Corps. He had attained the rank of Warrant Officer Class 1 and achieved his goal of becoming a Regimental Sergeant Major (RSM). During his time in the military Ian Frances attained very high grades from the Open University courses that he attended and on leaving the army he got himself a job in a local school. His teaching methods were classed as 'different' and although he had a very strict manner, his results were very hard to deny. He soon got a reputation as an excellent teacher and was 'headhunted' throughout most of his second career. He was due to take up a role as Headmaster in an illustrious Boys Grammar School in Oxford when he was investigated for bullying. The investigation was never upheld but his reputation was tarnished, and he eventually took his current role. Audley Grove was not a school for the more light-hearted of teachers and he needed all his forty-five-year work experience to run the school. He knew his ideas were becoming outdated, but he only had 18 months left before he could retire to the south of France and set up his Fishing School. Fishing was his one and only pastime and it enabled him to keep his stress levels down to a manageable level.

'Please sit Master Welling.' Greg gingerly sat down in one of the two chairs in front of Mr Frances desk.

'So, it has come to my attention that you have been involved in not one but two fights this week...'

Before Greg could answer, Mr Frances carried on. 'I have spoken to most of your teachers and they assure me you are a very intelligent young man who causes absolutely no trouble in class. I also know your father who is an outstanding contributor to this school and is an upstanding citizen. So, then why are you now the centre of attention deciding to fight at every opportunity?'

Once again before Greg could reply Mr Frances carried on. 'To be totally honest with you Welling, I need the names of the boys you had a fight with. If they are who I think they are then I'm sure you are aware that they cause me plenty of problems in and outside of this school and I need you to name them. It's funny isn't it Welling? Evidently there were lots of witnesses, but nobody can remember or saw a thing. So, the question is Greg, who were you fighting with?'

Greg looked at Mr Frances and then to the floor. He knew Mr Frances was staring directly at him and could feel the weight of expectation on him.

'I'm sorry Sir, but I can't tell you.'

Greg could feel his voice crumbling as he said it but he managed to finish his sentence before Mr Frances cut in, 'You can't or you won't, Welling?' came an angry response, 'You don't owe these boys anything. If you are afraid of retaliation, then I can promise you will be totally safe.'

'It's not that Sir. I just can't tell you.'

'Well I will try and jog your memory for you I hear you like to play football and are in the school team. If you decide to keep up with your amnesia, I will ban you from playing in the school team.'

Mr Frances' leant forward in his chair and smiled at Greg in a very smug way. He had heard how much Greg loved football and was convinced he had played his 'ace card'. Greg could never have imagined the course of questioning that had come his way this morning. He had presumed that Mr Frances knew that he had been fighting with the Barnes' kids and was just getting him in to tell him the error of his ways. He wasn't expecting to have to 'grass' on them, even if he did hate them.

'I'm sorry sir. I can't tell you.'

Greg was slightly more confident in his announcement even if he had very little reason to be. Mr Frances went mad. He rose from his chair and strode around his office explaining to Greg the error of his ways. For the next five minutes he managed to tell Greg all about his professional career and how he always followed the right path. Mr Frances walked around to behind his desk and took out one of his cherished canes. Waving it around his office like he was swatting flies.

He gave Greg one last chance to redeem himself. Greg felt totally overawed by his surroundings and the bully tactics used by his headmaster. He sat in silence wanting to shout out the names of Paul and Wally Barnes but for some unknown reason to himself he was unable. Mr Frances grabbed Greg by the collar and literally turfed him out of his office. Greg found himself standing in the corridor all alone, not sure of what had just happened. All he knew was that he had felt more emotions this week than at any time in his young life.

Greg returned to his lessons and spent the rest of the day in shock. After school Greg made his way to the sports hall to get changed for football training. Most of the boys were already there getting changed when he arrived. He found a space and put his bag down. The banter in the changing rooms was childish but good fun. Mr Rogers walked in and told everyone to be quiet. He looked around the changing room and caught sight of Greg.

'I'm sorry Welling but your no longer on the team. Orders from Mr Frances.'

An eerie silence spread around the room, all eyes once again on Greg. This was beginning to become a habit. Greg bit down hard on his lip but showed no emotion. He picked up his bag and left the room without saying a word. Mr Frances' threat had certainly come true.

Greg arrived home early, much to the surprise of Carol. Greg explained to his mum the conversation with Mr Frances and what had happened after school. She was understandably upset for her son and promised Greg that she would do everything possible to help him.

The rest of Greg's week was quiet. His stock had increased three-fold within his peer group and more kids than ever spoke to him now. Hazel was very friendly in class and a few more of her friends had acknowledged him in lessons. Paul Barnes was still an 'arse-hole' but he never pushed Greg too far, after all Greg had embarrassed him once. He couldn't afford to lose another fight; his family would disown him forever.

It was Friday afternoon and Greg were sitting in a double French lesson when he was once again summoned to the headmaster's office. Greg had two emotions running through his body. The first was relief at not having to sit through another minute of 'le chat or j'habit Torquay. The second emotion was of fright. His first visit to Mr Frances office was very prominent in his mind and it was not a pleasant memory. He entered the main building and gingerly made his way to Mr Frances office. He was amazed to see his father outside the office. He was sitting in his Chief Inspectors Uniform cutting an air of authority that even Greg found imposing. Greg sidled up to his father and acknowledged him with a small smile. He wasn't totally sure if he was in trouble or not. He was sure though that he would find out very soon.

The door to the office opened and Mr Frances appeared. He greeted David Welling with a smile and handshake that was reciprocated. Both David and Greg were ushered into the room. Mr Frances opened the discussion by explaining the events of Wednesday's meeting with Greg and his reluctant decision to prohibit Greg from playing for the school team unless he gave the names of the boys who he was fighting. David and Greg sat in silence until Mr Frances had stopped talking.

David Welling looked at Greg and in a quiet and endearing tone asked his son, 'Why won't you tell Mr Frances who you had a fight with and who beat you up Greg?'

'I don't know dad. It's not as if Mr Frances doesn't know the names, half the school knows. I just don't want to be the one who grasses them up. As far as I'm concerned, it's all over dad. If Mr Frances wants to get names, he's going to have to get them from someone else.'

Greg looked sheepishly at his dad not knowing if he had done right or wrong. He then looked his dad in the eye and asked, 'If you want me to say the names, I will dad. I don't want to do the wrong thing or for you to think badly of me.'

David Welling returned his sons stare. 'If you don't want to tell on them lads then that is fine by me. I'm not saying you are doing the right thing son, but I understand why. You can go back to your lessons now'. Mr Frances was livid.

'I don't think you understand the severity of the situation, David and I will let Greg know when he can return to his class.'

David Welling stood up. 'Mr Frances, is my son allowed to represent the school at football, yes or no?'

Mr Frances remained in his seat and looked at both the Wellings'.

'I'm afraid that if Greg's decision remains the same then so does mine.'

'In that case, Mr Frances, it is with regret that I resign my position on the Board of Governors.'

David Welling turned towards the door and ushered his son to the exit. They both left the office without another word spoken. As they entered the corridor, David turned to his son. 'I was looking for a way of getting off the Board of

Governors anyway'. He smiled and winked at his son, 'see you tonight son.'

CHAPTER 11

Greg spent all of Saturday with Mike as Torquay United were playing their penultimate game of the season away to Colchester. The two boys decided to go on a mammoth bike ride and spent nine hours out of the house. By the time they arrived back home they were cold, tired and very hungry. Carol fed them and Greg asked if Mike could sleep over. All was agreed and Greg and Mike had a great night mucking about and acting like young teenagers. They even managed to set up Greg's Scalextric set that had been in the loft for the last two years. Both boys woke up on Sunday morning still tired from their long day on Saturday. They got dressed ready to complete their paper-rounds. They said goodbye to each other and cycled to their respective shops. Greg completed his round and went back to the shop to read the papers. West Ham hadn't played the day before due to the FA Cup semi-finals taking place, however there was plenty of football that he could catch up on. He was looking forward to going to the Twent Fields and watching Heale Athletic play. Ross had promised him they would play his new formation and that they would practise it in training this week. He hoped Ross would honour his promise, but he wasn't raising his hopes.

Greg cycled to Twent fields and immediately caught up with Ray. He had been looking forward to seeing him and having a 'catch up'. In the last few months, they had become very close. Ray and Greg exchanged small talk for a while and Greg told Ray of his weekly escapades at school and of his father's intervention. Rays week was a little less interesting, but he always enjoyed listening to Greg. Greg noticed that the fields were filling up with players and supporters. He and Ray made their way over to the pitch where Heale would be playing. The Heale players arrived in good time, they seemed to have a spring in their step. As they arrived, they all acknowledged 'Cloughie' with a smile. Greg saw Wilko arrive and he headed straight towards Greg.

'Hey Cloughie' he waved a crisp five-pound note in his hand. His large grin disappeared the closer he got to Greg as he noticed the bruises still visible on Greg's face.

'What the fuck happened to you Cloughie?'

'Just school stuff Wilko.'

'Well here's that fiver I owe you and thanks again Cloughie. If there is anything, I can do for you Cloughie just give me a shout.'

He nodded at Greg and gave him a wink. On the other side of the pitch Ross was barking orders at the team. He had just handed out the kit and there was the usual scrap of bodies trying to get the best fitting pieces. Ross sent the team out to warm up and called 'Woody' over for a final brief.

'Cloughie, come over here son, I need you to be involved.'

Greg joined Ross and Woody and was briefed on the training that was taken in the week and the way they planned to form up and play. Greg was amazed at the amount of work that had been put into training and preparing for the match. Ross looked straight at Woody.

'This could all go pear shaped today Woody. It's your job to keep them lads motivated when things aren't working out. Between me and Cloughie here, we'll bark orders from the side lines and try to keep the shape of the team. I hope you're up for it, son.'

'Let's give it a go eh Boss.' replied Woody.

Woody joined his team-mates on the pitch and left Ross and Greg together.

'They've worked extremely hard this week Cloughie, they see something in you. You better make this team-talk something special'.

Greg looked up at Ross.

'I'm doing the team-talk'.

'That's right son, it's your tactics, all the players are fit and here, you pick the team and give the talk.'

'What, you haven't picked the team yet?' gasped Greg.

'Nope, I thought I would give you the pleasure. Today I'm your number 2. You better get a shifty on though, there's only 10 minutes till kick-off.'

Greg stood in silence scared to do anything, not knowing what to do. An old frail arm appeared around his shoulders and he knew immediately that it was Ray.

'Son, take some advice from an old man. Don't let your fears rule your head. Ross is giving you a chance to manage this bunch of idiots for the day. Grab the bull by the horns and go for it. What's the worst that can happen? They will lose, like they don't most weeks eh.'

He gave a little chuckle to himself before leaving Greg on his own once more. Greg took a deep breath and approached the players shouting at them to join him. It wasn't as much a shout as a schoolboy shrill and only a few of the players heard him. Greg looked at Ross who mimicked him to shout louder. Greg put his hands to his mouth, formed them like a megaphone and tried again, this time with a lot more meaning and gusto.

'If any of you want to play a game of football today, I suggest you gather round me now.'

That was a direct quote from his school football manager, but it was all he could really think of at the time. The players immediately stopped what they were doing, collected the five footballs they had been using to warm up with and surrounded Greg in a circle. Greg felt very intimidated as they all towered over him, so he asked them all to sit down. Now he was looking down at them he felt much more confident. Greg already knew what his idea of a best eleven was by watching the team play over the past few months and he formally announced the team. There weren't any surprises to the players which made the team talk a lot easier. The team already knew the formation and how they were expected to play. Greg didn't know what to say as this was his very first team talk, and all eyes were on him.

Wilo stood up and stood next to Greg.

'Lads were all here cos we love this beautiful game. We've all given up our time to be here so let's give this our best shot. I want to get better and I believe you all do to. If we give this weird formation a go what's the worst that can happen, we will lose again. Ross has been great letting Cloughie here,' he rubbed the top of Greg's head, 'show us something different. Cloughie is our little genius, I for one believe in him so let's go out there and win today, eh.'

There was a combined roar of fist pumping and back slapping as the players all stood up and ran onto the pitch.

Greg looked at Wilko and said, 'thanks Wilko, I didn't know what to say, you saved my bacon.'

'That's OK, Cloughie, you'll have them team talks down to a tee in no time.'

The game kicked off about 5 minutes late due to the late arrival of the referee. Heale started the game well, keeping the ball with the extra man in midfield and creating a few half chances. Out of the blue and against the run of play Albion were awarded a penalty for a freaky hand ball offence against Steve 'The Head' Weadon. 'Head' was so called as he was a big centre half who would head every ball that he could. He wasn't scared of putting his head anywhere, even if it did mean getting a studded football boot across his forehead. The referee was adamant that the ball had hit 'the heads' hand. He blew his whistle and pointed to the spot. Pete Northcott, the Heale goalkeeper dived the wrong way and it was 1-0 to The Albion.

Ross shouted from the edge of the pitch. 'Heads up lads, you're playing well, keep your shape'.

'Great shape.' came a shout from across the other side of the pitch, from The Albion management and subs gathered together. They were all laughing. The Heale players heard the banter and weren't best pleased but chose to ignore it. Heale carried on playing to the script and were by far the better team. The Albion were being outplayed and creating very little opportunities. Heale were testing Albions' goalkeeper at every opportunity and enjoying playing with more freedom. With five minutes left of the first half, The Albion got their first corner of the game. The ball was swung in and a large centre forwards forehead connected beautifully with the ball and it flew into the back of the net. 2-0 to The Albion. The Heale players trudged back to their positions.

'Keep your shape lads' came a shout from The Albion side of the pitch.

'What are you trying now? An Army formation 1-2,1-2, 1-2.'

A loud roar of laughter reverberated from them. Wilko ran over to where The Albion group were stood.

'If any of you fuckers keep up with that fucking banter, you'll have me to deal with after the match, I've had enough of your shit today already.'

He ran back to his position feeling aggravated that he had managed to slightly lose his self-control. The first half finished with no other score. Ross and Greg were waiting for the players at the side of the pitch with oranges and some squash.

'Over to you Cloughie' said Ross. The players were stood around trying to get to the 1/4 oranges and cups of weak orange squash. Greg asked them all to sit down and be quiet. They did so after a little help from Woody.

'That's the best I've seen you lads play all season. You have kept the ball well and created loads of chances.'

'Yeah but were still losing Cloughie' came the reply.

'How we gonna fix it?'

'Were not. You guys must go back out there and keep playing the same way. They don't know how to play against you and are lucky to be in-front. Don't get frustrated, you will score and then we will see who can shout from the side lines.'

Greg was enjoying his little speech and getting boisterous at the same time.

'Wilko don't get yourself wound up and sent off, we need eleven players to beat this lot. I don't want to lose this game, lets tear those fuckers apart.'

'I won't be having that language from my son.'

Greg looked behind to see his mum and dad. (They had turned up to the field to support Greg and see what all the fuss was about)

'Sorry dad.' The lads all laughed out loud.

Woody quietened the group and spoke softly. 'Cloughies right. I really enjoyed that first half apart from their goals. Cloughie's parents are here now and I for one don't want to let him down in front of them so, let's tear those fuckers apart.'

Another roar of laughter and lots of 'tearing fuckers apart!' could be heard before the players slowly made their way back on to the pitch. Greg looked at his parents and apologised again. They both smiled, (they knew he was growing up, too much like his uncles for Dave's sake).

'So, they call you Cloughie?'

'What role have you been given today Greg? asked his mum.

'I'm managing the team today, my tactics my decisions.'

David and Carol looked at each other, then at Greg and finally at Ross.

'That's right,' replied Ross, 'Cloughie is in charge today.'

The second half began with a flurry of missed opportunities for Heale. Ross had noticed that the players 'heads' were starting to drop because of their total dominance but with nothing to show for it.

'What's the plan Cloughie? Are we gonna change it or what?'

'I think we should give it another 10 minutes first Ross. If nothing happens, I will change a couple of the players but I'm going to keep the same formation, Albion can't get near the ball.'

With that a right wing cross was played to the feet of Gerry (Peas) Peacemore on the edge of the area, he controlled the ball with one touch before laying the ball on to Heales number 9, Roy (Sharpy) Sharp their striker who coolly slotted the ball past the Albion keeper, 2-1 and game on.

Wilko ran to the net and collected the ball, he wanted to get the ball back to the centre spot and get on with the game. The Albion keeper had other ideas and tried to hold on to the ball himself. Lots of pushing, shoving and insults were traded before the referee showed both players a yellow card.

Greg shouted over at Wilko, 'Wilko, calm down, we're back in the game, don't be getting yourself sent off'.

Wilko looked at Greg with a look of steel in his eyes and totally blanked him. Wilko was easily the best player on the park and was enjoying his role as the playmaker. He was, however, diving into most tackles and although he was going in very hard, his tackles were fair. Greg knew it was only a matter of time before one of those tackles was mis-judged and Wilko would receive another yellow card. Greg looked at the subs on the side lines and told Roger (Rog) Bast to warm up. Another sliding tackle from Wilko won him the ball. The Albion player rolled in agony as Wilko, left a little something on him. Wilko exchanged passes with Sharpy and coolly slotted the ball in the net 2-2. The Heale players were now totally running the game and focused on winning. Wilko ran past the Albion squad stood on the side lines, gave them a one fingered salute and hurled some abuse their way.

'Ref, sub' shouted Ross. All the Heale players heard him and waited with bated breath to see who the unfortunate player was to be brought off. They were all enjoying themselves and none of them wanted to be replaced.

'Wilko, Wilko' came a boyish shout. Greg was signalling at Wilko to leave the pitch.

'You're taking off Wilko?' was the response from Ross.

'He's going to get sent off, so I'm replacing him before we go down to 10 men Ross.'

'But he's our best player, I'll just calm him down Cloughie.'

Greg looked at Ross. 'Am I in charge or am I not? Don't give me a job to do and not let me finish it. I know I'm only a kid, but you asked me to do this today. If you want to take over then that's fine but don't treat me like your one of my teachers, this is not school.'

Greg couldn't quite believe that he had stood up for himself in such a manner but right now he was in his element and he wanted to see this game through.

'OK, you're in charge.'

Greg called Rog over. 'Rog, this game is ours now. I want you to sit a little deeper than what Wilko was playing. I don't want us to get caught on the break, so sit in front of the defence and keep that ball moving forward. If they haven't got the ball, they can't score.'

'Will do Cloughie.' Rog attempted to shake Wilko's hand on the exchange of subs, but Wilko was having none of it. He ran towards Ross and Greg, took off his shirt and threw it on the floor in front of them.

'I quit, I'm the best fucking player out there and you take me off, fucking ridiculous. I'll find a better club to play for, who hasn't got someone in nappies running it.'

Greg stood in silence, feeling tears in his eyes. He had never received verbal abuse like that from an adult before. He also liked Wilko and that made it even worse. As before, Greg felt an arm around his shoulders. This time though it wasn't a weak and feeble arm but a strong and powerful one. Greg looked up at his dad and managed to draw a smile.

'I don't think he liked that decision very much do you son?'

Greg smiled a bit more knowing his dad was there by his side. David Welling squeezed Greg's shoulder and returned to stand with Carol and Ray. Greg was now prowling the touchline. He was barking orders at the players, pushing them into positions when they drifted and was generally controlling the game from the side of the pitch. It was the most animated he had ever been in his life. David and Carol were witnessing something very new in their son. Sharpy had taken a very hefty tackle and was hobbling quite badly. Greg had got a message to him that there was only ten minutes left and could he last the time. A very big 'yes' was relayed back. Some great football by Heale enabled Sharpy to be put through one on one with the Albion keeper. Sharpy rounded the keeper only for his legs to be taken, foul. The referee immediately pointed to the penalty spot. The Heale players were ecstatic and rejoiced by slapping Sharpy on the back. Greg was trying his hardest to get the attention of the referee.

'REF, REF, REF. That's a blatant foul and yellow card. That's his second yellow card; he's got to go off. REF, REF REF.'

It was as if no one was listening. He hated being a kid. Greg ran onto the pitch. The ref was stood to the side waiting for the kick to occur, but Greg was having none of it. The Albion team and management were aware of Greg's interception and were also heading toward the referee. Greg reached the ref who was stood with his back to Greg. Greg approached too quickly and barged into the ref. The ref was none too pleased and turned around in anger.

'How dare you barge into me!'

'I'm sorry ref, I didn't mean to. Their keeper has already been booked and that was a deliberate foul. You must give him another yellow card? You have to send him off.'

By now most of the Albion players and officials had descended on the ref and were trying to defend their keeper and abusing Greg for trying to get one of their players sent off. The ref blew his whistle to quieten proceedings and joined his linesman at the edge of the pitch. Within a minute the referee returned to the centre spot where everyone had gathered. He first acknowledged that the penalty stood. Secondly, he was booking Greg for unsporting behaviour, he wasn't having anyone barging into him. Thirdly after taking advice from the linesman the Albion keeper was to receive a second yellow card and was being sent-off.

Greg quickly scurried away before any more abuse was fired at him leaving the ref to dish out a few more yellow cards to The Albion management for foul and abusive language. Greg noticed that Sharpy was still hobbling slightly and asked for another sub. He replaced Sharpy with a defender and pushed 'Peas' up front playing a 5-1-3-1 formation for the last five minutes. He believed that with only ten men, it wouldn't give Albion an advantage as they had already taken off a midfield player leaving them playing a 4-3-2. Sharpy was the normal penalty taker followed by Wilko.

Greg shouted to Woody. 'You take this Woody'. Woody wasn't a natural penalty taker but as captain could see why he was being asked. He gingerly placed the ball on the spot. He stepped back 5 paces and then ran toward the ball. He connected sweetly but did not angle it enough away from the replacement keeper who made a great save pushing the ball on to the post. The ball could have gone anywhere but rebounded to the feet of Woody who this time thundered the ball into the net. 3-2 to Heale. The last 6-7 minutes were played with Albion pumping long balls up field hoping for a lucky break, but it was very easily dealt with by the Heale defence. A few minutes of injury time came to an end before the referee blew for full time. Heale celebrated like they had won the FA Cup and The Albion gave them three cheers before sulking off. After some more back slapping and slurping of juice Ross gathered the team together into a huddle.

'Lads today was the best I've seen you play for years. I would love to say I'm proud of you, but it wasn't my doing. Young Cloughie here has that honour. Albion are getting promoted as league winners and you made them look ordinary today. I'm going to leave the rest of the talk to Cloughie as he deserves it.'

The players all cheered and decided to sit so they could hear what Greg was about to say.

'Not bad for beginners I suppose' and he allowed himself a little laugh. 'I'm so happy that you have all allowed me to do this today, it's a dream come true and Ross is right, you were all amazing out there.'

Lots of self-congratulations and back slapping took place before Greg carried on.

'I'm sorry to inform you all that Wilko has announced he is looking for another club and has resigned from the team.'

The players all looked straight at Wilko in shock. Wilko looked around at them all and laughed.

'I was only joking guys, I couldn't' leave you lot'.

'In that case Wilko,' carried on Greg, 'I fine you £1 for dissent, £1 for throwing your shirt on the ground for being subbed and 50 pence for being booked. I make that a total of £2.50.'

'Who fucking put you in charge?'

'Me,' shouted Ross, 'and you can all pay 50 pence fine for swearing in front of Greg's mum.

'On the subject of fines young Cloughie, I'm sure you attacked the referee and got yourself booked. That is also 50 pence fine'.

Everyone laughed at the thought of Cloughie attacking the ref.

'I'll pay his fine' shouted Wilko.

'That will take me up to £3.00. It will also pay back the abuse I gave him when I got subbed. I was in my own little world out there and I probably would have got sent off, you done well kid. Sorry for the abuse, but don't sub me again eh' and he winked and smiled at Greg.

'Right guys, training same time same place. It's the last game of the season. Let's go out on a high.'

The team slowly dispersed to their cars and made their way home or to the local pub. David and Sandra had already packed Greg's bike into the back of their car and were waiting to drive him home. Ross and his son 'Rushy' were taking down the nets and had already said their goodbyes to Greg so it was only Ray he needed to find. Greg spotted him at the far end of the pitch talking to an athletic looking man in a tracksuit. As Greg approached them the tracksuit wearing man shook Rays hand and walked off in the direction of Greg. Greg smiled as he approached but was shocked when the man stopped and held out his hand.

'Hi Greg, my names Mike', pleased to make your acquaintance'.

He held out his hand and Greg shook it weakly.

'Nice meeting you' Mike shouted as he wandered off towards the car park.

'I've just come to say goodbye Ray. Sorry I haven't spoken too much to you today, I was a little busy'.

'You've done an excellent job today Greg. Anyway, I've been with your mum and dad most of the time. I've been telling them all about your ideas and football knowledge.'

Greg hung his head not knowing how to acknowledge the praise.

'That man I was talking to and who said hello to you is a scout for Torquay United.'

'Oh, was he looking at anyone from our match, I reckon some of them could make it Ray.'

'Well he was Greg, but by the end of the game he only had his eyes on one person'.

'Who was that Ray, who was that'? Greg was excited to think that someone from the team could have the chance of getting a professional playing contract.

'It was you Greg, he was watching you'.

CHAPTER 12

School was entering the final four weeks of term and more importantly the school year. The weather was warmer, and coats had been replaced with jumpers. Greg loved the summer months as he loved the annual family summer holiday plus, he would hang around with Mike for the best part of the eight weeks.

The boy's 2nd year football team had an important game looming and one that Greg had very much hoped to be part of before his expulsion. They would be playing Plymouth Sound Comprehensive in the semi-finals of the Devon Schools Cup on Saturday. Unfortunately, they had been given an away tie, a not so favourable draw for them. Of the four teams left in the Cup, Audley were probably the least favourites. They had as many good players as the other three teams, but their tactics, training and teamwork were by far inferior.

Training was arranged for Tuesday afternoon after school and the team was to be announced at the conclusion. Greg had hoped that before his expulsion he would have been one of the two substitutes in the squad.

It was Wednesday morning and Greg was waiting outside of Miss Lamb's room for a double maths lesson. Greg spotted Mark Jenkins and Greg pretended to do an 'Ali shuffle' and feign a few boxing moves.

'Have a scrap with a school bully and you think you're hard as nails eh Welling.'

They both laughed.

'How did the training go last night? Same boring routines as usual eh, I'm surprised old Rogers even bothered showing up.'

'Well he might have Greg, but we didn't.'

'What you on about Mark, who didn't turn up?'

I take it you haven't heard pal. Pokey held a meeting straight after school last night and told us what had happened between you and old granddad Frances. He reckoned you showed real guts and balls to not name them lads as well as stand up to Frances. He also said your dad had resigned on the school of governors, but he wasn't overly sure of that. Anyway, we had a group vote and decided that if you can't play then we won't either.'

'You can't do that Mark; it's the semis of The Cup.'

'Yeh, there was a bit of arguing but Pokey got his way in the end. You should have seen Rogers face; he was fuckin' livid.'

The conversation was cut short by Miss Lamb, shepherding her class into the room. That was always a great standing joke among the kids.

Greg struggled to concentrate on any of the lesson and was pleased it was material they had already covered. It was only revision and he was quite good at maths. Why would the football team stand up for him? Most of them didn't really like him and he knew he wasn't one of the better players in the team. Word got to him that he was to report to Mr Harrison's classroom at 13.15, directly after lunch. Mr Harrison was Head of Year 2 and was one of the nicer teachers in the school. He was head of music and everybody believed he was 'gay', even though he had a wife and child. The stigma of a music teacher. Greg entered the corridor to the music rooms and looked up to see 12 boys causing quite a lot of noise and mucking about as usual. It was the year 2 football team. Greg approached them and a silence fell amongst the group.

'Look lads, I appreciate what you are doing for me but don't risk not playing on Saturday on my behalf. I would rather you play and me miss out, gods' honest lads.'

'See I told you, let's just say we made a mistake.'

'Shut the fuck up Owens, you're only worried he will take your place.'

Pikey had spoken! The door opened and Mr Harrison ushered the boys in. He spoke first, outlining the decision taken by Mr Frances. He reiterated that the decision was 'non-negotiable'.

'Sir,'

'Yes, Mr Pope.'

'If it's not negotiable, why are we here?'

'So that you can change your minds boys'.

'Well we won't, so let's go lads.'

Pikey walked out of the door quickly followed by the other eleven. The only person to stay was Greg.

'Sir, I've asked them to play but they won't listen to me, I'm sorry.'

'It's OK Welling, don't you worry, it will all get sorted out', but he wasn't so sure it would.

Greg arrived at school on Thursday morning unaware of the charades that were about to erupt. All the football team had by now informed their parents that they would probably not be playing in the Cup on Saturday because of their moral stance, or however they had put it.

Most of the fathers were avid football supporters and liked to watch their sons play football whenever possible. Although they weren't over convinced of the stance their sons had made, they sure as hell weren't going to sit back and let the game be void if they could help it. Mr Frances spent most of Thursday morning fending off phone calls from very irate parents. He tried his hardest to convince them that he was keeping up the school standards, most of the replies were that the school standards had 'disappeared years ago'. Even school Governors were getting involved. Finally, just after lunch, a small packet of crisps as his only nourishment, Mr Frances finally accepted defeat. The 2nd Year boys were the only sports team this year to have a chance of winning a trophy. For the entire world he really didn't want to back down, but parental and school governor pressure had finally got the better of him. He sent the word to Mr Rogers that Greg Welling was to be re-instated into the team immediately. He also expected success on Saturday, failure was totally unthinkable.

Saturday morning was a bit of a blur to Greg. He had to be at school for 08.30 to catch the hired school minibus to Plymouth. He was at the shop for exactly 06.00 hours. The shutters were still down. He completed his round in extra quick time and went straight home to eat some breakfast. He had no time for reading papers today. Carol had promised to drop him to school which came as a relief to Greg. The lads were all in a good mood and they all seemed happy to see Greg there. He knew that all other 12 players were better than him, but he would always be a good reliable sub if called on. The team had gathered outside the school gates as requested as the school was locked up for the weekend.

Mr Rogers appeared wearing a very outdated Admiral tracksuit that looked like it had been handed down from generations. There were a few sniggers and very quiet remarks but none that were heard by Mr Rogers himself, they weren't that stupid.

'Where's the mini-bus Sir?' shouted Pokey.

'Our usual one is in for a service so Miss Weer has a friend who has kindly lent us one for the day, she should be here any minute now.'

Smiles grew amongst the team. Miss Weer was a 22-year-old supply teacher who had landed herself a job at the school teaching English. She was very attractive and dressed fashionably. She was by far the most attractive teacher in school. Her boyfriend was a good- looking man called Darmian (Darmo). He was a farmer, working on Miss Weer's family farm and a keen sportsman. He had represented Devon youth sides in both Cricket and Rugby and was still considered an exceptional player now, even if his work did get in the way of training and matches.

A blow of a horn and a bright yellow minibus turned the corner and stopped in-front of the team. Advertised on both sides were 'Jennie's Play School'. The driver's seat was occupied by Darmo with Miss Weer sat beside him. There was an almighty sigh. Firstly, they would not be unable to openly ogle at Miss Weer as Darmo was now in attendance. Secondly, they would be turning up to the roughest school in Plymouth in a yellow play school minibus.

'You are having a fuckin' giraffe, aren't you?'

'Less of your swearing Poke.' shouted Mr Rogers.

He was though in as much shock and embarrassment as the lads.

'Hi, there,' shouted Miss Weer as she exited the now stationary bus. 'Sorry about the colour and all but we have been given the bus all day free of charge and Darmo has very kindly offered to drive us. Isn't it exciting? let's go kick some Plymouth butt.' and she stood beaming in front of the team.

Although the lads were horrified of the minibus scenario, they could not help but smile at Miss Weer's excitement and gusto. They all climbed on board and the happy yellow bus made the hour drive to Plymouth.

The roads were nice and quiet for a Saturday morning and the lads only noticed a few snide looks from overtaking vehicles. They were the biggest kids anyone had ever seen from a 'play-school'. Plymouth Sound school gates were open, and the minibus drove in and parked outside the gymnasium. The school was twenty years newer than Audley and had lots more modern equipment. News quickly spread within the Plymouth team that Audley had arrived, but the real news was their transport. All the players emerged from the gymnasium exit and stood outside laughing and poking fingers. The Audley players were provoked and were itching to get out of the bus and confront the Plymouth team, pride was at stake here. Mr Rogers was trying to calm the team down when Darmo quietly opened the driver's door and left the bus. He quickly approached the Plymouth team, his athletic figure making them look small and insignificant. After a small exchange of words, mainly from Darmo, the Plymouth players re-entered the gym.

Darmo made his way back to the van, 'Right, that's all sorted, over to you Jim.'

Mr Rogers thanked Darmo for sorting out the prior occurrence but was quite unsure as to how he managed to control a very animated group of lads so quickly.

Mr Rogers lead the team into some very posh looking changing rooms that had the word 'GIRLS' written on the door. In every away game you were put into the girls changing room, it wasn't supposed to make the players feel inferior, but it certainly did.

'I bet this is posher than Elland Roads changing room' joked Greg.

Everyone laughed apart from Pokey the only Leeds Utd fan in the team. Even he managed a smile as he returned a 'Fuck-off Welling.'

Mr Rogers had told the team to get changed and was rolling a cigarette when the Plymouth Sound football manager stormed into the changing rooms.

'Who is in charge here please?' he asked in a very concerned and authorative voice.

'That would be me.' and Mr Rogers walked over with his hand held out ready to shake it as pleasantries required.

The man ignored the hand gesture and replied, 'A word outside please.'

They both disappeared for a few moments before Mr Rogers entered again.

'I will be a few minutes gentlemen. Please stay in here and please keep out of trouble, we are in enough of it at the moment anyway.'

The boys all looked at each other mysteriously; they really didn't know what was happening. Mr Rogers appeared ten minutes later looking rather perplexed.

'Right boys, let's get down to business and talk tactics.' Greg rolled his eyes.

After the worlds' quickest team talk the players left the changing room and headed towards the football pitch. There were two football pitches and one rugby pitch. The one they would be playing on was used only for arranged matches and was of a superior standard to that of any they had played on before. They warmed up in their normal way, some boys kicking a ball to each other, some stretching and one firing a ball at Mark Jenkins. In all, they did what they wanted. Mr Rogers had named his normal team, 4 defenders 2 central midfielders, 2 wingers and 2 up front. Normally that would have beaten most teams as it was a powerful and skilful team, but Plymouth had a player who was already on Plymouth Argyles' youth set up and was destined for great things. Leo Cocker was of black African descent and his skills and power would be far too good unless they were abated. Greg knew it, if only Mr Rogers could see it too.

Greg was indeed a substitute, but he didn't mind. The others were better than him. He stood next to Mr Rogers and Miss Weer. He hadn't seen Darmo since they arrived at school. He was not allowed in the changing rooms as he wasn't a teacher or anything to do with the school.

'Where's Darmo, Miss, I haven't seen him for ages.'

'He's looking after the van Greg.'

'But he will miss the game Miss'.

'No more questions Welling.' announced Mr Rogers.

Later that day Greg overheard a slightly heated conversation between Miss Weer and Mr Rogers. She was defending Darmo for his actions earlier in the day. Evidently when he had approached the Plymouth sound players outside the gym, one of them questioned his masculinity. Having little diplomatic skills, he had offered to show all the boys how masculine he was by threatening them, suggesting he would 'knock them all out' there and then. All of them against him. His use of foul and in-appropriate language was also very much frowned upon. An agreement between Mr Rogers and the Plymouth manager was reached that Darmo should not be near the Plymouth players and he reluctantly sloped off to the confinement of the minibus and the entertainment of Miss Weers new cassette album of 'Boney M'.

It was a still morning and ideal weather for playing football. A good crowd had appeared with many of the Plymouth team's parents in attendance. Mark Jenkins parents had managed to make the trip from Torquay along with the Millers', Les the other central midfielder in the team and Mr Skullon (Richie, one of the two strikers) father.

Leo Cocker was a troubled lad who spent most of his time in and out of foster homes. He was well known to the local constabulary and would have been expelled from school if it not for his football skills. Plymouth Sound were proud of their history in the Devon Cup's, expecting years 1-5 to win it on an annual basis. They didn't like to lose.

Not long after the game had kicked off Greg recognised one of the faces within the sparse crowd; it was Mike, the man that had only introduced himself to Greg the previous Sunday. Greg excused himself to Mr Rogers exclaiming that he was getting cold and wanted to warm up. Mr Rogers flicked his hand away, Greg not knowing if that meant it was ok or not, he wasn't even sure if Mr Rogers had heard what he said. Mike was stood on the opposite side of the pitch on his own. He had written a few small notes into a tiny pocket size diary but nothing much.

Greg sidled up to him. 'Alright Mike, sorry to waste your time today but I don't think I will be playing, looks like you have wasted your journey.'

Greg was proud of what he believed was quick humour, something he hoped he had inherited from his uncles and allowed himself a small chuckle.

'Sorry to rain on your parade young Greg but you will be surprised to know that it wasn't just you I was here to have a little look at'.

They both laughed.

'Good footballer, isn't he?' as Leo once again made a great pass that cut through the Audley defence. This time the ball was met by a Plymouth forward for whom it was meant, and the ball was sweetly dispatched into the net.

'He's got a great technical ability Greg, as good as I've seen on any kid his age, all the scouts from Divisions 2-4 have had a look at him. It won't be long before the big boys in Division 1 make their way down to this part of the country.'

Greg and Mike watched as the Plymouth players first congratulated the goal scorer and then Leo. Greg noticed a rare show of character from the Audley team with Pokey clapping his hands and jeering on the team. They were being outplayed but were still in the match. Usually their heads would have dropped, and some internal bickering would already be in place.

'It's only 1-0 lads, let's keep at it' shouted Pokey.

'Who else have you come to see then' enquired Greg.

'A few names have popped up, so I thought I'd spend this morning enjoying a good school boy match. I've got the worse job in the world Greg. Do you know they even pay me to do this, sickening isn't it?'

'I'd love your job Mike.'

'You Greg? I thought you were going to be the next best thing in Management, sounds like you've got it all planned out,' and looked down at Greg with a little smile. 'Tell you what though, if you don't stop young Cocker out there you will lose this match. The reason why he is on Plymouth's books and not your Leeds or Liverpool's is because the bigger clubs aren't sure about his temperament. If you do go on to manage football teams in the future, not all the best players are the ones you need or want in the team. Today, Leo has all the time in the world to strut his stuff. When he gets heavily marked and is unable to play his way, he gets irate, then he becomes the troubled kid from the backstreets and starts fighting with the other team, his team and eventually himself. If he can't control that he will just become another excellent amateur player that slips through a very big net.'

Greg wasn't expecting such a lengthy diagnosis of the player but was pleased that Mike had the trust to tell him.

'It's fairly common knowledge amongst the scouting network, Greg but I'd appreciate it if you can keep it from your mates'.

'I won't tell a soul Mike, and thanks. I'd better get back; you never know they might need me'. Little did he know how true that would be.

As Greg was walking back towards Mr Rogers, Plymouth were awarded a free kick just left of centre outside the box. Mark was shouting orders at Tommy and Del his two central defenders as he was trying to set up his defensive wall. The referee blew his whistle and the ball floated over the top of the wall and landed in the top left-hand corner of the net. Leo cocker had scored a screamer and there was nothing Audley could do. Greg shouted encouragement from the side lines, but the Audley player's heads were dropping, and dissent was starting to show. This could turn out to be a long morning he thought. There was still 10 minutes left of the half and Greg was stood next to Mr Rogers listening to him tutting and generally slagging off his own players under his breath.

A strange lady was approaching them, and she looked decidedly disturbed. Mr Rogers and the lady moved out of earshot and talked for a few minutes. They then headed in the direction of Miss Weer whom they talked to for a further few minutes. Greg then saw the lady and Mr Rogers both head off in the direction of the school exit. Miss Weer walked over to where Greg and his fellow sub Andy were stood. She wasn't looking as bubbly as she did first thing that morning.

'Anything the problem Miss?' asked Andy.

'We could have a slight problem, but I'll let you all know in a minute. How long till half time?'

'A couple of minutes Miss.'

Greg and Andy were given some oranges and juice that had been provided by Plymouth Sound. They unwrapped the 1\4 oranges and put cups next to a large urn looking device that held the squash. The whistle blew to a very one-sided first half and the Audley team ambled their way over to where Miss Weer and the two subs were stood.

'Right boy's get some juice and oranges in you as I have some rather sad news.'

The boys quickly grabbed a cup each and faced Miss Weer.

'I'm sorry to have to inform you that Mr Rogers has had to leave. His mother has unfortunately passed away and he has had to leave with his dear sister. I really don't know the first thing about football, and he left me with no instructions to follow. I'm so very sorry.'

'Well that's us fucked then' exclaimed Pokey.

Miss Weer shot him an unapproving look but didn't follow up with any words.

'Not exactly' announced Rushy.

'You all know my Dad, right?' he looked around at them all and they all nodded back in Unisom. 'Well for the last couple of weeks, he's been taken a lot of advice from Greg' and he turned to face him. 'Before you all call me mad, Greg was in charge of Heale last Sunday and they beat Newton Albion. Dad said it was all down to Greg. We are getting our asses kicked out there and no disrespect to Miss Weer, if we don't do something we are going home with a thrashing.'

There was a lot of mumbling and shoulder movements before Pokey spoke.

'So, Greg, Ross lets you take charge of the team'.

'He did this week, yeah Pokey.'

'Fuck me, he must have banged his head in his garage or something'.

'Go on then Don Revie, do your stuff.'

Greg took a deep breath and told the players to sit down. A shout from the ref indicated 5 minutes till kick off.

'Miss Weer, I'm going to need a few more minutes than five. You couldn't go and chat with the referee, charm and stall him for just a few minutes more.'

'Greg Welling, I think that is quite dishonourable, but I'll see what I can do.'

She shot the team one of her bubbly smiles and went over to do her bit for the side and distract the ref.

'You're all playing really well. Leo Cocker is the only difference lads. Pokey, I want you and Les to man mark him. Plymouth play everything through Leo. Pokey, stick to him, niggle him, annoy him. When he stops getting the ball, he will get frustrated, trust me. Pokey you need to expect Leo to get in your face, don't retaliate mate, wind him up but don't retaliate. Les, your job is to protect Pokey, when Leo gets passed Pokey, be on him like a flash. He really won't like it. That means, we basically have no midfield. Lee and Darryl, I want you both to play upfront with Trev and Rich. You are going to have to track back when Plymouth are attacking and race up front when we are attacking. You are basically attacking full backs.'

'Attacking full backs. Am I a winger or a fucking defender Greg?'

'You're both Lee. You need to run more than you've ever run before. You're fit as fuck, just go for it. You guys are going to have to run for everything. Steve, Tommy, Del, Daz, every time you get the ball knock it long, cut out the midfield, Pokey and Les won't have time, they will be wherever Leo is and we want that ball as far away from him as possible. It won't feel right knocking the ball long but that will give us four on four and you strikers are better than their defenders. We could get caught out on the counter but it's the best plan I can think of right now.'

'Teams' shouted the ref.

The boys stood up and ran onto the pitch in a state of shock. What were they doing listening to Greg? The Plymouth Sound team strutted onto the field; the game already won. Where was the final being played, of yeah, Plainmoor, this year? Torquay United (Plainmoor), Exeter City (St James Park) and Plymouth Argyle (Home Park) all took turns in hosting the Devon Cup finals with Plainmoor this year's venue.

Plymouth kicked off expecting as easy a second half as the first. The ball was passed to Leo, Pokey and Les were on him in a flash. He evaded Pokey but was brought down by Les. The ref blew for a foul, but Greg was on the side of the pitch clapping.

'Good work lads keep him tight.'

This happened for the next ten minutes with Leo receiving the ball less and less. Leo, as expected started to get annoyed. Pokey was doing a great job at winding him up and even though Leo had threatened to give him an almighty slap after the match, he carried on. Pokey was confident that probably wouldn't happen and he could look after himself anyway, even if Leo was a big lad. The game became very scrappy with Leo's influence becoming less obvious. He still got the ball but not in positions that could hurt Audley.

He was now taking the ball from the defenders and trying killer balls instead.

Pokey and Les had noticed this and let Leo do this a few times. During an injury break they concocted a plan. Audley attacked and the ball went to the Plymouth keeper. He looked for Leo who had come deep to collect the ball. Leo was sure that he had time as his two-man markers had allowed him to collect the ball from the keeper on the last few occasions. Pokey and Les rushed at Leo, they had been standing closer than he thought. 'Man on' was shouted from players and staff of the Plymouth team and although Leo had enough skill and control to just about get the ball around Pokey. Les was too close and nicked the ball from him. He was stood near to the penalty spot with only the keeper to beat. He took a long hard look at the right-hand side of the goal and at the same time kicked the ball to the left. The keeper dove to where Les was looking, he had been sent the wrong way. This was one of Les' specialities as he loved to take penalties. Audley were ecstatic, Leo was furious. Leo stood and shouted at his players, it was their entire fault, obviously.

Greg could see the players were getting tired. Daz, the right back was stood near him.

'Daz, do us a favour, go down and pretend you're injured.'

'You what mate?'

Just do it pal, I need to speak to you guys.'

A few seconds later Daz collapsed on the floor as if he had been shot by a sniper. Greg almost laughed out loud to witness such a scene. He thought he might tell Mr Knight the drama teacher, he would be so proud.

'C'mon, Miss Weer, we are needed' and Greg grabbed her hand.

'Go and take care of Daz for me, tell him I only need a minute.'

She looked at him as if she didn't have a clue what was going on, which of course she didn't. 'I hope he's OK' she shouted.

Greg could only smile. Greg quickly got the rest of the team together.

'You're playing awesome lads. Who thinks they might not make it till the end of the ninety?'

'I'm fucked Greg, I've probably only got five to ten minutes left in me mate.'

Lee had run his arse off for the last 25 minutes and you could sense he was tiring. Greg was pleased that Lee had made the announcement; he didn't want to sub players unless he had to. Greg nodded to Daz who had made a miraculous recovery.

'Andy, warm up pal, you're going on soon. Watch how Lee is playing, you'll be replacing him.'

A few chances went missing for both teams and the game continued its scrappy affair. Plymouth still trying to play through Leo, Audley knocking the ball long at every opportunity.

Lee came over to the side of the pitch, 'I'm done Greg.'

'Ref, sub' shouted Greg.

Andy ran on to the pitch and Les walked off. He had never run so far in a match. The Audley substitution caused the Plymouth Manager to stride towards Greg and Miss Weer.

'Young lady, where is Mr Rogers?'

'I'm afraid he has had to momentarily leave us.'

'Then who is in charge of the team, rules state that at least one teacher is in charge and no outside influences are allowed'.

'Well, I'm in charge and I am being ably assisted by Master Welling here, who is also a substitute. I take it that no rules are being broken?'

'This is a very weird set-up and I don't like it'. The Plymouth Manager was getting very irate.

You probably won't like it even more now; I think we have just been awarded a penalty'. Miss Wear couldn't help smiling as she said it.

He looked across to see the referee pointing to the spot and being surrounded by Plymouth players. He was doubly disappointed as he had missed the whole incident and didn't know whether it was an incorrect or correct decision. After a few seconds the referee got control of the players and Les placed the ball on the spot. This time he looked at the left-hand side of the goal and stood with his hands on his hips. He then looked straight at the keeper and started his run up. He stroked the ball beautifully kicking it to the left-hand side, the goalkeeper diving to his right; he had 'done' him again. Audley was cock-a-hoop. They mobbed Les and ran back to their positions. Plymouth were looking for inspiration, either from Leo or their manager, they found neither. Greg was once again losing himself into his role and was the most animated person on the side lines. He was barking orders at the players and offering continued support to all of them. Mike, the Torquay scout had placed himself next to Greg. He was amazed at how much emotion and passion Greg had for the game and his team. The Plymouth manager was now also shouting and screaming at his team. He was ordering them into positions and had lost control of his emotions; he certainly didn't want a woman and a school kid getting the better of him today.

The Audley defence were now totally happy in just 'lumping' the ball up the field. Trev, Rich, Darryl and Andy were running their socks off up front and chasing every ball. The Plymouth defenders were struggling to cope and were now heavily reliant on their midfield to help them out. They looked bereft of ideas. Audley had a corner on the left side of the pitch. Daz drilled it into the penalty area. The Plymouth keeper came off his line to punch the ball but made a bad connection. The ball dropped to the feet of Les who swung his leg and hoofed the ball into the back of the net. 3-2 to Audley. They had five minutes to hang on and victory was theirs. Greg was trying his hardest to get the attention of the players, but they were too busy congratulating themselves.

'Concentrate lads,' he was shouting, 'concentrate.'

Leo was stood in the centre circle waiting to get the game started. The ball was quickly passed to him. He looked ahead and saw a gap in midfield that wouldn't normally have been there. He ran with the ball. Pokey and Les were caught unaware and were now chasing Leo rather than tackle him. He approached two oncoming defenders and feigned to shoot. With great skill he went between the two and found himself with only Mark Jenkins to beat. Mark came to meet him, but Leo had already pushed the ball on to his favoured left leg and shot past Mark, he had scored an amazing equalizer. There was great jubilation from the Plymouth team, staff and supporters. Leo had scored a 'worldy'.

Greg was ranting at the team. He could see they were all shattered and now had a few minutes to save the game. He wanted to shout instructions to them but there wasn't anything he could say or think of. All he could do was shout encouragement. Leo was desperate to get the ball and was shouting at his team to get it to him. Pokey and Les had other ideas and if they couldn't tackle him, fouled him instead. The referee warned them both that they were close to a booking but by then the game was over. The referee blew for full time. Miss Weer wasn't sure whether to be happy or sad. Greg didn't have a clue what was happening next.

'You need to go and speak to the referee Miss, I'm not sure what is happening now.'

'What do you mean Greg?'

'You're the Manager Miss. Remember, we don't have Mr Rogers.'

Miss Weer wandered over to see the referee and Greg approached the players who were lying on their backs.

'What's happening Greg. I couldn't run a bath right now'.

Les was totally done in.

'I'm not sure lads, Miss Weer is over there now talking to the ref. Whatever happens lads, you were super out there today.'

Greg felt proud as punch of his team-mates and of the way they had fought against a very good Plymouth team.

'If its extra time Greg, count me out.' Les really was out on his legs.

Miss Weer returned to where the boys were lying.

'Please bare with me lads, evidently the cup rules for a semi-final are that it goes straight to a penalty shootout. Does that make any sense?'

Greg was quick to get the team to their feet.

'Right lads, you've had an amazing game. We've got a great chance to make it to the finals. Get yourselves switched on, start stretching and keep warm, I'll find out what the format is. Pokey, get them ready'.

He was almost ordering Pokey what to do. Greg wandered over to the ref.

'Excuse me ref, what end will the penalties be taken from?'

'I've already explained that to the young lady'.

'I know ref, but she is only helping out and it would be easier if I knew.'

'Are you the Captain, son?'

'No ref, as of now I'm the Manager.'

The ref looked down at Greg and smiled, 'Course you are son.'

Greg was not at all amused.

'I suppose I'm too young, am I? Are you going to tell me or not'?

Greg felt himself getting angry and knew he sounded rude.

'Who do you think you are talking to young man?'

'I only asked you a question, Sir.'

Greg was trying not to upset the ref but he wasn't doing a good job.

'Well, like I told the young lady, the penalties will be taken from the roadside of the pitch. I will need the names of your 5 penalty takers, preferably in the next minute or two'.

He then turned his back to Greg and wandered over to the Plymouth team manager. Greg ran back to the team.

'Miss Wear is right, it's straight to penalties, no extra time.'

'Thank fuck for that' shouted Les.

'I need five volunteers right now, who's up for it?'

Les was first to put his hand up, a renewed vigour had masked his face. Pokey was quick to follow as well as Trev, Rich, Lee and Darryl. Greg looked around for Miss Weer who in her wisdom had decided to keep out of the proceedings especially as she didn't understand them.

'I need a piece of paper and pen please Miss'.

'He's after your telephone number Miss' laughed Tom Chant.

He was quite relaxed, no penalties for him to worry about. Miss Weer produced a small, pretty pink notebook with matching pen. Greg nearly snatched them without noticing the femininity of them.

He looked at the players, 'Right, Pokey first up followed by Rich, Trev, Darryl and finally Les. You all got that?'

They all nodded apart from Lee.

'Why ain't I taking em? I'm as good as anyone else!'

'You're also knackered Lee'.

'So is Les.'

'Do you want to take Les' place?'

'Course not he's our best penalty taker.'

'Sorry pal, it's what I've decided.'

'Well I'm not happy, that's all I can say.'

Greg felt a little isolated but was relieved to hear the referee shout across that he required Audley's list. He had already received Plymouths' and was enjoying a joke with their manager, they looked friends. Great, Greg thought. He ran over to the ref and handed over a scruffy list of names. He then ran back to the players.

'I really don't know much about penalty taking but I once read from an autobiography of a player that once he had picked the side he was going to shoot; he would never change his mind. Mark, I have no advice for you. You are an amazing keeper, do what you do when you practise with me cos you always save my penalties.'

'That's cos your crap at taking them' he replied and the whole team laughed.

A whistle was blown, and the referee called for the two Captains to join him. A coin was tossed, and Pokey returned to the team.

'We're going first, I won the toss.'

Both sets of teams made their way to the half-way line. The Plymouth players all seemed to know what was going on which was in stark contrast to Audley. Greg was getting asked questions from all the team, evidently, he was now the font of all knowledge although he knew about as much as them. The Plymouth keeper had placed himself in the centre of the goal and was waiting to face the first penalty.

'Over to you Pokey' shouted Greg.

Pokey walked towards the penalty area and then suddenly stopped. He had never been involved in a penalty shootout before and for one of the very first times in his short football career found himself lacking confidence. His confidence was shot a little more when the referee called him over.

'You'll want the ball young man.'

He felt his face redden and could hear laughter from the Plymouth team behind him. Pokey tried to compose himself, but the goal was now looking very small and the keeper had seemed to have grown. He took four steps back, ran up and blasted the ball. No direction, the ball flew high over the crossbar. It was probably one of the worst penalties he had or ever would take. The walk back to the team seemed to take forever and with his head down he mouthed 'sorry' before slumping onto the floor behind the team.

Mark was on his way to the 'nets'. Greg knelt beside Pokey.

'Hey mate, you might feel like shit right now, but the lad's need you now. I know they've let me take control, but they respect and trust you a million times more than they do me. You need to get back with them otherwise we are doomed.'

Pokey looked Greg straight in the eye.

'When the fuck did you become a philosopher Greg? You sound like my bleeding dad.'

Greg stood up and joined the team. They were looking a little despondent.

'C'mon Mark, you've got this.'

The players looked around and saw Pokey stood next to Greg.

'Sorry again lads, crap penalty. Hopefully you lot can pull me out of the shit.'

Leo was up for Plymouth and took his penalty with aplomb, sending Mark the wrong way. Rich, Trev and Darryl all scored with their penalties as did the Plymouth players following them. Les knew he had to score otherwise it was all over. Les as always was full of confidence. He connected with the ball as well as ever but stood in horror as the ball flew towards the goalpost. It was as if the world had stopped still as he saw the ball hit the inside of the post. The ball then flew inwards towards the centre of the goal, in the direction of the keeper. It hit the keeper on his shoulder and rolled over the line, goal. Les turned and looked towards the team. He gestured with his hands and body that it was just as he had planned, looking as cool as always. He was though, feeling ultra-lucky and relieved. All Plymouth had to do now was score and they had won. Mark hadn't really got near any of the other four penalties he had faced. In training he was always saving them and was always very confident. Today he was guessing what way he thought the player would kick rather than rely on his instinct and try to follow the ball. Greg walked towards the goal with him.

'Mate, do what you do in training, trust yourself.' Mark nodded but didn't reply.

He stood in the goalmouth and made himself look as big as possible. The player put the ball on the spot but didn't look confident. He turned, approached the ball and then placed it to Mark's right hand side. Mark watched the ball and dived to his right. He managed to get a solid hand to the ball and push it away to safety. 4-4 on penalties. Now what? Mark was celebrating with the team, but Greg had already made his way towards the ref. The Plymouth Manager and Greg both approached the ref at the same time.

'OK, it's now sudden death. We will take penalties until someone misses. The players that have already taken penalties are illegible to take any more, is that understood?'

Greg felt that this news was being directed at him as he was sure the Plymouth manager was fully versed in procedure.

'Where is your teacher young man?'

The Plymouth manager was stood, hands on hips looking decidedly unhappy.

'She's over with the team Sir, did you want to talk to her?'

'I thought she was in charge and if she is why are you here?'

'I'm just helping out Sir.'

'Where is Mr Roger's? I thought he was only away for a little bit! This is very untoward, I'm not happy.'

Greg stood for a while, not knowing what to do. He decided that re-joining the team was probably his best bet.

'Right lads, we're going to sudden death. Those that have taken penalties can't take them again. I need more volunteers.'

The raising of hands wasn't so quick this time. Lee was first to put his up, followed by Steve, Daz and Del. The only person not to volunteer was Tim; he still didn't want anything to do with penalties. Mark also offered to take a penalty if needed.

The ref called Greg over.

'Same format as before young man, your team are first up. Are you ready? We've all got things to do this afternoon?'

'We're ready ref.'

Greg shouted over to Lee.

'You're up Lee, smash that ball into the back of the net'.

Lee was still knackered but was pleased to be involved in the shoot-out. He felt confident in his own ability and was still slightly pissed off with Greg for leaving him out of the original five. Lee placed the ball on the spot and had no problem converting his kick. As he turned and celebrated the referee blew his whistle. He ordered the kick to be re-taken, the ball had evidently not been placed on the spot correctly. The Plymouth manager had complained to the referee who had upheld the complaint. Greg and the team were livid. They couldn't believe that the ref had listened to the Plymouth manager. Greg ran and faced the referee.
'How can you re-order a spot-kick? You blew the whistle to let us take the kick. Surely you would have noticed if the ball wasn't on the spot correctly. You have to let the kick stand.'

'I don't have to do anything son, my decision stands'.

'Well you're a cheat' shouted Greg in frustration.

The referee reached into his pocket and pulled out a red card. He held it in front of Greg and said in a very authorative voice, 'You are off son. I will also be reporting you to your headmaster, I resent your remark as I am certainly not a cheat. I demand you apologise at once.'

Greg just looked at the ref and turned away. The team had been watching all of this in silence and no one could really believe what was going on.

Greg walked up to the team, 'It's over to you lot now, good luck lads.'

He walked over to Miss Weer, who by now was wishing she had never got herself involved in any of this whole episode.

'Sorry Miss, I'll get my stuff from the gym and meet you at the minibus. Darmo probably needs the company anyway'.

With that he slowly walked away from the pitch and towards the gym.

Lee placed the ball on the spot. He looked at the ref, 'Is that ok ref?' The ref nodded.

'Are you sure ref'? he spat the words out.

'If you want to follow that other young man into my book, I suggest you just get on with it'.

'Yes ref, just checking'.

Lee once again faced the keeper. Pick your side and don't change it, Greg's words ringing in his ears. He ran up connected well and the ball was placed to the right of the keeper, advantage Audley. Mark ran to the goals. He was bouncing up and down and very animated. He wanted to get into the goal and look confident. He also knew that the next set of penalty takers weren't as confident as the one's prior. Watch the ball, watch the ball, believe in yourself. He was in the zone. The Plymouth player ran up to the ball. He was looking to Marks right. Was he trying to 'con' him or was it penalty nerves? Mark shuffled a little to his right but was concentrating on the ball. The ball was kicked hard and flush, to Marks right. He leapt full stretch and pushed the ball round the post. The game was over, he was the hero. He ran towards the players who in turn were running to him. There was an almighty 'bundle' as the team bonded into a mass of hysteria.

Greg had watched the final moments from outside the gymnasium. He was now dressed in his tracksuit and thought that he wouldn't be noticed. He didn't know the rules on being sent off at school, he didn't really know the rules on being sent off anywhere to tell the truth. Greg longed to join in the celebrations but didn't dare; he was probably in enough trouble as it was. Miss Weer was ecstatic and was doing a stupid jig on the side lines. Mark, Les and Richie's parents had joined her for the most part of the match and were all jumping around; it had been a superb performance by Audley. Miss Weer wandered over to where the Plymouth team were gathered. The players were understandably upset, and Leo had already returned to the changing rooms, disgusted by the loss.

'What a great game' she announced.

It was all the Plymouth manager could do to not shout back at her. He grunted and turned his back.

'How very rude' she remarked.

He turned to face her, 'Rude, rude. You come down here, your boyfriend threatens my team. Mr Rogers disappears leaving you and an upstart in charge to run the team. That same upstart also manages to get himself sent off for abusing the referee. You put two players to man mark my best player and continually foul him and you wonder why I'm rude!'

Miss Weer composed herself, smiled and sweetly replied, 'Sore loser.'

She returned to the celebrating Audley team.

Inside the gymnasium, the girls changing rooms were full of boyish banter and high spirits. With the absence of Mr Rogers and no male teacher to keep an eye on them, the boys were having a great time. It took the arrival of a Plymouth Academy teacher to calm matters down and usher the boys back to the minibus. Greg had already briefed Darmo on the outcome of the match and had received warm praise from Miss Weer on her arrival. Greg could see, and hear the lads approaching the minibus. He got out and waited for them to reach him. In one quick un-organised movement they rushed him and embraced him in a boyish scrum. It took a good minute before he could come up for air, his hair and tracksuit a crumpled mess.

'Lads, lads, quiet.' Pokey calmed the team down.

'Greg, you were awesome out there today. I don't know where or how you come up with your ideas but credit to you, you got us through today. You were the best player out there and you didn't even kick a ball.'

He put his arm around Greg, 'Well done Revie'.

Greg looked at Rushy. 'You can't be Don Revie and Brian Clough' replied Darryl

The trip back to Torquay was one of Greg's best journeys of his young life. The team were all asking him questions about his 'superior football knowledge' and were being genuinely nice to him.

'Whose autobiography was it?' asked Les.

'What you on about' replied Greg.

'You said that you had read an autobiography of a footballer who took penalties. Who was it?'

'Greg looked a little embarrassed as he replied. 'To be totally honest lads, I've never read an autobiography of anyone. You all looked really worried about the penalty shoot-out, so I just made it up'. They all laughed together, pretty much all the way back to Audley Grove.

CHAPTER 13

Greg's newfound fame was quite unnerving for him. He was used to being quite invisible at school but during this term time all that had changed. Conversations that he would have been excluded from were now an open forum with kids even asking for his opinion on matters he knew very little about. Even girls were acting differently around him, and he had it on good authority (Hazel) that some of them found him 'dishy'.

He still managed to make time for Mike who had struggled with Greg's newfound fame. Mike was used to having Greg to himself and wasn't keen on sharing him with the rest of the school year. He was however happy for Greg and didn't begrudge him his newfound popularity.

News had also got back to David and Carol. During a rare family evening meal together, Alison told her parents of Greg's recent heroics. He was asked to repeat what had happened on that fateful Saturday. They both sat in silence while Greg told his story. He left out a few facts, more out of respect to them than lying. He did however, relay most of the story to the best of his knowledge. After he had finished there was an uneasy silence as no one knew what to say. Alison was stunned as the story Greg told was even better than the one, she had heard at school. She was also receiving extra attention from some of the lads in her year who were using Greg as an excuse to talk to her. For that she was eternally grateful to him.

The yearend school discos were nearing and talk in school was all about what people were going to wear. Greg had only ever been to birthday parties before where the dress code didn't matter, you just wore what your mother put you in. He was now very conscious that he had nothing to wear to a disco. 'Ska' music was very popular, and everyone was dressing like the bands of the time: Madness, The Specials, The Selector and The Beat were just a few.

Greg was asked by his mum if he could accompany her into town on the Saturday morning. Greg had plenty of other ideas what he could be doing on Saturday morning, but Carol was quite adamant. He really didn't know why she couldn't just go with Alison; they almost always went shopping together on Saturdays. The weather was awful, it was supposed to be spring, but the rain was chucking it down. Greg trundled through the town walking slightly behind Carol and Alison. The last time he had been into town was with Mike and apart from a few select shops he had no idea of what most shops were apart from those that Carol and Alison shopped in. They stopped outside a shop that he didn't recognise and then Carol and Alison entered. Reluctantly he also entered, at least he would be getting in out of the wet. Greg immediately noticed that this shop was very modern, and all the mannequins were dressed in the most up to date clothes. Greg looked at his mum and then at Alison. He wasn't sure what was going on.

'Your sister has informed me that you are planning to go to the school disco and that if you wear the clothes that I would pick out for you, you will probably get bullied for the whole of next year. I also haven't a clue what you want or like so Alison has come along to help me get you an outfit for that disco, how does that sound?'

Greg looked around the store and for the first time in his life had a buzz for shopping. In that split second, he got why his mum and sister loved shopping so much.

'Wow, thanks mum,'

'Don't thank me Greg, thank your sister, it's her idea.'

'Thanks sis, love you.'

Alison smiled, 'C'mon bruv, let's get you kitted out.'

'Just one thing you two, your dad knows we are here. He just doesn't know how much clothes cost these days, got it?' She smiled at her two children.

'Got it' they replied in unison.

It was the last two weeks of school. The entire end of year tests had been completed and the lessons were much more relaxed. It was going to be a busy week; the football final was on Thursday afternoon and the school disco Friday night.

It was Monday lunchtime and Greg was playing football on the school playground with the normal crowd. Suddenly a large group of older kids walked through stopping them in their tracks. At the head of the gang was Wally Barnes, he was heading straight towards Greg. Greg's initial thought was to run but he just sat and watched the mob get closer. He felt sick to the pit of his stomach especially as this visit was totally unexpected. Wally stopped in front of Greg. Greg noticed that Wally was sporting two bad black eyes; probably caused by the broken nose he had been given.

'You lot, fuck off, I need a word with Welling.'

The playground emptied quickly leaving Greg alone with Wally and his gang.

'One of your footie mates paid me a visit the other day Welling. Evidently, he wasn't happy with the way I dealt with the matter of you and me brother. He said I needed to apologise to you, which I fucking won't. He also said I had to promise you that my family won't touch you again. That I can do, so you'll get no more shit off us lot. OK? Don't think about gobbing off though, my patience won't last forever, got it?'

Greg looked at Wally, he was serious.

'I've got it Wally, thanks.'

'Don't thank me Welling, thank your fucking mate.'

With that, Wally turned and walked away, followed by his flock. Greg just stood and slowly stopped shaking. Gradually the football crowd returned to the playground with everyone wanting to know what Wally had wanted. Greg kept it to himself, but he really wanted to shout it from the rooftops, something he knew wouldn't be wise. He knew Wally and his siblings would keep their promise, but he didn't want to test out their resolve.

Football training was booked for after school on Tuesday. The team all turned up on time, no-one on detention for once. There was a buzz around the changing room. Mr Jenkins had told everyone to turn up but not to get changed. He had only seen a few of the boys since their win in Plymouth and wanted to speak to them all. He entered the Gym looking very pleased for himself.

'Right lads, I'm pleased to tell you that we've been allocated the home changing room at Plainmoor, great news eh.'

The team looked at each other and sort of acknowledged that good news.

'I've decided that you don't need to do any more training. I'm going to read out the team for Thursday and go over a few tactics.'

Once again, the team looked at each other but this time they looked at Greg, they all laughed. Mr Rogers quietened the lads and announced the team, no surprises, it was the same team that beat Plymouth.

'Any news on Exeter Academy Sir? How do they play? Anyone we need to keep an eye on?'

Lots of questions fired at Mr Jenkins by Pokey.

'I really don't know a lot about them young man. If we just play to our strengths, we should be fine.'

'Is that the extent of your tactical knowledge sir?' replied Pokey.

'Watch your lip young man. We've done very well so far so I can't see any reason to change it now.'

'How are we gonna set up then Sir?' asked Pokey.

'We will set up as we always do. Now if you have no other questions, I will see you here at three o clock on Thursday.'

That week Greg and the football team felt like stars, especially to the year 2 kids. By the time 3pm came on Thursday they were all buzzing. They made their way to Plainmoor (in the normal minibus) and walked around the huge pitch while Mr Rogers and a representative of Exeter Quays Secondary Modern tossed a coin to see who would get to pick which end they wanted and who was to kick off. The ground was eerily silent, and Greg hadn't realised how big the ground looked from pitch side. He felt nervous and he wasn't even playing. The boys wandered around the pitch for a while taking in their surroundings before making their way to the changing rooms to get ready for the biggest game of football in their young lives.

The changing rooms were spotlessly clean and painted in yellow and white, the colours of Torquay United. There was an unnerving smell of ralgex or some other muscular pain spray. Mr Rogers had entered the changing rooms a few minutes before the lads and laid out the strip onto hangers and onto the benches. He sometimes detested his job but today was different, he was proud of this team but found it hard to show it, this was his best way of letting them know.

Exeter Quays were a big powerful team with no visible weaknesses. They had comfortably got to the final and even though Audley had beaten Plymouth in the semis were now favourites to win the final. A lot of their players were having trials for Exeter City FC and had high hopes of carving out a football career.

The team started to get changed and the mood quickly swung from excitable to serious. Mr Rogers wasn't big on speeches or team talks so left the lads to get changed while he went outside for a fag. Pokey was the first to speak.

'Right Greg, how do you think we should play these muppets today?'

Everyone looked at Greg expecting him to have a detailed report put together.

'I've never seen them play before Pokey. I don't know anything about them. I don't know how they will set up. All I'm good at is reading the game, you guys will have to play your normal game till half time and then I might have an idea.'

'Fuck me Greg, I thought you were a genius. It looks like it's back to the old Audley way then lads.'

Mr Rogers re-appeared after his nicotine fix. He tried his hardest to give a 'Churchilian' type speech, but it pretty much fell on death ears. The referee entered the room and gave a five-minute warning. He also laid out some ground rules about discipline, behaviour and bad language.

Walking out onto the pitch was an amazing experience. Greg didn't know if he would ever have this opportunity again, so he cherished it. He had already spotted his mum, dad, sister and Mike, who had somehow managed to get Greg's parents to pick him up. He then spotted Steve, Graham and Danny sitting a few rows behind. He didn't realise they were coming and felt proud to have such good mates. Hazel was also there with some of her friends and he sought of hoped she was there for him, even though he probably wouldn't play. There were about 200 pupils from Audley that had made the short trip across town plus about 50 kids from Exeter Quays. Along with parents, teaching staff, scouts and a few odds and sods there was about 350 people in the crowd. They made an amazing noise when the teams appeared, and both sets of teams seemed to grow a few inches in height.

Pokey got the option of heads or tails and as usual he chose tails, he liked to be different. The coin fell on a head and Exeter chose to kick toward the away end. There was no logic in this decision as all the supporters of both sides were in the seated Popular Side. Even Pokey had no idea what he would have done.

The first ten minutes were very cagey with both teams having a few long-ranged shots but with no clear-cut chances. It was a real stalemate, both playing a 4-4-2 and cancelling each other out. Rushy and Lee had hardly touched the ball and were both getting very frustrated. Pokey was having a good game as usual but apart from that mistakes and poor passes were prevalent. With 30 minutes gone Exeter got a corner. Their team was bigger than Audleys and a powering header from their centre back duly put them in front. There were a few chances for either side in the next 15 minutes but at half time it was a disappointing 1-0 to Exeter.

For the last 10 minutes of the first half Greg sat in the technical area frantically writing down notes. He had come up with a game plan but wasn't sure how he would be able to execute it, one because Mr Rogers wouldn't agree to it or two because he also had to sell it to the players.

The whistle went for the end of the half and both sets of teams made their way down into the changing rooms, such a lovely change from sitting on the side of a windy, cold pitch. Mr Rogers was waiting for the lads when they entered the room.

'Well to be perfectly honest lads, that's one of the worst halves I've seen you play. It's a good job Exeter have been as bad as you, they won't be that bad next half.'

The boys quickly tucked into the rather large orange 1/4s and orange juice which was so much nicer than they were used to. Mr Rogers approached Greg.

'I'm aware of what happened in Plymouth and your input into the team winning. I'm not sure what I can do now to help the team, have you got any ideas? I saw you scribbling notes for the last ten minutes or so.'

'I do have one idea Sir, which I think may change the way we play. If you and the team are happy, I would like to give it a go.'

Mr Rogers called for silence and explained Greg had a change of tactics.

'I really believe we can win this game lads. We just need to play to the width of the pitch. If you trust me, I want to play a tactic that Terry Venable's uses quite often but it means a different way to play again. It's like a Christmas tree, 3-5-2.

The team were still quiet which was good news. Tommy, Del and Steve, I want you to play as a back three. Tommy on the centre left and Daz centre right. Tommy you stay centre. Steve and Lee, you are both playing as wing backs. You need to bomb up and down the wings, hug the touchlines. Don't worry so much about the opposition, let them worry about you. Pokey, Les, your both in centre midfield.'

'What about me?' piped up Rushy.

'I want you to play in the middle also. Let's crowd the midfield and get hold of the ball. Get the ball down the wings. You'll also have to track back and help the defence, but you are all fit enough to do that. Trev and Rich, keep getting yourselves into the box, hopefully you will get on the end of one of the balls the lads are going to get to you. This could all go belly up lads and I've only seen this shape on telly but bare with it, it could work.'

'This isn't another one of your autobiography stories, is it pal?' joked Mark.

A nervous laugh was made by all but deep inside all the players were bricking it. They were about to play the second half of a Cup Final in front of the biggest crowd they had played in front of including friends and family and they were about to try out a new formation for the second game running. It was left to Pokey to have the final say.

'Lads, Greg pretty much got us here last week so let's go out there and try this. We are Audley after all.

Exeter Quays were already out on the pitch when Audley appeared. They were looking super confident and formed up ready for kick off. Audley lined up as if they had never played football before and Greg had to shout at Steve and Lee to move closer to the touchlines. They didn't look confident. Audley were struggling to cope with their new formation when Exeter scored their second goal. A corner came over from the left-hand side and it was headed in by their striker. Greg tried his hardest to get himself heard but his voice wasn't strong enough in this large stadium to make that much of an impact. Audley kicked off with only 5 minutes of the second half gone. They quickly adjusted to their new playing style and started creating chances of their own. It was only down to the Exeter goalkeeper why they hadn't scored. The three in midfield were now dominating possession and Steve and Lee were causing the Exeter full backs all sorts of problems. Exeter Quays made their first substitution, bringing off a striker and replacing him with a midfielder. They had hoped that would stop Audley having as much possession. Greg knew that Exeter were 'shutting up shop' and hoping to get through the game without probably scoring again. He knew that Audley needed to score soon, or it was game over. There was no point in substituting any of the team as the best players were already on the pitch.

Exeter were now getting the ball more often but were struggling to create many chances as their lone striker was being well guarded by the Audley defence. In a moment of madness, Tommy went to head the ball and handled it instead. The ref automatically blew his whistle and pointed to the penalty spot. Tommy hung his head and tried his hardest to deny his offence, but everyone had seen it and he knew himself it was a penalty. The Exeter Captain placed the ball on the spot and turned his back on Mark Jenkins. Mark was jumping up and down and hoping to get lucky. Could he be the hero again? The Exeter Captain turned and ran slowly towards the ball. He looked at the right-hand side of the goal and kicked the ball to the left. Mark watched which way the ball was travelling but it was struck so well that he could only get his fingertips to the ball. 3-0 to Exeter Quays.

The Audley players were trudging back to their positions looking totally deflated. Greg called Pokey over to the side of the pitch. Mr Rogers was sat totally unanimated in his seat; the game was lost.

'Pokey, push Tommy up front and you sit in defence. We are going to play a 3-4-3 so you basically need to get that ball into the box.'

'I can't defend Greg; I'm shit at the back.'

'Pokey, we are 3-0 down, what's the worst that can happen? Just get the ball in the box.'

Pokey quickly relayed the instructions as best he could. They kicked off and passed the ball around before 'lumping' it into the box. The 'area' was now occupied by 3 Audley strikers and 4 Exeter defenders. It was a goalmouth scramble and Tommy somehow poked his leg out and connected with the ball. It rolled into the net. The crowd who were now very quiet cheered but in a resigned way. There was only five minutes left and it was too late for a come-back. The Audley players didn't celebrate. Tommy grabbed the ball and ran back to the centre, placing the ball on the spot. Audley were ready to go. Understandably, Exeter took their time but were warned by the referee. They kicked off and tried to keep the ball. They knew that if they kept calm, the Cup was theirs. Audley won a throw-in and the ball was thrown to Pokey. He passed the ball to Lee who went on another mazy run down the wing. He went past the defender and crossed the ball into the box. Rich was unmarked on the penalty spot and coolly slotted the ball passed the keeper. The Audley fans were now a lot more animated and were causing plenty of noise in the stand. A ruckus happened in the goalmouth when Rich tried grabbing the ball to get it back in play and the goalkeeper tried holding on to it. It was all 'handbags at dawn' and the referee warned both Rich and the Exeter keeper. Greg was jumping up and down on the touchline and had now been joined by Mr Rogers. Even he was shouting encouragement at the players. The Exeter Manager was barking orders at his players who were in 'shell-shock'. Five minutes ago, they were cruising to the Trophy and now they were facing an equaliser.

'How long have we got ref?' shouted Pokey.

'Enough time to kick off young man' came the reply and blew his whistle to get the game underway.

Exeter looked edgy and none of their players looked like they wanted the ball. Les nicked the ball off an Exeter player and did a quick one-two with Rushy. He was now striding towards the goal, there wasn't a lot on, so he decided to shoot. He struck the ball with great commitment and saw it head goal wards. The ball flew past the Exeter keeper and thundered onto the goalpost. Everyone in the stadium stood still waiting to see where the ball would rebound. The ball landed at the feet of an Exeter defender who gladly booted the ball into the stands. The referee put the whistle to his lips and blew it, calling time on the game. The Exeter players were jubilant and were hugging each other in sheer ecstasy. The Audley players fell to the ground, they had worked so hard to get to this final only to fail at the last hurdle. Greg felt totally deflated until an arm appeared around his shoulder.

'Well done son, you did a good job today.' It was Mr Rogers.

Greg didn't know what to say apart from 'Thanks Sir'. He just wanted to join his team mates on the pitch.

The Trophy was awarded to the Exeter Quays Captain with the Audley players having to watch them celebrate. It was even worse listening to them celebrate in the changing room. Audley knew how Plymouth must have felt now. The atmosphere in Audleys' changing room was very low. The lads made small talk and took advantage of a hot shower, so much better than the lukewarm ones they got at school. That was at least one small bonus. They were all pretty much changed when Mr Rogers appeared.

'You all look so disappointed but I for one are so proud of you lads. You have gone from an argumentative set of individuals into a great team, and I mean team. You showed great team spirit out there today, especially at 3-0 down. Now, when you leave here in a minute, go out with your heads held high, you have nothing to be ashamed of. Just make sure that next season you get revenge on these guys and win the Cup.'

CHAPTER 14

Friday at school came and went without much drama. Greg received quite a lot of praise from his circle of friends but most of the buzz was about the up and coming school disco that night. Hazel had asked Greg if he was going and seemed quite pleased when he agreed he was.

Greg was collected from school by his mum as she had booked him in for a haircut. Normally she cut his hair, but Alison had convinced her to take Greg to a professional. The Wellswood Barber was owned by Colin, who had been cutting Gents hair for over 30 years. He also cut David Welling's hair. He didn't normally take bookings, but he was doing this as a favour to David. Greg and Carol arrived just before 4pm. Colin was waiting for them and greeted them in his normal jovial and happy way. Greg's hair was quite unkempt although he combed it often. He sat down in the large barber chair and was covered by a black gown.

'Right young man, what can I do for you?'

Greg had never been asked what type of haircut he wanted before; he usually got what he was given.

'I don't know Colin. I've never really thought about it.'

Luckily Carol was on hand to help.

'Greg is into all that new music; Madness I think he likes.' She was talking as if he wasn't there. 'Could you just give him a haircut that is modern and in fashion? Please Colin. Nothing to wacky though please.'

Colin smiled and went to work. He chatted to Greg as if he had known him all his life and made Greg feel at ease. When he had finished, he applied a small amount of hair gel and announced Greg ready for partying. He had transformed Greg's appearance with some scissors and clippers.

The school disco was being held in the gymnasium. A small 'tuck shop' had been erected where some of the teachers would be selling soft drinks and snacks. It started at 7pm and Greg had arranged to be there at that time. Unfortunately, his dad had arrived home late from work, so he arrived 30 minutes late. The music was loud, and Greg noticed that the gym was full. He didn't want to enter alone but he had no choice. Nerves started getting to him. A few weeks ago, he wouldn't have been bothered about going to the disco or not and now he was worried about going in on his own. He wasn't used to being any sort of centre of attention. He did though, feel amazing. For the first time in his life he felt like a million dollars. He was wearing a white Fred Perry polo shirt and a tapered pair of two-tone trousers. Braces were attached to his trousers and were worn over the top of his Fred Perry. He finished his look by wearing a beige Harrington Jacket. A pair of pristine white socks was covered by shiny black loafer shoes. Greg certainly looked 'the dog's bollocks'.

He wandered through the gym trying to find someone he knew. Everyone he passed seemed to stop and take a second look; it was as if no one recognised him. Greg caught sight of Hazel who was stood with a large group of her friends. He headed her way, but only to ask if she had seen any of his friends. Hazel saw Greg and her eyes widened.

'Hi Greg, you look, well you look so different, amazing even'.

Greg Blushed and thanked Hazel. 'You're looking good yourself' he managed to squeeze out of his nervous mouth.

They both stared at each other with a strange smile on their faces but not knowing what to say. Greg had known that he liked Hazel but now he really liked her, in fact Hazel was the first girl he had ever fancied. Time stood still for what seemed like an eternity but was in fact for only a few seconds. Suddenly all of Hazels friends appeared and started flirting around Greg, they hadn't realised how handsome and trendy he really was, until now. Hazel and her friends were all dressed to kill and had spent hours getting themselves ready for the night. Most of them wore jump suits which were in the height of fashion. They were all donning BIG hairstyles. Some looked like they had had overlarge rollers in their hair for weeks making their hair as full as possible. Some of the girls had "crimped" their hair which gave the impression and texture of a crinkle cut chip. Hazel had gone for a high, wide and curly perm that was pushed away from her face. She looked beautiful.

Greg loved the attention, but deep down was still a shy young man. He was trying his very hardest to act natural when in fact he was very much out of his comfort zone. Hazel was getting quite irate with her friends and although she didn't want to admit it, she was very jealous of those who were all trying to get Greg's attention. Greg caught sight of Mike and made his apologies to the girls as he left to join him. He tried to catch Hazels glance, but she was by now in a full-blown argument with two of her friends.

The disco was a success for most involved. Apart from Pokey punching someone in the toilets for pushing him everything passed off peacefully. Everyone had made a great effort to dress up and to get on with one another. The girls danced to all the pop music without being joined by the boys, dancing wasn't a boy thing. However, when a two-tone record was played the boys immediately broke into some form of dance trying to impress the girls. The boys didn't class that as dancing, they were strutting their stuff. Greg had gone to the 'Tuck Shop' to get a couple of cokes when he bumped into Hazel. He had spotted her a couple of times during the night, but they had always been in the company of a friend or two which made it impossible for him to have a quiet word with her.

'Have you had a good night Hazel?'

'Yes, thank you Greg, it's been good fun. What about you?'

'Yeah, it's better than I thought it would be. I've never danced so much in my life. Hopefully I haven't made too much of a prat of myself!'

'You've certainly got all the girls talking, you are the topic of the night, and no one can believe how good you look. You could have the pick of most of the girls in here.'

Greg could feel his face redden, embarrassed by the situation. Without thought Greg asked, 'So if I picked you what would you say?'

He regretted asking the question as soon as he had said it, but it was too late. He had never asked a girl out (even if it was in a roundabout way) before. He had also never faced rejection from a girl before and was now envisaging what that would feel like. He started to apologise when Hazel leant forward and very gently kissed him on the lips.

'I think I'd say yes' and she stepped back. Greg's smile went from ear to ear and he felt emotions that he had never felt before. The awkwardness re-appeared between them and they once again stood and stared at each other. Hazel was the first to break the silence.

'I'll see you at school on Monday Greg Welling. Have a nice weekend.'

She went to leave but Greg stopped her.

'Does that mean we are boyfriend, girlfriend?'

He sounded almost desperate in his question, but he really wanted Hazel to say yes. Hazel turned her back on Greg and started to walk off. His heart felt heavy and his emotions were in turmoil. Just as Greg was about to turn away himself, Hazel turned around, blew Greg a kiss and nodded her head in a very definite yes. Greg now had a girlfriend, although what that meant he didn't have a clue.

CHAPTER 15

Today was always one of the best days of the year for Greg. It was Saturday, but not a normal Saturday. Today was FA Cup final day. Greg completed his paper round and Carol cooked bacon rolls for the family. Greg commandeered the television in the lounge and took the chair directly in front of it. BBC and ITV provided hours of non-stop football coverage. The foreplay was often the best part of the magical day. There were special features such as the team trip on the coach, a visit to the teams hotels, clips of the teams songs (which were always pretty bad), meet the players, pitch walk by the players and also a goal of the season competition. There was even a pre-recorded clip showing the two fastest players in the League racing each other for the glory of fastest player. At 1445 the players emerged from the tunnels and appeared in front of their fans, to an amazing chorus of noise and flag waving. Today, Arsenal were playing Manchester United and there were a sea of red and white flags and scarves waving around the enormous crowd. Greg's biggest wish was to watch West Ham play in a Cup Final but for now he would enjoy this game. It was very rare to get to watch a live football match and he was in his element. The players lined up and were introduced to FA Officials and a member of the Royal Family. Finally, the whole stadium stood and sang to 'Abide with Me', a song Greg would grow to love as he grew up. The game was a great spectacle with Arsenal winning 3-2. Greg felt a tinge of jealousy watching the Arsenal Captain lift the Cup in front of 40,000 of his own fans. Greg couldn't quite get his head around why the losing fans would leave so soon after the game but, in many years, to come he would get to understand. The Arsenal players wandered around the large Wembley pitch passing both the Cup and lid among each other. It was an experience they would never forget.

After the game, Greg grabbed a football from the shed and kicked it against the back wall practicing his ball control and volleying. This also allowed Alison to take control of the television for a few hours before David and Carol watched the Saturday night classic, 'The Generation Game'.

Sunday was the final day of Heales' season. They were playing Buckland Vale who were near the bottom of the league and already relegated. Greg arrived at the Twent fields early. He felt part of the team set-up now and loved being in the company of the older men; they treated him like an adult which made him feel very grown up. Ross was putting the nets up so Greg wandered over to give him a hand. They exchanged small talk for a few minutes before Ross explained how training had gone in the week. They both agreed to play the same formation as the previous week as it had worked, and Buckland would not be aware of the tactics. The players turned up in good time and in good spirits. They loved their Sunday football but were also looking forward to a bit of time off, as were their partners and wives. Ross held the team brief and asked Greg if he wanted to add anything which he didn't.

The game was a triumph for Heale who had their best result of the season and won 9-0. Buckland couldn't get to grips with Heale's formation or skill and were totally outclassed. Greg hadn't noticed that Ray had been joined by Pete. They were having a good chat on the side lines and Greg was intrigued to know why Pete was there. After the game, Greg was invited to the end of season awards that were to take place in the Bull and Bush pub near Ross's house. It was to take place the following Sunday evening and was to be held in the rear function room. Ross had cleared it with Carol for Greg to go but he was only allowed to stay for some food and the awards presentations. Carol didn't want Greg witnessing anything untoward and had made Ross promise to look after Greg.

CHAPTER 16

Greg arrived at school ready for the final week. This week tended to be relaxed with all yearly tests now completed. The teachers were all as excited as the pupils to get into the school holidays and had also 'chilled out' somewhat.

Greg took his seat in registration and sat down next to Hazel. They both smiled at each other without talking. One of Hazel's friends blew an imaginary kiss at them both which set the whole class into raptures. Paul Barnes was making some distinctly rude gestures towards them both which they tried to ignore. They both sat and blushed awkwardly until Miss Howard eventually turned up, late as usual. The commotion died down as the register was taken. Greg slid one hand under the table as did Hazel. Their hands found each other, and they sat in silence, enjoying the secrecy and touch of one another. They arranged to meet at lunchtime for fifteen minutes. Their hearts were fluttering.

They met outside the Science block where it was always quiet. They sat on some dry grass holding hands. Greg leant over and gave Hazel a kiss. It was a little awkward as he was very inexperienced but that didn't put him off. Hazel responded and their kissing became more relaxed and comfortable. They eventually came up for air when a few pupils walked past and started making obscene remarks. Greg went to stand up as most of the remarks were aimed at Hazel, but she stopped him.

'Greg, cool down.'

'I think we are going to get a lot of this so just ignore it, If I can you can, OK?'

'Ok, but that doesn't mean I have to like It.'

They then carried on where they left off.

The rest of the week carried on the same. The fifteen-minute meet up increased daily until Thursday lunch when they spent the whole time together. They were inseparable and very much in love.

Friday was 'non uniform' day and Greg wore most of the clothes he wore to the disco, replacing his two-tone trousers with some skinny jeans. He once again felt special and walked straighter and taller than normal. He realised that looking good was good for his ego and he vowed to himself to ensure that as much as possible he would take care of his appearance. He agreed to meet up with Hazel in the following week and they had also agreed on a date at the roller-disco in Torquay. It was held every Saturday night in the Pavilions on the sea front. He didn't have permission from his parents, but he couldn't see it being a problem.

Greg walked home with Mike who was staying the night. They had a great night mucking about playing Subbuteo and Scalextric. They listened to the latest 'Top 40' hits which Alison had recorded. She had done what most teenagers did and sat in front of her cassette recorder on a Sunday afternoon pressing record when the music was on and pressing pause, trying to cut out the speaking. She had become quite good at it and had mastered the art of recording music.

Carol drove Greg to the 'Bull and Bush' and walked with him to the function room situated in the rear of the pub. Most of the players and their partners were there and she felt a slight unease, although her upbringing held her in good esteem, and she showed no fear. She caught sight of Ross and headed in his direction. The air was full of cigarette smoke and a distinct smell of Aramis aftershave who Carol couldn't work out from whom. Ross greeted them and Carol stayed and talked for a few minutes not wanting to seem rude.

'I'll pick you up at nine Greg.'

It was just gone 7 so that gave Greg two hours. Greg was introduced to all the player's girlfriends and partners who all made a fuss of him. Ray was an honoured guest and Greg managed to catch up with him just before the awards. Everyone sat down around neatly arranged round tables. A finger buffet consisting of an assortment of sandwiches, sausage rolls, vol au vents, cheese and pineapple sticks and chicken drumsticks were placed on each table. It was quite a treat. Ross had placed a small platform in the centre of the room and had also plugged in a microphone so he could be seen and heard over all the noise. Silence was ordered and Ross started by thanking everyone for attending. He introduced Ray who was the special guest. Ray was really enjoying himself and now felt part of a family once again. He was sat next to Greg who was a little miffed not to get a mention. Greg never noticed Pete arrive and he was duly ushered up to the platform alongside Ross. Ross announced that Pete owned a Newsagent Shop in Torre and would be sponsoring the team as of next year. 'Pete's Newsagents' would be emblazoned across the front of the football shirts and in return Pete would pay for the new strip plus practice and match balls and training bibs.

The team were overjoyed, and Pete announced that they would have a say in the design of the new kit. It was a good start to the night. Ross kept the theme light hearted and handed out awards for the most booked player, Steve 'The Head' Weeden, worst trainer, Pete Northcott and biggest troublemaker Wilko. They all received gifts worthy of their awards which were graciously received by the recipients and audience. The main award though was for Player of the Year. In third place was Roy 'Sharpy' Sharp who was the team's top scorer. Second place went to Rog who had a brilliant season in centre midfield and the winner went to Wilko. The votes were by the players themselves, so it was a fair result. Greg was chuffed and Wilko took his reward as well as giving a pissed but well-presented speech. After managing to get Wilko back to his seat Ross announced that he had one final piece of information for the team. At that time, he asked for 'Cloughie' to join him on stage. Greg reluctantly joined him and felt shy again. He looked around the room and saw smiling faces everywhere and within seconds had his confidence back. Ross happily relayed the story of how Greg had been watching games from the side lines to now being nick-named 'Cloughie' and being an integral part of the team make-up. He also announced that he had been with the team in some capacity for 22 years and that now was time for him to slow down a little and spend more time with his wife Laura. A silence came over the room with no-one quite sure what he was saying.

'So, what I'm proposing is this. I will still take training every Tuesday evening and I will manage the team for all away games.'

'What about the home games you tosser' shouted Gerry Peacemore.

Ross looked at the players and put his arm around Greg. I want my Assistant Manager to manage those games. Greg looked up in horror. It was fun helping but managing a team on his own, no way. There was plenty of small talk in the pub until Ross quietened them all down.

'I need to start slowing down guys, but I can't give it all up, not yet. So, I've found a solution. If any one of you doesn't think that young Cloughie here hasn't got the knowledge nor isn't the future of this club then your disillusioned. I obviously need to clear it with 'Cloughie's' parents, but I need to vote on this guy. So, all those in favour?'

Slowly but surely hands started to rise. First up was Wilkos followed by Pete and Rog. More followed until only one hand remained down, it was Woody, the Club Captain.

'All those against.'

Ross looked at Woody but he never raised his arm.

'What about you Woody, you can't abstain?'

'I'm not sure boss, he's a great kid and will go places but it's an awful lot to ask of a person so young. Is it fair on the young lad? How is he going to cope when we get beat and we take it out on him, he could be scarred for all his life'

'I don't know how he will cope Woody, let's ask him.'

All eyes focused on Greg, not for the first time in the evening. Ross handed the microphone over to Greg. Greg nervously took control of the microphone and spoke. It was going to be the first time he had heard his voice aloud.

'Thank you for having faith in me. I don't think I'm special, I just love football. If my mum and dad allow it, I would love to help manage you. Woody, I really don't know how I will react if you all shout at me, I will probably cry' and he laughed, joined by the players. 'However, I will try my hardest to find out ways to win games so that you never have to shout at me. I hope that is ok.'

Woody looked straight at Greg and gave him a nod and a thumbs up. That was it, all settled then.

Greg spent the next 45 minutes eating sausage rolls and drinking Coca-Cola. He was sat next to Ray and Pete talking mainly about football and sometimes about grown-up stuff, which he found slightly boring. Nine o'clock soon appeared and Ross waited with Greg outside until Carol turned up. They said their goodbyes and Greg got into Carols car, an Austin Mini Metro. Greg hated the car. Carol had traded in her Morris Marina, which was an even worse car than her new car. The Metro was bright green and the worst shaped car Greg had ever seen. He hated being picked up in it and wished Carol had collected him in David's Ford Granada which Greg loved. It was a big square shape and very modern. Because it was a Ghia X it was a lot quicker than the Metro and had a far more executive interior, Greg always felt rather special in his dad's car.

Greg got into the Metro.

'Did you have a good night love?'

'Yes, thanks mum, it was a great night. I think Ross is going to give you a call next week.'

'Why what did you do?'

'Oh, nothing mum! They have asked me to be the assistant manager next season.'

Carol laughed but realised Greg wasn't laughing with her.

'You're serious aren't you Greg?'

'Yes mum. They want me to manage the team for the home games at Twent. They need to know if you and dad will give your permission. Ray will be there to keep an eye on me, and I think Pete will also as he is going to sponsor the team. What do you think mum? Can I?'

'I will have to speak to your dad and see what he thinks. It's a big thing though Greg, they are asking a lot from a 14-year-old. It all depends whether your school- work suffers or not'

'It won't mum I promise. Do you think you can talk dad around?'

'I can't promise anything Greg, but your dad and I will talk to Ross and we will make a decision. You really have made a big impression on that team haven't you, young man'

CHAPTER 17

Greg loved the summer holidays. He got to spend an awful lot of it with Mike which was amazing. They had so much in common that whatever they did, they did in unisome. He also had two 'dates' set up with Hazel before he went abroad with his family. He was really taken by Hazel and enjoyed being with her. She was good fun, for a girl! The Wellings always took a family holiday every year. This year they were travelling to Spain and staying in the popular resort of Benidorm.

The Wellings' first family holidays consisted of a week somewhere within the UK. They had visited the Isle of Wight the Lake District and more recently Jersey. Last year was ten days in Majorca and this year was to be a full two weeks away. They were staying in a four-star hotel on full board and the hotel was placed right on the sea front. There were kids' clubs on site with lots of facilities for the whole family to participate. Greg loved family time; he even had a great relationship with Alison on holiday, they found each other's company quite enjoyable. The only thing he missed was not having Mike with him; they would have had such a laugh. A week into the holiday and Greg had turned a lovely bronze colour, mainly from him jumping in and out of the large family pool and being in the sun all day, he never used a towel to dry off. At dinner, David told Greg and Alison that they were all to have an early night as the family were off on a day trip and were leaving the hotel very early in the morning. The Coach was leaving at 6am and wouldn't arrive into Barcelona until 11 am. Greg's eyes lit up. The coach was going into Barcelona central and dropping off guests, which would include Carol and Alison, who were going to spend a girlie day shopping. The coach was then going to make its way to the Camp Nou where the rest of the tourists would be offered a guided tour around the home of Barcelona Football Club. Greg struggled to sleep during the night, he was so excited.

The trip to Barcelona was boring, although Greg slept at least half of it due to his broken sleep the night before. The coach arrived into Barcelona and made its way through the streets to its drop off point. The city was enormous, and Greg couldn't help notice the different style of buildings compared to those at home. He was really impressed so far and hoped the Stadium wasn't going to disappoint. It was only a short ten-minute drive before Greg could see the outline of the stadium coming into view. He was itching to get off the coach. The driver reversed into a coach lane and turned off the engine. Greg was the first off the coach and stood in awe of the great stadium. The biggest stadium he had ever been to was Portsmouth's Fratton Park. He had been taken there as a young boy by a family friend. He could still remember quite vividly the ground and had happy memories of the evening. They had sat very close to Alan Ball who was about to become Pompey's new manager. Greg only wished he could meet Alan Ball now, a World Cup Winner. He would have thousands of questions to ask him. A tour guide appeared and ushered the small group towards the stadium. He was Spanish but spoke perfect English. The group advanced towards the stadium and were blown away by the glass frontage of the stadium, it looked amazing. The tour was to last for just over 2 hours and would consist of a visit to the changing rooms, trophy room and the clubs very own Chapel. Greg tried to understand the religious thing but couldn't quite appreciate why any club would want its own 'little church'. David promised to try and explain things in more detail on the coach during their trip home. The highlight of the tour was walking out into the open stadium and viewing the near 100,000 seats, all neatly arranged in the club colours. It was the most impressive thing Greg had seen in his young life. The tour guide explained that the ground had just undergone an expansion adding VIP lounges and a new press area. A third tier was to be added to the stands in participation for the 1982 FIFA World Cup. The stadium capacity after the expansion would take the capacity up to 120,000. Greg was stood high up in the stands and thought the pitch looked small, although he knew it wasn't. His mind wandered off and he imagined himself standing on the touchline as the teams ran out in front of a raucous crowd, with himself as Manager. Greg was brought back to the real world by the tour guide informing them that the tour was nearly over. Greg asked the guide if he would mind taking a photo of himself and David. Greg had already nearly used his roll of 32 photos and according to his camera he had two left. He sidled next to his father and they put their arms around each other. Two magical snaps were taken, photographic memories Greg would never forget.

With the tour over, Greg and his dad made their way back to the coach. David Welling admitted to Greg that the stadium was the most impressive he had ever visited. He had been to Wembley and to his beloved Twickenham, but they paled into insignificance compared to what he had just visited. They both agreed that they had had a great afternoon and had enjoyed spending time together. They were more alike than they thought. After collecting the girls and sightseers from Barcelona they headed back to Benidorm. Carol and Alison had purchased a few items and they all exchanged stories of their day. David was sat next to Greg and began explaining the importance of religion to the Spanish and how Catholicism worked. He was engrossed in his own little story when he realised Greg was very quiet. The reason being was that he was fast asleep. Another day perhaps.

CHAPTER 18

With the two-week summer holiday over, Greg was pleased to be back in Torquay. He spent the majority of the next four weeks with Mike whilst also meeting up with Hazel for a kiss and cuddle. He was enjoying his meetings with Hazel more and more. The weather in Torquay was pretty decent so much of his days were spent down the beach. Greg had turned a great colour on holiday and liked to run around the sand in just his shorts, showing off his bronzed tan. His body was starting to fill out a little more and he wasn't the scrawny little kid he used to be. Mike was also very happy to go down the beach with Greg. Hazel and her friends were down there often as well and Mike liked a couple of them, he was hoping he had a chance of making their acquaintance a little better in the future.

Football training for Heale was due to begin in mid-July. Ross had asked all the players to keep up some form of training during the summer break in order to keep up their fitness levels. Some took this request quite seriously, but most didn't. They took the weekend breaks to catch up with friends, family and the local boozer. The census of opinion was that the football season was long enough as it was without having to train in the summer.

The first training session was on its normal Tuesday night and the whole squad was ordered to attend minus those away on holiday or working, which was only two of them. Greg had been given permission to attend by his parents and Carol dropped him off at the school. There were people everywhere and many faces Greg didn't recognise. He wasn't even sure if he was in the right place. Greg spotted Ross and wandered over to where he was standing.

'Hi Ross, are we sharing this training session with another team?'

'Oh, hi Cloughie. No son, this is the new squad. You have made a bit of an impact on the Sunday league scene, there are six players that have asked to join us this year plus we are taking on John Poke, Mark Jenkins and Lee Pier from your school. Most of the new players are of a good to very high standard so the competition for places will be extremely strong. We have applied to run a second team in one of the lower leagues and Pete has very kindly offered to pay for extra kit. All of the new players have heard about the way you can change tactics and formations and want to try playing in a different way, your famous son!'

Wilko ran past Greg and winked. Many of the players quickly acknowledged Greg; they were all pleased to see him.

Ross called all the players together.

'Good evening. I hope you have all had a great four weeks off and are fully refreshed. I also hope you have kept your fitness levels up cos if you haven't you will get found out these next few weeks. I'd like to welcome all the new faces here today and thank you for wanting to join our team.

There are also a few young faces here as well. Remember lads, these guys are still very young, but they've got loads of potential. Please treat them with respect and vice-versa lads. Finally, to all the new guys, I'd like to introduce you to Cloughie. For many of you, he is the reason why most of you are here today. Remember he is only fourteen so curb your language if it's aimed at him. Also remember that he is my assistant manager so what he and I say goes. If you don't like it, you know what you can do! Anything you want to add Cloughie?'

Greg was starting to get used to speaking to large groups and even though he was nervous knew what he wanted to say.

'Hi guys. I wasn't expecting to see so many new faces, well any to be honest and it's nice to see a few school mates here, so welcome to you all. I know Ross will have a training plan for the next few weeks which I believe will be mainly fitness training. Once he believes you are fit enough, I would like to try out some different training methods that the big European teams use abroad.'

'Are we gonna be Real Madrid now Cloughie'? Shouted Woody.

'Well, the way I see it Woody, if it's good enough for them I reckon it's probably good enough for us.'

Ross broke up the squad into different groups and had them all doing different exercises with a short break in between. Whilst that was going on, Greg was explaining to him about

4 a side matches and the importance of keeping the ball, looking after it like you owned it. Real Madrid believed in having the ball all the time, if you've got it the other team can't score. Lose the ball; get it back as soon as possible. Ross listened intently.

'Where did you get all this info from Cloughie?'

'I read it Ross. It was in one of my magazines'.

'Wow son. You really do love this game, don't you?'

CHAPTER 19

There was now only two weeks left of the school summer holidays and this year had been the best summer Greg had ever had. Spain, Barcelona, Mike, Hazel, the beach and football training. Wow, was life good.

Greg was still doing his morning paper round and ritual of reading the papers. He arrived at the shop as normal and in his cheery way greeted Pete. Pete was always very pleased to see Greg but today he seemed very stand-offish. Greg wasn't sure if it was something that he had done so loaded his bag and left the shop. He completed his round in the normal time and returned to the shop to read the back pages. Pete was still very quiet so as soon as Greg was done, he left. It was just gone 9am when the Wellings' doorbell rang. Greg answered it and was very surprised to see Pete stood at the door.

'Hi again Greg. Is your mother or father in?'

'They're both in Pete although dad is off to work in a little while; do you want to speak to them?'

'Could I come in Greg, there is something I need to tell you, but I would like your mum or dad present.'

Greg shouted upstairs for his mum or dad to come down. Carol came trotting down and was as surprised as Greg to see Pete stood in the hallway. They went into the lounge and sat down.

'Firstly, Greg, I'm sorry for how I was with you this morning, I'm just not good at this sort of thing'.

He looked awkward and uncomfortable as he spoke.

'Yesterday evening I had a telephone call from Ray's daughter telling me that Ray was in Torbay Hospital. I'm afraid he has had a massive heart attack.'

'He's OK, isn't he? He's still alive?' Greg's voice was shaky and quiet.

'I'm afraid Greg, he isn't awake, and they don't think he will survive past today, I'm so sorry.'

'No, that can't be right, he's really fit for an old man, he will be OK, you'll see.'

There was desperation in Greg's voice now.

'I'm so sorry Greg, he really is in a bad way, you should prepare yourself for the worst'.

That was more than enough for Greg and he ran out of the room and made his way to the safe haven that was his bedroom. Carol and Pete carried on talking for a few minutes before Pete left. Carol left Greg in his bedroom; she wasn't sure what to do or say either.

The drive to the hospital only took 10 minutes but it seemed to take forever. Greg didn't know whether he wanted the journey to last forever, so he didn't have to go or for it to be all over and he was in the hospital sat next to Ray. Carol parked in the hospital pay and display and mother and son made their way to the Intensive Care Unit. During the drive to the hospital Carol had explained to Greg the reason for intensive care in hospitals. She had tried to be as vivid as possible as her first visit to an ICU had been a very overwhelming experience and she was well beyond Greg's young age at that time. As they entered the ward, they were greeted by a chirpy nurse who had just started her shift so was still in good spirits.

'Hi, could you tell us what bed Raymond Giles is in and would it be possible to visit him?'

The nurse looked at her register. 'Are you relatives?'

'No, we are family friends.'

'Raymond is in bed number 8. I'm sure you're aware of Mr Giles condition. We ask that you only spend ten minutes with him please.'

Carol and Greg both nodded and tentatively made their way across the ward to bed number 8. No matter what Carol had told Greg, he wasn't prepared for what he saw. Ray was lying in a single bed and his arms and chest were attached to tubes and wires leading to all various types of machines and emergency equipment. He was dressed in a hospital gown and looked very thin. Greg thought that he had aged 10 years over night.

'Would you like 5 minutes on your own Greg?'

'I don't know what to say to him mum.'

'I'm sure you'll think of something love. I'll be in the family room when you're finished, OK.'

Greg sat next to Ray and stared at his friend, he looked so vulnerable but also so peaceful.

'We started football practice this week Ray. There are lots of new players, even some of my school mates are in the squad. We will have two teams this season; you'll have more matches to watch this year. Oh, and guess what? Dad and I went to the Nou Camp in Barcelona. It was amazing Ray. You should have seen the stadium. It was so big and 'all-seated. Even dad was impressed!' Greg took hold of Ray's hand. Tears were running down his cheeks.

'Please be OK Ray. I know you will be alright, you have too. I need you with me on a Sunday. I need you to stay alive, please Ray, please.'

Carol appeared at Greg's side. She was worried for her son and decided to make sure he was ok on his own. Even though he was growing up so quick she still knew he needed her support.

'Ready to go Greg?'

Greg turned around, his face awash with tears. 'Yes mum'.

Greg stood up and let go of Ray's hand. Carol put her arm around Greg and gave him a hug. She leant forward and put her hand on Rays.

'Goodbye Ray,'. Greg looked at Ray. 'See you in a few Sundays time Ray'. He meant what he said; he just didn't know if he believed it.

As Greg and Carol walked away strange noises started reverberating from one of the machines attached to Ray. Within seconds a large group of nurses and other medical staff appeared. They wearing apparatus around their necks looking totally professional but also very concerned. They quickly pulled a curtain around Ray's bed to award Ray some privacy whilst they started the unenviable job of trying to revitalise his body. Carol and Greg stood in silence while all the commotion went on around them. Carol asked Greg if he wanted to go home or stay in the family room, he chose the latter. They sat in silence for around ten minutes. Greg could see nurses buzzing around the ward and for the first time in his life, he closed his eyes and prayed to God. He had done so as a kid but only because he was asked to do so. This time was different, he wanted to save Ray, and this was his last and only option.

'Please God, don't let Ray die, he is such a nice man. He has daughters and grandchildren who love him. I love him. Please God don't let him die.'

He opened his eyes and saw Carol staring at him. She knew what he had just done but this was a private moment between Greg and his God, whoever he presumed it to be. Their silence was interrupted as the door to the room opened. A woman in her late 40's walked in looking tired and emotional. She looked as if she had been crying.

'I'm sorry for interrupting,' she apologised. 'My father has had a heart attack and they are working on him now; I don't think he will survive' she sobbed.

'Please don't apologise, you aren't interrupting anything. Is your father Ray?'

Intriguingly the lady looked at Carol.

'Yes, Ray is my dad, who are you?'

She sounded ruder than she meant but she wasn't expecting to meet anyone in the hospital. Shirley had travelled down from her home just outside of Bristol the day before and was staying at Ray's house. She was already on her way to the hospital when Ray had taken his turn for the worst. Her sister June was on holiday in Scotland and was due in Torquay the following day.

179

'My son is called Greg; he has become quite good friends with your dad. They watch football together on a Sunday morning.'

Through the pain and grief on Shirley's face appeared a smile.

'So, you're the young man my dad talks about all the time. He has really become very fond of you. Every time I call him, he talks about your time together watching football; he looks on you as a grandson. Thank you for being there for him.'

The door opened again, and an official looking man entered the room. He looked hot and sweaty and it was obvious he had been working hard. Carol and Shirley could sense what was coming but Greg was unaware.

'Do I have the daughter of Ray Giles in the room?'

'Yes, that's me' came a quivering reply.

'Would you like to go somewhere more private?' he asked.

'No thank you. We are all here for my dad. How is he? Is he still in a bad way? Can I see him?'

"Your father suffered another heart attack about 20 minutes ago. We have been working on him since that time. Unfortunately, we have not been able to resuscitate him and sadly your father has passed away. I'm so very sorry for your loss'.

Shirley collapsed into the seat behind her and wailed in distress. Greg didn't really understand what the doctor had said but was aware of the outcome especially with the hysterical emotional actions of Shirley. He stood in the middle of the room and sobbed. Carol put both her arms around him and held him tight. Caught up in the emotion, she cried with him.

CHAPTER 20

Greg put on his school trousers; they were the only black trousers he owned. His crisp white school shirt followed and then his black school shoes. School wasn't starting for another week so dressing in these clothes felt weird. A slight knock on the door was followed by his dad. David Welling dressed in his ceremonious uniform was carrying a black tie. He stood in front of Greg, lifted Greg's shirt collar and tied the black piece of cloth around Greg's neck. He gently lowered the collar and tightened the tie, straightening it at the finish. He did all this in complete silence; nothing he could say today would make Greg feel any better.

The Crematorium was only 10 minutes' drive away. David and Greg arrived in good time. The service was at midday and Ray's family weren't expecting a big turnout. Most of Ray's friends had passed away already and only a few family members from Bristol were due. There were a few cars in the car park and Greg could see Pete and a few faces that he didn't recognise. He couldn't help thinking how sad it would be to die with no friends or family in your life. Cars started to enter the car park in quick succession and Greg wandered if they were arriving for another service. He then realised that he recognised the people getting out of the cars. It was the Heale players. They were all wearing their new football tops. At least 15 of the players turned up including Ross. Ross had got in touch with the players and told them of the date of the service. It was their idea to wear the tops, they thought it would have put a smile on Ray's face. All the players acknowledged Greg and passed on their condolences to him. It was as if he was related to Ray. Greg felt like he was in a way. This was the first funeral Greg had been to and he hoped it would be the last for a long time. David Welling had volunteered to go with Greg. Carol was still quite emotional and didn't think she could control her emotions, especially when Greg became emotional as well.

The small crowd were gathered near the crematorium gardens when they were shepherded towards the main entrance doors. Greg could see some large black cars driving slowly up the private road towards the building. The first two cars stopped in front of the gathering and Ray's family got out. Greg recognised Shirley who was with her husband and children. Greg presumed the other family was Ray's other daughter. The two cars pulled away leaving space for the hearse to pull in. Greg had never seen a coffin and he could feel his lip quiver at its sight. A strong arm appeared around his shoulder; it was his dads. Greg didn't know how his dad could sense it, but he really appreciated that support. To the side of the coffin and at the rear were Wreaths with the writing 'DAD' and 'GRANDAD' in beautiful bloom. The two son-in laws emerged to the rear of the hearse followed by two elderly gentlemen. Greg later found out they were Ray's good friends. The congregation made their way into the crematorium and stood in silence. Music was playing in the background, but Greg realised it was from an era he didn't know. The four pallbearers carried the coffin passed the gathering and laid it to rest at the front of the room. An order of service was sitting on the bench and Greg picked it up. There was a picture of Ray on the front cover with him dressed in military uniform when he was in his early 20's and a picture of Ray and his late wife on the back.

The service started with the Officiate welcoming everybody to the service and saying some kind words about Ray. He then asked the congregation to stand and join in with the singing of Ray's favourite song, 'Abide with Me'. The words were on the second page in the order of service. Music began and the congregation joined in singing. It was poignant to many of the service, especially those football lovers and most sang with conviction making it all the more special. Greg felt an immense sense of pride but didn't know why. Ray's son-in-law approached the lectern. He spent the next ten minutes narrating a wonderful eulogy of Ray's life, from childhood to death. Although Greg was sad, he enjoyed listening about Ray's very colourful life, much of it unknown to him and probably most of the congregation. There was one final song, 'The Lord Is My Shepherd'. Greg didn't know the hymn so just listened to the words. It seemed that everyone else knew it and it was also sung with gusto. As the hymn neared the end, the coffin began to move. Greg hadn't realised that it was on a small conveyor belt and as it moved backwards curtains began to slide sideways until the coffin had disappeared and the plush red velvet curtains were fully drawn. Emotion overcame Greg once again. Tears welled up in his eyes which he could not prevent from dropping onto his cheeks. He was never going to see or speak to Ray ever again and that was so difficult to accept. Once again, the strong arm of his father wrapped around his shoulders. He was so pleased that his father had attended with him, it made his sorrow a little easier to bear.

The Officiate finished the service with a lovely closing speech and invited the congregation to leave. They would be walking out to one of Ray's favourite songs. Greg was unaware until today that Ray had been born in London and had followed Chelsea as a kid. He had held affection over them all his life, he just never really let people know. As the mourners stood to leave 'Blue Is the Colour' started to play through the crematorium speakers. The mood amongst the gathering lifted immediately, everyone had a smile on their face, including Greg. 'Blue Is the Colour' is the football song associated with Chelsea and was written and released in 1972 to coincide with the club's ultimately unsuccessful appearance in the League Cup Final of that year. Outside the room was a lined floral arrangement from previous funerals plus Ray's. Greg walked past and read all the ones addressed to Ray. They all had loving words, and Greg knew Ray would be sorely missed. Greg didn't know that the club had all 'chipped-in' together and purchased a wreath, all in the colours of the club. It stood out amongst the other flowers arrangements and Greg was proud to be part of such a caring small family club.

The 'Wake' was held in a function room in a local pub close to the crematorium. Most of those that attended the funeral were there as well as Greg and his dad. The adults all had an alcoholic drink in their hands and looked like they would be having a good few more before leaving. A finger buffet had been laid on and Greg tucked into sandwiches, sausage rolls and pastry things called vol-au-vents that were very nice. Shirley went over to Greg and introduced her sister June. They stood and spoke for a long time about Ray which Greg enjoyed. The two sisters made their excuses and re-joined their families. Greg asked his dad if they could go home, it had been a long day and he was mentally drained. Greg went over to where the team were sitting. They were in good spirits and were having a good laugh. Greg wasn't sure if it was being disrespectful to Ray and his family or not. David Welling had already explained the idea and reasoning behind the wake but getting drunk didn't sit too well in Greg's eyes. The team all said goodbye to Greg and wished him well, they knew how 'cut-up' he was.

Greg skipped dinner, the buffet had filled him up and he really didn't want to socialise with anyone. He was lying on his bed reading an old Shoot Annual when a knock came, his dad came straight in.

'I'm so very proud of you son. Going to any funeral is difficult but your first one is always the hardest, especially if its someone you are close to. You were very grown up today.'

'I cried through most of it dad' he laughed.

'You cried because you cared, and Ray was your friend. Just because you're a man it doesn't mean you can't cry.'

'But I've never seen you cry dad.'

'Just because you've never seen me cry Greg, doesn't mean I never have'.

David Welling sat next to Greg and for the third time that day gave Greg a hug, but this time with two arms. Greg responded and for a few seconds they held each other close. David broke the embrace, stood up and started to walk out of the room. He turned and looked straight at Greg.

'I love you very much son.'

'I love you too dad.'

CHAPTER 21

Going back to school wasn't a big deal to Greg. He had enjoyed a great 6 weeks or so and had crammed so much into such a short space of time. Going back to school meant that he could see more of Hazel, something he still really enjoyed. The professional football league season had already begun so all the talk in school between the boys was who was going to win what, the early 'bets' were that Liverpool were 'odds-on' to win everything.

The school football season wasn't due to start until January. The Rugby season was due to start as soon as the school year started but this was of little interest to Greg. The school football season was always a short season with lots of games played in a very short succession. Last year this annoyed Greg as he couldn't wait for the school season to start but now, he was very pleased, it gave him more time to concentrate on Heale Athletic.

The first day back to school was always a fun time. Greg always used to wear exactly what his mother had provided and never thought anything different. This year was different. For the first time he had volunteered to go school uniform shopping with his mum. He picked out black trousers that were a good length and not too wide in the leg, he couldn't stand flared trousers. His school shoes were black loafers, something his mum wasn't keen on him wearing but were cheaper than the 'hush puppies' she normally bought him. He found some white shirts that fitted him properly and a grey jumper that he thought looked pretty cool. The school policy on uniform was quite relaxed so Greg knew that although all the other kids would be wearing black jumpers, he would get away with wearing a grey one. He also liked the idea that he would stand out in a crowd, something he was feeling more confident about as time went on. Greg had been taught at an early age to tie knots and he was good at making his school tie the right length. This year he had decided to tie the thin end of the tie around the thick piece and tuck the remaining thick piece inside his shirt leaving a tiny knot and a thin tie. Greg's final 'piece de resistance' was his new coat. It was in fact a Donkey Jacket that he had purchased in an Army and Navy Store. This purchase was by far his favourite but also the most difficult to persuade his parents to buy. They knew Greg needed a new coat and would have much preferred him to wear the more normal 'snorkel parkers' that many of the kids wore. They couldn't understand why Greg would want to wear a coat that council workers wore. They didn't understand fashion, that was all.

Greg strutted into school like a peacock showing off to the peahen. He had been to see Colin, The Wellswood Barber on the Saturday before and had a very stylish cut that he thought made him look good. Even though he was going to school he felt that he was going to the disco on the last day of term.

Greg's new form teacher was Mr Pimm. He was recognised as one of the better and nicer teachers in the school. His subject was History which he somehow made interesting. Greg was already aware that Hazel was not in Mr Pimm's form which he was totally pissed about. He used to love his little chats with her in the morning and holding her soft hand under the desk. He was intrigued who he was going to be put next to this year, especially as he didn't get to pick. Greg entered his classroom and looked for his name on a desk. Written in big black bold text on a small piece of card was the name G WELLING. Next to it was a card with the name T MASON. Who was this T Mason, he had never heard of him. Greg sat down to his empty desk. The other kids all sat down at their desks being very noisy as ever. A few minutes later Mr Pimm entered with a very, pretty young lady by his side. He pointed to the desk where Greg was sitting, and she walked over and sat down. Greg smiled at her and she responded with her very own smile. Greg could see all the other kids in the class staring at her and knew she must have been feeling very awkward.

'Hi, my name's Greg, what's yours?'

'I'm Teresa, everyone calls me Tre. Me and my family have moved down from Bristol. We have bought a B&B in Torquay and have been here for about 5 weeks.'

Greg had never spoke or met anyone from Bristol before and couldn't help but smile at her 'funny' accent. For the next 15 minutes Tre asked as many questions as she could about the school, the kids in school, leisure activities, boys and anything she could in between Mr Pimm explaining what was going to happen for the term. After putting their timetables together, they both realised that they were in quite a few classes together. Greg had promised to show her to all the classes that they were in together and to point out the friendlier girls who would be able to show her around when he wasn't able to. During all this, Greg forgot to mention that he had a girlfriend.

The next lesson for Greg was maths, which was also Tre's, Hazel's and Mikes. Greg volunteered to walk Tre to the class and show her some of the school at the same time which she quickly accepted. Greg felt very comfortable talking to girls now, he was no longer awkward, and tongue tied like he used to be. They arrived at the classroom having taken a slight de-tour around the school. Hazel was stood outside the class with her friends. She was hoping to get a few minutes with Greg before they went in. The look on her face when she saw Greg and Tre together was priceless. Greg walked towards Hazel, happy to see her.

'Hi Hazel. Meet Tre. She has just moved to Torquay from Bristol, so I was just showing her around'.

Hazel looked at the pretty girl stood next to Greg and managed to raise the falsest smile she could. At that time the bell rang, and the class entered the room. Once again, small cards with names on them were placed on desks. Greg was placed next to Mike, which was a bonus on one point, they could have a laugh but on the other they knew that they wouldn't learn too much. Tre was placed next to Hazel. Hazel was one of the nicest girls in the year and was put next to Tre to make her feel welcome. That would have been a great idea if Greg wasn't Hazel's boyfriend, and if she wasn't jealous.

CHAPTER 22

Greg had attended Heale's last training session the week before. He had the squad playing four-a-side and one touch football. Ross had introduced the same session the week before that and had limited success in implementing it. Greg knew exactly how he wanted the session to go and got the very best out of all the players. They enjoyed playing football and Greg's ideas about possession football.

The first game of the season was a home tie with Dartmouth Academy. They had been promoted the season before and had some very promising players. Ross and Greg turned up at the fields half an hour before the player's, they had a difficult team selection to make. Ross had offered to attend the first home game to support Greg and then home games were all Greg's.

Two of the new players Jason (Jase) Myles and Ginge Maine had shown great skill and presence at training and had come with glowing tributes. Jase was a quality central defender and would make a great central partnership with Steve 'The Head'. He was 'two-footed' and comfortable on either the left or right of defence. He was a tremendous acquisition. Ginge was a tricky winger who had an abundance of tricks and skill. He had two problems though, firstly he would beat a player, then he would go back and beat him again. Secondly, he was very slight. He would easily get knocked off the ball and unless the referee was sympathetic to wingers could easily get lost in a game. On his day though, he was a match winner. Greg had decided to start with a solid 4-1-3-1-1, Greg knew it was a bit defensive but didn't want to go 'gung-ho from the off. Pete Northcott was in goal. Neil Fielld and Graham Woolcot were left and right defence with The Head and Terry in the centre. Sitting in front of them and protecting the defence was Rog. Ahead of him in a 3-man midfield were Wilko, Peas and Woody. Greg had given

Ginge 'license to roam' in front of the midfield leaving Sharpy up front.

The players arrived in good time. Greg had implemented a new warm-up routine where the players would be in small sections doing either warm-up exercises or a small keep ball exercise. He had witnessed both Arsenal and Man Utd doing this before the FA Cup Final and really liked what he saw. He had been given permission to record the game on the family's new VHF Video Recorder. These fantastic machines had only just appeared in the electrical stores and Greg was over the moon when his dad arrived home with one that he had purchased from Dixon's electrical store. Not only could you record programmes, but you could watch videos instead. Greg had already hired out many football videos and had scribbled down reams of notes. He also recorded MOTD and played it back in slow motion. He had also spent many hours watching silly movies with Mike as well.

This year every player had been given a full strip, home and away. They were to keep the strips for the season and with a change from last year were to wash and dry them themselves. Players would get fined for turning up in dirty or untidy kit. After the players had finished warming up, Greg gave his first team talk of the season. He reminded them of how the last season had ended and what he expected from the team this year, PROMOTION.

It was all about keeping the ball and getting it back when they lost it. The team lined up in their formation, this time they looked comfortable with the shape. They all looked very smart in their new kit. Pete was stood close by and looked proud of the new kit and that his little shop was now a small advertising model. He hoped that it might bring in some extra trade; he would need it to pay for the outlay of the strip. Greg had also come up with another idea a few weeks earlier. He had asked Ross that if a player was either injured or suspended for a match, they go and watch the next team on Heale's fixture list. Greg's idea was that if he had information on how the team played and what positions their best and worse players played, he would have an even better idea of how to beat them. Ross wasn't sure if that was ethical. Greg didn't really know what that meant; he just believed it to be very smart. After some thought Ross agreed and this week Mark Jenkins had volunteered. Heale's next opponents were Buckland Utd, a quality team who had been relegated from the Premier Division last year. It had been 15 years since Heale had been in the top division and this was their main mission every year. Buckland were playing away to Chelston Vale, only a stone's throw away from Marks house. He had been given a good brief by Greg and was aware of his duties.

Heale played a good first half and deserved to be 2-0 up at half time. They had 70% of possession and kept the ball well but lacked penetration. The players were pleased with their contribution and were all smiles walking off the pitch. They grabbed some juice and oranges and sat down. Greg wandered over.

'Right guys, well played out there. I'm going to make a few changes for the second half. I want us to create more chances, be a little more ruthless.'

'But were winning easily and are playing well.'

'I know Wilko, but I just don't want to win, I want to win big. We're going to switch to a 3-5-2 formation, we've played it before and practised it a lot in training. Head, Jase and Tel (Terry Prentis) you're going to play as a back three. Rog, as before sit in and protect. Wilko and Woody in front. Peas and Ging on the wings. Sharpy up front with French (Ben Mustard). Unfortunately, Neil you're off for this half. You played really well.'

'That's OK Greg'.

Heale took the second half by storm. Wilko and Woody ran the midfield, Peas and Ginge terrorised the wings and Sharpy scored a second half hat-trick to go with his two goals in the first half. Add to that a Rog penalty and a Wilko free-kick, 7-0 was a great start to the campaign. Greg and Ross were packing up the nets and balls when the Manager of Dartmouth approached.

'Your guys were amazing out there today.'

He was looking straight at Ross when talking.

'That's one of the best performances I've ever seen by a Sunday League team. I'm sure you'll take this League by storm.'

'Thanks, but it's only the first game of the season, I'm sure they'll be some tough times ahead.'

The Dartmouth Manager looked straight at Greg; he wasn't expecting the reply to come from him. Ross continued to pack the nets quite happy to let Greg do the talking.

'Sorry son, I was talking to your dad.'

Ross stopped what he was doing and looked up.

'Oh, he's not my son, he's my assistant manager. In fact, he made all the decisions today, I'm just here as it's the first game of the season.'

The Dartmouth managers' face reddened somewhat before making his apologies and leaving. Greg and Ross both laughed. They knew that their arrangement was totally unique.

Mark and Greg had arranged to meet on Monday morning before school began. Mark had written lots of notes and had a detailed dossier on the best players and their positions. He had enjoyed compiling this but found it difficult to watch so many players and concentrate on the game. It was at this time he realised that Greg had a special talent. He pointed out to Greg that Buckland were a very good team and had won the match 5-0. They had few weaknesses and were managed by Tommy Atkins. Tommy was renowned in the local Sunday Football leagues. He was in his late sixties and had managed many clubs winning lots of Trophies along the way. He had come out of retirement this year to help

Buckland get promoted back into Division 1. They were known for being one of the best teams in the area and hadn't been relegated for over 30 years until last year. Last year had turned out to be a disaster for them and after losing their last 3 games were relegated on the last day of the season. They were hoping the skill, experience and knowledge of Tommy would get them promoted at the first attempt. They were indeed strong favourites to be promoted as champions. Mark tried to explain that although they seemed to play a steady 4-4-2 formation, the second striker would drop deep into midfield if needed when the opposing team were attacking leaving just one up front. Their strengths were counter attacking at pace catching the opposing team off guard on most occasions. Four of their five goals had come that way.

Greg thanked Mark for his hard work and hoped to see him at training the following night if he was allowed. Greg made his way to class and sat next to Tre. She had made some new friends during the week and had met up with them at the weekend. She was a lot more relaxed than the previous week. They both enjoyed catching up about each other's weekend and were genuinely interested in each other's stories. Greg really liked Tre, just like Hazel, she was good fun. He couldn't see why Hazel and Tre didn't like each other. He had an awful lot to learn about the female species.

Greg had come to a compromise with his parents over Heales football training. He could attend training which was from 7-9 pm on Tuesdays' but he had to have an earlier night on Saturdays. Greg was OK with this as he could set the video recorder, so it recorded all of MOTD. He could then watch it when he returned home from his paper-round on Sunday morning. Alison never got out of bed before 10 so he had ample time to watch it before heading off to football. All the players had turned up for practice and Greg spent the first 10 minutes going over the previous game, which was 90% positive and the other 10% was based on constructive criticism. The next 10 minutes was based on the brief given by Mark. Greg explained about the idea of a scout at every match and the purpose for it. He explained how Buckland set up and how they used their speed to counter attack. Whilst Greg was doing this, Ross was setting up cones and goals for the training session ahead.

The session was very constructive. Once again 4 and 5 a side games had taken place plus attacking and defending scenarios set up by Ross. The final 30 minutes consisted of defending against counter attacking teams and attacking such teams. The player's commitment was great, and everyone was aware of their roles within the team. Greg couldn't wait to pick his wits against old Tommie.

CHAPTER 23

It was 'The Gulls' second home match of the season. Greg had missed the opening home game of Torquay United's season to illness; he had picked up a stomach bug and was afraid to go to the match in case he unwillingly shit himself during the game. He knew it would have been an awfully long walk home with brown stained trousers.

He met up with Steve, Danny and Graham near the ground and they all grabbed a burger and coke outside the stadium (it was cheaper than inside). Greg hadn't seen any of them since before the summer holidays, so they had lots to catch up on. They were all engrossed in Greg's story of the Nou Camp and its magical aurora. Greg also told them about Hazel, Ray and Heale. He didn't realise what a full life he had until he told his mates. The three boys also told Greg of their summer holidays but none of it was as exciting as Greg's. Torquay were playing Crewe Alexander, recently relegated from Division 3 and now in the depths of Division 4 with 'The Gulls'. Torquay had won their opening home league game and drawn their last two away. It was a good start and at least they were unbeaten. It was still only early September and the sun was still high in the air making it feel like an extended summer. The boys appreciated the nice weather as they knew that later in the season, they would be stood in the same spot wearing boots, gloves and scarves whilst stamping their feet to keep warm. There was a very good crowd even though the travelling Crewe contingency was quite scarce. It was over a four-hour drive and a long way even for the most committed of fans. The game was an edgy affair with little action at either end. The hot weather seemed to be draining both sets of players. Greg hoped it wouldn't be this hot tomorrow. The four boys huddled around Steve's radio. Greg was worried as his beloved West Ham was playing away to Liverpool, the League and European Champions. Both teams had started the season well, but Steve and Danny were a lot more optimistic than he was, even though he didn't let them know. Aston Villa were at home to QPR who were bottom of the league. Graham was confident of an easy victory. The commentary game was the North London derby between Arsenal and Spurs which was presently at 2-2 and a real 'hum-dinger'. The boys were certainly enjoying that match more than the live show in front of them. The radio signal had been poor, so the boys were struggling to catch the scores. It was half time at all the grounds, and they were transmitted to Anfield where a shock result was on the cards, Liverpool 0 West Ham 1. Evidently it was all Liverpool, but West Ham had scored a Julian Dicks penalty on the stroke of half time. Greg was beyond jubilant and started to give Steve and Danny lots of boyish grief. Danny was also 'cock-a-hoop' as The Villains were 2-0 up. The four lads hoped that Bruce Richo would make some changes at half time, the team needed freshening up. Both teams re-appeared, Crewe had brought on a wide player for a central midfielder whilst 'The Gulls' had no changes. The crowd tried their hardest to liven up the Torquay team, but the second half was just as flat. Crewe got on top of the game and before Bruce decided to make changes were already 2-0 to the good. Torquay pulled a goal back in the final ten minutes, but it was too little too late. To make matters worse, Steve's radio had packed up; he had forgotten to replace the batteries. A 'schoolboy error' he was rudely reminded by the others.

The crowd had started to disperse with a few minutes to go but as always, the lads stayed to the end. This way they always got to hear the full time results over the stadiums loudspeaker system. The referee blew his whistle and

Torquay had put in a miserable performance and lost their first game of the season 2-1. It wasn't long before the full-time results started coming through. Spurs had beaten Arsenal 4-3 whilst QPR had come back to draw 2-2, Graham was livid. Greg, Steve and Danny waited for all the other results of four leagues plus the top Scottish League. Evidently there had been an incident at Anfield that had delayed the game for 5 minutes.

'We now have the final score from Anfield, Liverpool 5 West Ham 2.'

Kenny Dalglish had come on as a second half substitute and helped himself to an 18-minute hat-trick. Steve and Danny couldn't help re-paying Greg all his wonderful banter that he had so willingly given out just over 45 minutes earlier. Between them they pretty much destroyed him on their walk home. Oh, what fun being a West Ham fan, not. Why couldn't his family have come from Liverpool? Life would have been so much simpler.

Although the arrangement was for Greg to only attend home matches he desperately wanted to go to as many games as possible. His mum and dad had agreed to monitor his schoolwork every fortnight and if this wasn't suffering, he could attend the games. It was also under the proviso that Ross collected and returned him home. Greg loved his role within the club and felt at ease around the players, they all respected what he wanted to do. Ross collected Greg and they made their way to Buckland. Buckland was a small hamlet in Dartmoor, and it took about 45 minutes to get there. The weather was once again sunny and hot, and the two managers spoke about fitness levels within the squad. They had already decided on the formation and tactics but on reflection decided to drop Rog and replace him with another of the newer players, Steve (Horny) Hornbrook. Horny was only 21 and a lot fitter than Rog. Rog was a great player, but the two managers wanted speed and fitness, something Rog was working on. Rog was one of the oldest players in the squad and was never the fittest. He realised, now more than ever that if he wanted to stay in the team his skill alone wasn't enough. He was 'pounding the streets' in the evenings, something he had never done. He wanted to be with the club if and when it got promoted. He had been with Heale since his last year at school and had a long-term love of the club.

When Ross and Greg arrived at Buckland, they both agreed how nice it would be to play at a proper ground. Most of the clubs in the top Sunday leagues had their own little ground and social club. Heale used to have its own ground and social club but due to financial difficulties had to release their ownership. Their old ground was now used by a local Rugby Club, which was also struggling financially. There had been talk of Heale re-leasing the pitch and social club for the summer and the Rugby Club using it in the winter meaning income all year-round. The small social club needed some TLC, but it was big enough for purpose. Apart from promotion, this was the next big step for the club, getting back its full identity.

Buckland was a nice little ground with a smart social club and small but clean changing rooms. Tommy Atkins was already at the ground with some of his players. Greg and Ross walked over and introduced themselves.

'Hello, Tommy good to see you again.'

'Hello Ross, likewise.'

Ross and Tommy had crossed paths on a few occasions before, mainly in cup competitions with Tommy's teams always coming out on top.

'And who is this young man, your son?'

'No Tommy, this young man is called Greg; he is now the assistant manager of the club.'

'Yeah, course he is' laughed Tommy, and he walked away.

'Catch up with you later Ross, and good luck; your boys will need it today.' If that wasn't enough motivation for Ross and Greg, then nothing was.

The Heale players turned up at different times, all in good spirits. They were ushered into the small away changing rooms ready for a brief. Whilst getting changed Ross announced the team sheet. There were a few strange looks when Rog was announced as a sub, but no one said anything. Greg re-explained the formation and how he wanted the team to play. He reminded the team of the training they had practiced on Tuesday evening and the need for patience, especially on such a hot day. Greg's plan was to 'turn the tide' on Buckland. Although Heale's new philosophy was to look after the ball and get it back as soon as possible when lost, this was not the case today. He wanted Buckland to have the ball and Heale were going to get them on the break. He had the team set up to look attacking hoping to throw Tommy off-guard. The referee blew his whistle dead on noon and the match began. Buckland applied pressure and Heale allowed them. Heale were very disciplined in defence and with ten minutes gone had made a steady start. Buckland attacked but this time one of the central defenders pushed too far up field. Woody stole the ball and pushed hard and fast up field. The Heale players pushed forward in unison using their new found tactics and had opened the scoring with a neat finish by Sharpy. Whilst Heale celebrated Buckland looked shell-shocked.   Tommy was shouting instructions from the other side of the pitch. Greg had decided early that he wanted to be far away from the opposing manager. He wasn't particularly bothered by what they were saying and planning, he didn't want them to know what he was saying and planning. Greg and Ross shouted encouragement from their side of the pitch.

Buckland carried on applying pressure and Heale carried on defending well. Buckland had a few half-chances to score before getting caught once again on another quick break by Heale. Heale had already caused numerous problems on the break and now they found themselves 2-0 down. This time 'Horny' was on the end of a precise through ball by Wilko and he had scored on his debut. Tommy was going mad at his defence but, they were just getting caught by swift counter attacks. The referee blew his whistle for half time and both sets of players made their way to their respective sides of the pitch. Normally the changing rooms would have been used but as the weather was so nice, they decided to make the most of it and sit outside.

'Awesome performance lads. That's not how I'd like us to play football, but you were all totally professional in that half. I'm not going to change anything for now but I'm sure they will. Their manager has been around a very long time and will have a trick up his sleeve. If I can spot it and I need to change the shape and players I will. Otherwise it will be the same as before.'

'Thanks for that Cloughie, but I'm in charge today remember' remarked Ross.

'Oh yes sorry Ross, I got a bit carried away.'

'Well Ross, what are we going to do for the second half?' asked Woody, he looked a bit worried that both Ross and Greg may have different ideas.

'Oh, exactly same as what Cloughie said' and he laughed out loud. 'He's the tactical genius; I just carry the water bottles.'

The team all laughed and laid back in the sun for a few minutes deserved rest. Greg looked across at the Buckland team. Tommy was very animated in his actions and Greg could hear most of what he was shouting. Indiscipline and poor ball control were what he was most upset about.

As the teams lined up for the second half Greg tried to analyse Buckland's formation. It looked as if they had sacrificed a midfielder for a striker. Greg presumed that they were planning on giving up some possession and try and counter attack, like Heale had done to them. Greg asked Rog to warm up. After a quick 5-minute stretch and run Rog was back next to Greg. Greg passed on instructions to Rog, he in turn was to pass them onto Woody. This was all done in a slick way that had also been practiced in training. Rog came on for 'French' and both teams pretty much cancelled each other out for the rest of the game. Tommy used up the other one substitute that he was allowed but to little effect. At the final whistle the score remained 2-0. Ross and Greg wandered over to the other side of the pitch towards Tommy. Ross held out his hand which was weakly shaken by Tommy.

'You boys did a good job on us today, shame you play boring football.'

'Oh, we play great football, we just played a different way today. Next week will be different again that's for sure. It was nice meeting you Mr Atkins.'

Greg put out his hand to Tommy. Tommy was taken aback by the young man's brazen attitude and had no intention of shaking his tiny scrawny hand.

'I look forward to beating you guys next time we meet' was his only reply.

Greg removed his hand and turned away from Tommy. 'Good luck with that' he said as he and Ross went to join the celebrating team.

CHAPTER 24

It was now 8 weeks later, and things were going well for Greg. He was excelling in his schoolwork without having to work too hard. This was great as he didn't want to be known as a 'swat' or class creep so he took in as much information as he could and completed his homework as soon as it was delivered. He had realised that he could digest information easily and had the ability to hold on to it. This he used to his advantage at both school and with his football. He and Hazel were still together but they were seeing less and less of each other. Greg was totally wrapped up in his football which took up Tuesday nights, Saturday afternoons and most of Sunday. He and Mike still spent a lot of time together leaving an afternoon here and there plus time at school. Hazel was maturing into a beautiful young woman and was after a bit more in a relationship than what she was getting. Greg knew this but at his time in life couldn't accommodate her.

Heale were unbeaten in the league after 8 games and were playing great football. Their last match was a 4-2 win over Starcross Utd. The game had been played away at Starcross and although they had conceded two late goals had been well worth their win. This afternoon was a Devon Cup match and they had a home game against Brixham AFC. Brixham were in Division 1 and lying in third place, only 3 points behind the leaders.

Sometimes the Twent pitches were all occupied meaning that there were a lot of people hanging around the vast area. On this occasion though only one other game was taking place. It had only just kicked-off and had a handful of supporters, mainly family watching. It was still 15 minutes to kick off and there were people stood around the pitch that Greg or Ross had never seen before. The players had just started their now very refined warm-up when Greg spotted one of the new faces in the crowd; it was Mike, The Gulls scout. He was stood next to a gentleman that Greg recognised but didn't know where from. Greg knew he had a few minutes to spare so he quickly ran across the pitch.

'Hello young man, I wasn't sure you would recognise me again, now your famous'.

'Hello Mike, have you come to watch a decent game for once?'

Greg was so pleased with his come-back that he laughed at his own joke. Both men joined in the laughter before the other man spoke.

'Cheeky fucker.'

'Pleased to meet you too, I'm Greg but everyone calls me Cloughie.'

'Mike's told me all about you Cloughie, thought I'd come and take a look myself.'

'Yeah, you and a load of others, are they all with you?'

'No, I think there is a fair few from Brixham and I do believe some are from the local papers. Heale are starting to get headlines.'

It was just then that Greg realised where he recognised the man from. Greg saw him every other Saturday sat in the dug-out next to Bruce Ricoh. He was The Gulls assistant manager and his name was Jay Pinner.

'Got to rush, nice meeting you Mr Pinner. See you later Mike', and with that he ran back across the pitch to where the team were finishing their warm-up.

Greg had asked 'Taff' to watch Brixham in their last match. They were big and strong and had no apparent weaknesses. Taff was an ever present at training but never got a game. He was a defender but was well below the standard needed to play for Heale. Nonetheless he was extremely liked amongst the squad and loved being part of the set-up. He was always willing to do anything for the good and benefit of Heale. The only thing that he could find as a weakness was that they didn't look as fit as they should. He wasn't sure if this was a big point, but it was the only real thing he could come up with. It was at least something Greg could use to his advantage. They played a regular 4-4-2 and didn't deviate that much from it during the game. Greg had decided to play his trusted 3-5-2 formation as he was convinced none of the teams, he faced were watching them play so he had a tactical advantage. The players were used to the formation and enjoyed playing that way. Greg knew he could easily change it if everything went 'pear shape'.

Everything did go wrong in the first 20 minutes of the game. Brixham seemed to know how Heale were going to play and put an extra man in midfield, disrupting Heale's flowing football and making them look ordinary. Greg tried his hardest to get the players to change shape, but they were looking dishevelled. At 2-0 Brixham looked comfortable and odds-on to win the game. Greg knew he had to do something drastically or watch his team get a hiding. He grabbed Woody as he ran past.

'I need to change formation Woody.'

'Gotcha Cloughie.'

Within a minute Woody was lying on the floor complaining of a twisted ankle. The referee called on the trainer who happened to be Greg. Within a minute or two Greg had relayed his instructions to Woody who in turn had informed the players by code. Greg was still working on codes to pass on to the Captain without having to get him to feign injury. Greg had decided that a solid back four was needed but he now couldn't afford a defensive midfielder as Heale were now chasing the game, so he had three central midfielders with two high wide men and Sharpy up top. This was very attacking and another Brixham goal would finish the game. Luckily, the change worked, and the effect was there for all to see. Heale got hold of the ball and started to play football. By half time it was 2-1 and they were back in the game. The second half was as good a Sunday League game as you would see. Heale equalised and applied pressure looking for the win. Both teams had chances in the end 2-2 was a fair result. There were no replays in the cup competitions so extra time and penalties were the order of the day. Greg watched the Brixham players walking off the pitch. They were truly a great team but did look slightly tired. The Heale players were walking towards him but he didn't want them to look sluggish.

'Run in guys, quick as you can' and he clapped like he was enticing a dog in with a ball. The players looked confused but did as they were asked.

'What's with the rush, Cloughie?'

'I'll explain everything in a minute Woody. There isn't much squash left but get as much as you can.'

The referee came over and explained that it was 15 minutes each way and if no team was in front at the end then penalties would be taken. Once the referee had left, Greg and Ross only had 5 minutes left for a team talk. Greg explained what 'Taff' had told him about Brixhams fitness and why he believed Heale was far fitter. He demanded that the first half of extra time would be as 'high tempo' as they could make it. Brixham wouldn't be expecting it or ready for it. Greg asked every player if they felt fit enough to do as he asked. This was 'The Cup' something Heale had not won in over 20 years and he wanted to be part of their history, he challenged the players to be part of history as well. Woody had been struggling with a groin strain for the last ten minutes and gingerly announced that he probably wasn't fit enough to play the way Greg wanted. This was the first time in his career he had admitted such a thing, but the team were more important than him right now. Greg looked straight at Rog who had been left out of the team for the fourth straight match.

'You fit enough Rog?'

'Am I ever Cloughie? Bring it on.'

His tracksuit was off, and he was away warming up before he even managed to finish his sentence.

'Let's show Brixham how good we really are. That ball is ours, keep it if you can and get it back when you lose it.'

'Finally, lads, don't walk back onto the pitch, run on like you haven't played a second of football today. Let them think we are fit as fiddles.'

The referee shouted over to the teams for them to make their way on to the pitch. Brixham had a last 'hurrah' and wandered slowly to their positions. Greg held his players back, much to the annoyance of the ref who stood with his hands on his hips staring at Greg and Ross. Greg released the team and they sprinted into position, jumping up and down on the spot when they arrived at their destination. The look of surprise could be seen by all the Brixham players and staff. Greg caught sight of Mike who just smiled and nodded, he appreciated a bit of 'gamesmanship' when he saw it.

Heale started the half with a super attitude and chased down every ball with great determination. During a swift attack, Brixham broke away and scored a super goal. It was against the run of play and hard on the Heale players. Rog was the one to 'fire up the team'. Heale kicked off and Rog was the first to get hold of the ball. It was a new Rog, slimmer, fitter and more focused. He was always a good player, but he looked even better today. Heale had a good ten minutes and scored an equalised on the stroke of half time. This made Greg's team talk so much easier. He praised the players and asked for 15 minutes of the same. He was convinced that if they carried on playing the same way they would win. The next 15 minutes was as good as any you would see in Sunday league football. Both teams played great football and attacked at will. They both played the game with true sportsmanship. Only one team managed to score a goal and avoid the lottery of penalties. Brixham had a corner which was taken long. A strong header by a Brixham defender was heading towards goal before Pete Northcott dove to his left and pushed the ball on to the post. It kindly rolled back towards him and nestled in his arms. Instantly he jumped up and saw Sharpy and French had remained up front. He kicked the ball quickly towards his two strikers. Brixham had pushed most of their players up hoping to score the winning goal. Sharpy ran towards the oncoming ball and outjumped his marker. He got enough of his head on the ball to knock it onwards. French had already realised Sharpies plan and had gambled on Sharpy winning the ball. French took one touch and smashed the ball into the net past the despairing Brixham keeper.

Mike and Jason were the last of the crowd to leave the pitches. They approached Greg. 'Great game today Cloughie.'

You have a good quality team there. Your boys beat one of the best teams in the Devon League today, and well deserved I must say.'

'I got it very wrong today at the start but I'm still working on my tactics. I'd love to come and watch The Gulls train and pick up some tips.'

'We may be taking some tips from you, young man if you carry on playing like that.'

Greg had learnt over the last few months to take compliments without getting too embarrassed, but today was different. He was taking a compliment from a full-time professional coach and his face reddened because of it.

'See you again soon young man, good luck for the rest of the season although something tells me you probably won't need it.'

CHAPTER 25

Greg had spent more and more time on his football and less time with Hazel. He had been due to meet up with Hazel on the previous Friday night but cancelled it at the last moment, he had agreed to meet up with Mike instead. Greg got to school early on Monday, he understood he had to apologise to Hazel and that he had some serious "sucking up " to do. She was always with her close friends, so he always knew where to find her. He wandered round to the Geography blocks situated at the rear of the school. Greg spotted Hazel's friends but could not see her. As he approached the girls, he could sense unease among them. He smiled and greeted them politely as he always did, they were a nice group and always pleasant to him.

'Where's Hazel?' he said in his pleasant way.

There was no reply but one of the girl's eyes wandered between two of the stand-alone classrooms. Greg passed the girls who tried to stand in his way. He could see two figures standing close to each other, very close. As he approached the two figures, he noticed one of the figures was Hazel and the other a fifth former named Tom. They had just finished kissing when Tom spotted Greg. Greg ran at him full pelt and knocked Tom to the floor before he could defend himself. It wasn't a punch, more a full-blown push. Tom was a big lad who played rugby for the school and Torquay Academy. He was nearly 16 and not far off 6ft tall. He would have "wiped the floor" with Greg in a normal fight and rose quickly to prove it. Hazel jumped in between the two, she was now crying.

'I'm sorry Greg; I didn't want you to find out like this.'

Greg stared at Hazel, he could feel emotion rising to his eyes, he knew he had to turn and run before everyone could see the tears his eyes. He ran straight out of the school gates, passing lots of school children entering the school. He didn't know where to run to and eventually found himself in Chappell Woods at the same spot as his infamous fight. He sat down and cried, sobbed even. He didn't know if it was because he had just lost his girlfriend or for the fact that someone had just stolen his girlfriend from him, he was indeed jealous. He would also have to deal with the fact that everyone would know about him and Hazel by the time he returned to school. He decided to head home for the day, a stomach bug would be his white lie but would also bide him a few hours. He also knew that Tom could be on the hunt for him and he didn't want to be in that position again.

Greg walked into school the next day believing that everybody would be looking at him, but he was happily surprised. He met up with some of his classmates who didn't even mention a thing. His ego had been getting the better of him and he was pleased that he wasn't the centre of attention which he obviously thought he was. At register he sat next to Tre as usual. She was looking as beautiful as ever and they had their normal morning chat. Tre was aware that Greg and Hazel had split and told Greg that she was pleased, she might be able to talk to him now without getting 'daggers' from Hazel. Little did Greg know it but she had her own plans for him.

CHAPTER 26

Greg returned to the shop after completing his paper round. Mandy had been in the shop first thing so when Greg arrived back, he was surprised to see Pete.

'Morning Pete, did you have a lie-in this morning?'

'Yeah, it's been a busy week'.

'Me too Pete! I've got some great news. Dad spoke to the Chairman of Torquay Saints Rugby Club. They are happy for Heale to ground share with them as it will also save them money. We need to come up with money for goalposts and to pay for ground maintenance. Dad has volunteered to do a raffle at work, and I have spoken to all the guys at training. They are all going to do their own fund-raising and raise as much money as possible. We also must pay for the upkeep of the club bar, which also needs re-decorating. It's going to take a lot of money, but dad reckons we can do it'.

'Well count me in young man; what do you want me to do?'

'Dad reckons you could have a little collection pot on the counter, and you could ask all your customers if they could help donate.'

'I think I could handle that Greg. When are you hoping to have all the money raised?'

'I want us to be playing in the new ground at the start of next season, in Division 1. Ross reckons I'm mad, but he also reckons we can do it. Wouldn't it be good to get the old ground back instead of playing our home games at Twente fields?'

The Gulls were at home to Bury that afternoon. Bury were a good footballing team and Greg knew they would cause Torquay all sorts of problems that afternoon. As per Saturday routine Greg met up with Steve, Danny and Graham. The boys chatted as usual about their week and the game a head. As they were chatting Greg spotted Jay Pinner walking around the pitch. Greg ran to hoardings at the edge of the pitch and shouted out to Jason. Jason spotted him and wandered over to Greg.

'Hi Jay. Do you think I could do a collection at the ground one Saturday? Heale are trying to get back to the old ground we used to use years ago, and we are trying to raise money. Do you think I can? Please.'

'It's not something that we normally do Greg, but I will speak to the boss. We are at home again next week in the FA Cup. If you can get here at 1 o'clock I will let you into the ground and take you to see the Chairman and Bruce, if he isn't too busy.'

'Thanks ever so much Jay. Oh, and good luck for today, I think you will probably need it.'

Greg was right, Torquay were totally outplayed that afternoon but with the help of some very sturdy defending and extremely poor attacking by Bury they managed to hold onto a 0-0 draw. All three boys walked home happy that afternoon having learnt that their respective teams had all won.

Heale were at home to Buckland Athletic on Sunday. Buckland were struggling at the bottom of the league and had lost to a lower league team in the Cup a week earlier. Ross had announced that he wouldn't be attending, and Greg was now getting used to being in charge. Everything was in place, the nets were up, corner flags in place and Greg had already chosen on his starting team. He had decided on a few changes and with a few players carrying knocks or suspended Buckland was as good a team as any to make those changes against. Players started turning up, all in good spirits. Those that had hardly played in the season were excited to play and to prove their worth to the team. Wilko turned up but was not in his tracksuit, he was wearing his work clothes.

'Sorry Greg, I'm not gonna be able to play today, I've got to go into work. I've got no choice. You'll beat these muppets without me that's for sure.'

Wilko was going to be a big loss but there were plenty of others that could replace him. He apologised again before heading back to his car.

 Rog appeared to the side of Greg. 'Alright Cloughie. Bad news, Woody isn't very well so he won't be coming today. He's picked up a bug and is losing bodily fluids from both ends. He sends his apologies and says to have a good game today.'

Rog then wandered off to get changed and warm up, oblivious to Greg's dilemma. A dilemma it certainly was. Without Woody and Wilko, Rog was the only recognised central midfielder. 'Peas' had already been left out due to injury, so Greg was in a pickle. He took out his notepad and frantically started to jot down some ideas.

Greg ordered all the players to warm up, even those that had no chance of playing, or so they thought. Greg was so relieved that the application to play a reserve team was submitted too late for this season and the new Heale Reserves wouldn't be playing until next season. He called the players in early from their warmup and sat them down in front of him. He spent the next five minutes explaining how he wanted the team to play and the formation of the team. The formation was defensive for the standard of team they were playing but the players hadn't been told the team sheet yet, they weren't 'privvy' to the information Greg was about to give. Many were wandering where the rest of the players were though. Greg announced the team. Many eyebrows were raised when the inclusion of two fourteen-year olds was included, Pokey and Lee Pier. Pokey and Rog would play as a central two with Lee and Ginge on the wings. Adam Colyer, one of the new players to join in the close season, a sixteen-year-old kid with an abundance of talent was going to start, playing slightly in front of Rog and Pokey and just behind the lone striker French. Sharpy had also been given day off to recover from a slight hamstring injury. The formation was a 4-4-1-1. Greg gave as good a team talk as he could about being top of the league and believing in their own abilities, but he didn't really believe it, he knew they were in trouble today. It really was men against boys. Greg knew that Pokey and Lee were nervous. They were two of the most vocal kids in the school team but today they looked like 'fish out of water'. Greg pulled them both to one side.

'Just imagine you are playing for the school team today. Don't let the Buckland players bully you'.

Pokey and Lee nodded and re-joined the team for the final warm up. Greg called over to Rog who joined him on the side lines.

'Pokey and Lee are great players for their age, but they are really nervous. You need to look after them today Rog, don't let them hold on to the ball, they will get knocked off it. You are going to have to run a few extra miles today pal.'

Rog pulled in his stomach, flexed his biceps and replied, 'never been fitter Cloughie, you can rely on me'. Greg knew that to be true and just hoped that would be enough.

Greg couldn't help smiling when the teams lined up. Buckland had some athletic looking players in their team and a few older players nearing the end of their Sunday league career. Heale looked like they had just grabbed the first eleven players off the street and put a kit on them. Greg could feel the eyes of the Buckland manager staring at him from across the pitch. He knew that they thought he was taking the piss out of them for fielding a weakened team, he only hoped he hadn't used that in his team talk.

Heale kicked off and passed the ball around trying to let everyone get a touch of the ball to calm any nerves they may have. The ball was lost a few times but won back very quickly. Pokey was having an early influence and although being one of the smallest players on the pitch becoming more vocal by the minute. He took possession of the ball in the centre of the pitch and lost his marker. He drove forward, played a 1-2 with French and hit the ball with full force 20 meters away from goal. Like a bullet it flew into the back of the net giving the Buckland keeper little chance. Pokey wasn't a natural goal scorer, so his celebrations were slightly over the top, but it was only to be expected. With only five minutes gone it was 1-0 to Heale. Buckland kicked off and immediately lost the ball. Once again Pokey got the ball, but he passed it quickly to Rog. What seemed like seconds later was an off-ball challenge on Pokey that wiped him out. He hit the floor in agony as the opposing Buckland midfielder trotted back to his half. Nearly everyone watching saw the late tackle apart from the referee.

The Heale players went mad and a big melee occurred in the centre of the pitch. There were lots of pushing and shoving with verbal abuse thrown in for good measure. The referee managed to take control of the teams and called both Captains together. He explained that as he never saw the tackle, he was going to dismiss the whole incident and that the next player to overstep the mark would be booked. Rog was livid and continued to argue with the ref which eventually got him an unwanted yellow card. During all the drama Pokey had his ankle strapped and was running freely.

The game re-started with both sets of players on tenterhooks.

Only the more experienced and hardened players wanted to keep the ball for fear of retribution by the opposing team. The game was evenly matched, Buckland were winning the 50-50 balls because of their size but Heale were quicker, sharper and a lot fitter. The speed certainly contributed to Heale's second goal. Lee Piers was not having a great game and was getting closely marked. He got the ball and for the first time lost his marker. He passed the ball to Adam who feigned to shoot, only to pass to French who coolly slotted the ball passed the oncoming keeper. It was only a few minutes to half time, and they were now 2-0 to the good. Greg was trying to calm them down from the side lines and get them to concentrate for the last few minutes of the half. Buckland kicked off and pressed forward from the instant. They caught Heale slightly 'off-guard' and just as their number 7 was about to shoot he was brought down on the edge of the area by Rog. Rog got straight up and grabbed the ball trying to defend his actions and to let the ref know that the ball was his target and not the player. Unfortunately, it was no avail. The referee reached into his pocket and produced a second yellow card, quickly followed by a red. Rog continued to argue his case but was obviously getting nowhere. All the time Buckland were lining up the free kick and Pete Northcott was trying desperately to line up his wall and organise the defence. The referee signalled that it was a direct free kick and the Buckland Captain lined up to strike it. Instead of trying to curl it over the wall he slid the ball forward and to his left. This was a well-practised free kick and a Buckland winger ran on to the ball quickly squaring it into the box for a now unmarked striker to easily put the ball in the net. Heale had been caught out and Greg was seething, surely, he should have been made aware of this free kick strategy from the scout who watched them play last week. What was the point of someone going to watch the opposition if they weren't going to gather all of the necessary facts, he thought?

The referee blew for half time and the players ambled over to where Greg was standing. Things had happened so quickly in the last few minutes that he genuinely didn't know what to do. He told everyone to chill out for 5 minutes and take in some juice and oranges.

Greg looked around at his depleted squad. He wished Jason Myles wasn't away at a wedding or that he hadn't asked Horny to watch their next opponents. How good would he have been right now?

'Right lads. Taff go warm up. You're gonna play central defence alongside Terry. Head, I want you to slot into midfield alongside Pokey.'

'I can't play in midfield Cloughie.'

'You can now Head. I've got no-one else. Lee I'm bringing you off pal. Pokey, Head, Ginge, you guys need to stay tight in a three-man midfield. Adam sit just in front and French you are going to be alone up front. I don't think you will get much of the ball but just put yourself about as much as you can.'

'Got it Cloughie.'

'This is going to be a really tough 45 minutes lads. They will be buoyed by their last-minute goal and us going down to 10 men.'

'Yeah sorry about that lads' sighed Rog.

'They have got the extra man and will take advantage of that and we need to use our speed and fitness. Let's keep it tight and try and get something out of this game.'

Buckland kicked off and immediately went on the attack. Heale defended well but could only clear the ball hoping to get it to French. French was a quality player but was getting exhausted running for every ball with little support arriving when he got it. With 20 minutes gone it was still 2-1 and Buckland attacking at every opportunity. Pokey was having a great game and trying to get the ball as much as possible. He took a pass from Terry and turned to lose his marker. He was instantly chopped down and once again left writhing on the floor in agony. It was the same player as before who had committed the foul but this time the referee had witnessed it. He ran over to the player and showed him a yellow card. Greg let the emotion of the day get the better of him and shouted at the referee.

'That is his second terrible challenge, he should be sent off. If you had had your glasses on the first fucking time ref, you would know that.'

A quiet enveloped the pitch as the referee approached Greg. 'I don't usually do this but for your cheek and bad language, I'm giving you a yellow card'.

'So, I get a yellow card for swearing and that lump of a Buckland player gets the same for hacking down a player twice.'

'Don't' push me young man, if you think you can do my job, you're more than welcome to try.'

'Well I probably wouldn't get it cos I don't wear glasses.'

As soon as Greg had said it, he regretted it. He had been told before that his quick-witted humour could get him into trouble and now was probably that time. The referee stared at Greg. He didn't know what to say or do so he reached into his pocket and pulled out another yellow card and once again a red one.

'I suggest you go away young man and take a little walk. You can have nothing more to do with this match, do you understand me?'

'Yes ref.' Greg looked at the team who were looking at him in a stunned silence. He walked away knowing that his actions could well have cost Heale any points today. Pokey limped off; he would not be playing any more part in the rest of the game. His ankle was swollen to nearly twice its size. French who was stand in Captain, tried to organise the team. Adam dropped back into midfield and he would stay up as a lone striker. It was now 11 versus 9. Buckland attacked at will and eventually got the equaliser with 10 minutes to go. Heale's players were 'out on their feet' and running on empty. They looked to the side-lines for inspiration, finding none. Desperation set in and they did everything possible to deny Buckland scoring again. With injury time looming Buckland had a corner and pushed every player up. French was also defending so Buckland weren't worried about a break- away goal. The ball was swung in and was met by the head of the big Buckland striker. The ball headed goal bound and passed the stricken Pete Northcott. Instinctually Neil Field dove and pushed the ball away. He jumped up trying to persuade the referee that he had headed the ball but this time the referee had spotted the infringement. Once again, a red card was pulled from the pocket of the referee's shirt and Neil was sent off. Heale were now down to 8 players. The big Buckland striker gathered the ball and placed it on the spot. After hearing the refs whistle, he calmly ran and side footed the ball past Pete and into the net. Buckland had won 3-2, even if it was against 8 men.

As soon as the game was over Greg wandered back to the pitch, making sure he kept away from the referee. The team were slumped on the floor, no words coming from their lips.

'Great effort today guys, you all played magnificent. I'm sorry the result wasn't what we wanted but this is only a little set-back.

As Greg was talking, he noticed the referee coming towards him.

'I will compose a thorough report of today's incidents and forward them to the Sunday League Committee. I'm sure your club will be hearing from them very soon. Goodbye'.

And with that he walked off. Greg knew that this wasn't going to be the last time he had to worry about the matter.

CHAPTER 27

It felt as if Saturday had come around quicker than normal. Greg had attended training on the Tuesday night and had felt awkward explaining himself. Firstly to Ross and then to the rest of the team! They had already learnt about the facts through talking to each other, but Greg felt dutiful to go over them with the team. He apologised for his sending off admitting that his actions were unacceptable whilst the other players sending offs were basic football occurrences. He also apologised to the team for losing their unbeaten record which he felt totally responsible for. Ross was really understanding and had taken great comfort in the fact that they had nearly pulled off a shock win with 3 kids and only 8 players left on the park. The feedback about Lee, Adam and especially Pokey was really promising. He did warn Greg that there would be some form of fine for not only him but the two other players plus probably the club itself.

Greg had been allowed to call Steve, Danny and Graham to tell them he would meet them in the ground later that afternoon. Telephone calls were strictly forbidden from the house unless authorised by David or Carol as the bills were so high. Some of Greg's friends had locks put onto the house-phones to stop them using them. Greg arrived at the ground at 12.45, fifteen minutes early. It was just gone one o'clock when a young lad not much older than Greg approached. He was wearing a very bright yellow 'high vis' jacket.

'You Greg?' Greg nodded. 'Mr Pinner has asked me to come and get you, we gotta be quick though.'

Greg had been going to the ground for a few years and still loved the fact that it was an actual Football League ground, one of only 92 in the entire country. Obviously, there were many more grounds but only 92 teams had that privilege. Greg followed the young man and they entered the Club Shop. Jay was stood in the foyer and thanked Greg's usher for collecting him. Jay shook Greg's hand and offered him a yellow, white and blue scarf, 'Brand new this season, compliments of myself.'

'Thanks Jase, my scarf is about 3 years old and getting a bit tatty, I needed a new one.'

He was genuinely happy with his new present. Jay explained that the players had already started turning up and they all had to be at the ground no later than 13.15 hours. They would have a small meeting with the manager confirming their individual fitness before he announced the team. A series of massages and personal warmups would take place before the players would take to the field for their main warm-up. They would then return to the changing rooms for a final five-minute brief by the manager before returning out onto the pitch five minutes before kick- off.

'The boss is probably in the changing rooms now if you want to wander through and meet a few of the players if you wish.'

'Yes, please Jay, that would be great.'

Jay led them through a corridor and entered the changing room. The intense smell of Ralgex (a heat spray for muscle relief) overwhelmed the room. Greg thought he would feel nervous in front of the players that he watched every fortnight, but he was quite relaxed. A few of the players nodded at Greg not knowing who he was but just being polite. Greg didn't realise how big some of them were or how athletic they looked until he was close up to them. They all looked super fit. Greg spotted his favourite player, Les Lawrence, a big centre forward who had been at the club for a few years.

Greg sidled over to Les, 'Are you going to score today Les?'

Les looked up at Greg and smiled. 'I sincerely hope so young man.'

'Who have we got here today Jay?'

'This young man here Les, is the assistant manager of a Sunday league team in Torquay called Heale, everyone calls him Cloughie.'

Les laughed but soon realised that Jay and Greg were looking very serious.

'And how is your team doing this year, Cloughie?'

'Oh, we're top of the league, but we lost our first game last week. We are going to get promoted this year back to Division 1'.

Les looked at Greg knowing that he meant every word.

'So, what brings you to the ground today and why the VIP tour?'

'I come to every home game with my mates. I'm hoping to get to speak with the Chairman today. I am going to ask if I can do a collection at the ground one match day.'

'And what is the collection for Cloughie?'

'Our club plays its home games at a council owned field in Torquay; we lost our own ground many years ago. We are trying to raise enough money to ground share with a local Rugby club which was also where we used to play years ago. We haven't got enough money to do so yet, so all the players and staff are trying to raise money, even my dad.' Greg felt a hint of pride as he said that.

'Would you like to come and watch us one Sunday? We've a great team and play nice football, it's not all kick and run'.

Jay jumped in on the conversation.

'Cloughie is a football nut Les. He has a knack of reading the game and being able to change it. He likes his team to play 3-5-2',

'Like a Christmas tree' Greg interrupted.

Les sat nodding his head. He had never met this kid before, but he liked him already. He even wanted to watch his team play. Bruce Ricoh interrupted the conversation. He wanted to address the squad. Greg said goodbye to Les and wished him well for the match. Les stood and shook Greg's hand.

'Nice meeting you young man.'

Greg and Jay left the changing rooms and headed towards the Chairman's Office. The Chairman was an elderly gentleman who had been at the club for twenty years. He had put a lot of his own money into the club but was now looking for a potential investor to buy him out. Jay knocked on his door and waited for a reply. 'Come -in' replied a soft elderly voice.

'Len, I'd like you to meet Greg, he's one of our loyal fans and the lad that I told you about last week.'

Greg moved forward and held out his hand to the Chairman. 'Hello, Mr Batson. Pleased to meet you.'

'You too young man and you can call me Len. I'm told you're a football nut and are helping to manage a Sunday league team, is that correct?'

'Yes Len, Heale Athletic, we've got some great players. I reckon one or two could get in Torquay's team.'

'How do you think we will do today?'

'I'm hoping we will win today but it sort of depends on our tactics, Bruce is quite defensive, and I think at home we should be more positive, get at them.'

Greg realised that he had sort of slagged off the manager of a club that the chairman had hired, what a great start to his charity appeal. Len laughed out loud.

'Say what you think son,' and carried on laughing. 'You can leave us for a little while Jay, I think Greg will keep me amused for a little while yet.'

For the next 30 minutes Len and Greg talked football. Greg was very pleasantly surprised at how much football knowledge Len had (although being a football Chairman he should be well versed) and was engrossed in how the day to day running of a football club went. Len was also blown away by how much enthusiasm Greg had for the game and his love of three things: West Ham, Heale Athletic and Torquay United. Probably in that order he presumed.

Les looked at his watch. 'I'm sorry Greg but I have to go and meet the Chairman of Bognor Regis, etiquette and all that'.

(Bognor Regis played their football in one of the lower leagues and had done well to qualify for the FA Cup 1st Round proper).

'That's alright Len, my three mates will be waiting for me anyway. We always come together.'

'I have an idea Greg; go find your three friends. What are their names?'

'Danny, Steve and Graham'.

'Go find Danny, Steve and Graham and come back to the Main Stand. I will make sure you are let in. You can all watch the game with me. I do believe that you haven't actually come to the point of why you asked Jay if you could meet me and now, I'm totally intrigued.'

Greg felt slightly embarrassed as he had just spent thirty minutes with Les and had totally forgotten to ask him if he could do a charity collection. He was enjoying Lens' company very much and he reminded him of Ray in many ways. Greg jumped up from his seat, thanked Len and ran out of his office pronto.

The four boys were back at the Main Stand within ten minutes. Greg had run all the way to meet his mates and explained what was going on in seconds. The four boys reached the Main Stand and Greg approached a Match day steward and gave him his name. The steward wandered off and returned within a minute.

'You're to follow me lads, The Chairman is waiting for you.'

They were led to the seating area and the steward pointed to where Len was sitting. He instantly spotted Greg, stood up and waved the boys over.

'Nice to meet you lads, sit down and enjoy the match, were about to kick off.'

Greg sat next to Len and in between breaks of play Greg talked to Len about Heale's idea to ground share and the need for finances. The half-time whistle was blown, and Greg and the boys were invited to join the two Chairmen for drinks and nibbles. They were 'buzzing' for some food and drink. The two Chairmen spent most of half time talking and left the lads to their own devices. They tucked into the free food and drink and caught up with the half time scores via the video player on BBC 1. It was very posh in the Executive lounge. With a few minutes to go before kick- off they all returned to their seats.

Len turned to Greg, 'What did you think of the first half Greg?'

'Pretty boring really. I don't think a team had a shot on target, no wander its 0-0. Bognor have set up for a draw, they will fancy beating us at their place, they would have a sell-out crowd, and it would probably be in mid-week. I think they would probably beat us as well; we need to win today! Bruce should be more attacking. Bognor's left and right backs are very slow, we could easily manipulate that. Les Lawrence is also playing up front on his own, every time he wins the ball, he has no one to support him, he needs a partner up front. Bognor are playing with one up front also but with 5 in midfield, they aren't interested in scoring, just stopping us scoring. Also, their number 7 is their best player but he was limping for the last ten minutes and if you look closely his ankle is heavily strapped. He won't last long so we could capitalise on that also'.

Greg stopped talking. He looked at Len who was just staring at him.

'I watched the same first half as you kid but didn't really notice any of that, just that it was boring.'

'When I watch a game Len, I also watch the players at the same time. Evidently, it's a knack that I have, I thought everyone did it but obviously not.'

'So, do you think my manager is any good then?'

'Mum says he was a great player in his time, a Scotland legend she says but I don't think he's a great manager. Sorry.'

'Oh, don't apologise Greg. I'm not going to sack him because a teenager who I've just met thinks he's not very good'.

'Oh, that's good then' replied Greg.

'Well not yet anyway' and Len flashed Greg a cheeky grin.

The second half was a dreary affair. Bruce threw caution to the wind and put on another forward and attacking midfielder, but Bognor just defended deeper and put everyone behind the ball. At the final whistle the Bognor players celebrated while The Gulls players walked off to a chorus of boos. The fans weren't happy, a good crowd had turned up to watch and hope to see their team progress to the next round. The rewards for getting past rounds 1 and 2 in the cup were that the top two divisions joined the party and you could find yourselves with a home tie against a Liverpool or Arsenal. True dreams. Torquay should have beaten Bognor and be waiting for the next draw hoping for a nice home tie and one step closer to a dream tie, not dreading a journey along the south coast to play a replay against a non-league team.

After the match the four boys joined Len in his box for after match refreshments. Len disappeared for ten minutes to go and see the players, he did this win, lose or draw. They did play for him after all and he liked the interaction with them. He returned to the box and spent another 5 minutes with the Chairman of Bognor who was very upbeat about his team's performance and their chances of winning the replay. Len returned to the four boys who were now full up from the feast they had just devoured. They tucked into the food as if they would never get another meal and left very little for anyone else that may have turned up. They were all happy, West Ham had travelled to Birmingham and won 2-0, Aston Villa had beaten Everton 1-0 and Liverpool had thrashed Man City 4-0. Len grabbed Greg by his arm and politely moved him away from his three pals. They weren't over bothered as they were deep into club loyalty talk.

'Greg, I am sorry, but I will not be able to allow you to do a collection at the ground. If I let you do it, I would have every Tom, Dick and Harry wanting to do it. It would be like opening a can of worms.'

Greg's disappointment was plain to see.

'I do have an offer for you though. You probably don't know this, but I own a building company. If you ever get the money to return to your ground I will send in my guys and fix up the Club Bar, free of charge, up to a certain price obviously.'

Greg couldn't hide his delight. He pumped his fists (something he never did) and shouted out 'YES' much to his embarrassment when everyone turned around to look at him. He was about to hold out his hand to shake Lens' but instead hugged him instead. It was a natural reaction but took both him and Len by surprise. Greg quickly released and hoped that he hadn't overstepped the mark.

'Well I wasn't expecting that young man. I have one caveat though. When you eventually become a well-known football Manager, I want you to come to this club some time in your career.'

Greg laughed and nodded. 'Can I add a caveat too?' Len tilted his head and made a facial gesture as if to say, 'try me'.

'You have to attend one of Heale's games.'

'I think I can do that. We need to shake on it, Greg, to bind the deal'. Greg shook Lens' hand as strong as he could.

CHAPTER 28

Greg received an Official letter in the post. The only post he ever got was birthday cards from his relatives in London and this was no greetings card. He opened it knowing what it was. He was 'invited' to attend a hearing at the Devon FA. Because he was a minor an extraordinary meeting was being held on Saturday at 10 am. He was to be present with an accompanying adult. Greg had asked Ross if he could go with him, he knew his father was working and he knew Ross had a good standing in the Devon FA.

Greg dressed as smart as he could, and Ross wore a smart pair of trousers and jacket. They arrived at the Headquarters in plenty of time; this allowed Ross time to prep Greg for the meeting.

'They are going to warn you of your actions on the park, they may even fine you but may find that difficult as you are a minor. Just hold your tongue Greg; I will try to speak for you.'

Both were called into a room where three men were sitting at a long table in front of them. The man sitting in the middle of the other two stood as they entered the room.

My name is Mr Oakenfell, Chairman of the Devon FA. You must be Gregory Welling'.

Without waiting for an answer, he looked at Ross.

'Good to see you again Ross.'

'You too Dan.'

Greg and Ross were ushered to their seats and sat facing the panel. Dan began by introducing the other two men, Den Morley, secretary and Jon Blatchferd, finance. He then explained how the proceedings would take place and in what format. He then read out the referee's report on the match in question. It sounded a lot worse than it was and Greg started to feel quite nervous. He hadn't really worried what the outcome of the hearing would be as he didn't feel the crime was that punishable but listening to the referees report he had changed his mind. After finishing the report Dan asked Greg if he wanted to reply. Ross quickly jumped in.

'I would like to speak on Greg's behalf please Dan.'

As Greg was a minor the FA knew they were on muddy ground and had limited experience in dealing with these matters.

'I feel that although Greg's actions were out of order most of the occurrences were of my doing. I left Greg on his own to manage the team and even though there were extra-ordinary circumstances that led to his sending off, I believe if I was there we wouldn't be sitting here now. Greg is very sorry for his actions and promises that it won't happen again, and he will apologise to the referee in question when he sees him next'.

Ross had been to a few hearings during his prolonged career and knew that a bit of 'arse licking' always went down well. After sitting in silence for a good minute Dan took off his glasses and lent forward on the large table.

'Gentleman, we have a problem here. I somewhat agree that if you were at the game in question Ross the incident wouldn't have happened, but you weren't there were you? And if my facts are correct you won't be there for at least half of the matches in the season, leaving Greg, a minor to run/manage the team. I think we know what does and could happen when you are not there. I, we, are not happy or indeed know if we are legally allowed to let a minor run one of our clubs without adult supervision.'

'But our paperwork states that I am manager and Greg assistant manager.'

'We know what your paperwork states Ross,' and Dan picked up a folder and flapped it in the air,' but we also know that isn't totally true. I would say you are most definitely joint managers and we know your arrangement.'

Ross started to sit uneasily in his chair they knew an awful lot about him, Greg and the club, where did they get their information from?

'We have decided not to fine you Greg but are going to fine the club £30.00 for the misdemeanours of the match. That also considers the three sending's off. We will also not take any action against the other two players as we believe they were unfairly represented on the day by your club. We are uncomfortable with the fact that we have a minor in charge of one of our senior teams and that he doesn't know how to obey the FA rules. We have decided that we are going to suspend you Gregory Welling for two matches and you are not to attend those games, even to watch. We are also in agreement that Gregory is to be struck off the Manager list as he is too young. He will be allowed to attend future matches and help the manager running the team but will not be able to perform any management duties with the club until he reaches the age of sixteen. If we believe Heale are ignoring this rule, we will implement more fines or stronger measures if needed. That is our final decision.'

Ross opened his mouth as if to argue but was cut short by Dan.

'That is our decision Ross, there is an appeals procedure if you believe our decision is unjust'.

Ross sat dejected in his chair; this meeting had not gone the way he believed it would. Dan put his glasses back on and looked at Greg.

'I do believe this is the right decision young man. You are far too young to be given the responsibility of running a football team'.

He spoke almost patronisingly. Too often this past year Greg had been in tears and he couldn't wait for the day when he could control his emotions, today wasn't that day. Greg stood from his chair; he was shaking.

'I know I was out of order last week and I apologise, but what you have just done isn't fair.'

Ross tried grabbing Greg's arm, but Greg pushed it away.

'No Ross, sorry. You sit there in your fancy jackets and ties and within ten minutes have just ruined my life. I love managing Heale and being with the players. I love football. Everyone calls me Cloughie. I read a book on him the other day and he thinks the FA are a waste of space, well I totally agree with him. He quoted that "When the FA get in their stride, they make the Mafia look like kindergarten material". 'Fuck you all.'

With that he kicked his chair and ran out of the room. He was very quickly followed by Ross.

CHAPTER 29

Greg attended the next training session and Ross explained the outcome of the meeting. The players were furious and wanted to know who was going to take charge of home games now Cloughie was unable to or allowed. Ross had asked his brother-in-law, Dave Waters to become Assistant Manager. Dave attended nearly every game and used to play for Heale in the early 70's. He was an astute person who would carry out instructions effectively. Ross and Greg had decided to write down the proposed starting line-up and formation at training and then leave Dave to make any changes or substitutions as he saw fit. The players had tried to talk Ross into attending the home games, but he had his orders from the other half, and he had promised her. She had been a football widow for far too long. He would carry on taking training and Managing the team at away matches only. The players weren't over happy at the news of Dave becoming assistant manager in place of Greg but accepted the decision. Greg promised to attend all training sessions and apart from the two suspended matches be at as many games as possible.

That was until he received his second letter. It was once again addressed to him and was very official. Greg opened it hoping the FA had had a change of heart and were reversing their decision. How wrong could he have been. In a very strongly worded document, it read that after his 'outrageous and very immature outburst' he was to be indefinitely suspended from attending any of the Heale games apart from being in audience. If he was to be caught in any capacity helping the team, Heale could be fined, deducted points or both. His young life really had ended.

CHAPTER 30

October and November came and went; Greg celebrated his fourteenth birthday with his family but declined a party. His schoolwork had started to suffer, and his teachers had seen a negative side to Greg's personality. So much so that David and Carol had been asked to attend the school to speak to Greg's head of year, Mrs Mills. She had witnessed Greg go from a top of the class student to someone who didn't care about his marks or disciplinary standards. David and Carol had both seen a dramatic change to Greg since his suspension but hadn't realised it had spread to his schooling. They were quite shocked to hear what Mrs Mills had to say, and quite embarrassed.

Greg still spent a fair bit of time with Mike, but they had gone from being childish young men to boyish, rude teenagers. They had little regard for other people's property when they were out and were not afraid to answer back to elders who tried to point out the errors of their ways. Greg was pretty much the main instigator with Mike going along with things for the laugh. Greg had also teamed up with Tre who was also a negative impact on him. She smoked when she could afford to and was always trying to get Greg to try. He had declined up till now, but he knew her charms could get the better of him one day. Her parents were liberal and let her stay out later than Greg could. If she was out with Greg, she would get him to push the boundaries as far as he could. In all, Greg had become a bit of a loose canon away from his football environments.

Greg was still going to all home games of 'The Gulls' even if they were playing awful football and in the wrong half of the table. They had been dumped out of the Cup by Bognor and Bruce was still in charge but for how long was anyone's guess. Greg hadn't been to a Heale training session in weeks and had only been to Twent fields once. Heale had won their game but Greg was frustrated at how they had played and that he could have no influence on the game. He knew that all the referees were looking out for a schoolboy within Heales ranks and he wouldn't be hard to miss. He couldn't jeopardise Heale's season for his own gain, as much as that was killing him. West Ham were playing OK. They were sitting in mid-table and Greg liked the look of the team, lots of youth backed up with some good experience. Heale had dropped to third in the league but had a game in hand due to still being in the Devon Cup. They were playing Plympton on Sunday who were playing great football and top of the league. Greg had decided to go but try to keep a low profile.

It had rained all week and the pitch looked waterlogged. Greg would have tried his hardest to get the game called off as you could not play football on a mud bath. Unfortunately, he knew that the game would go ahead, and it wouldn't be beneficial to a team that liked to play football, Heale were in trouble before the game even kicked off. For a December morning it was fairly warm, and Greg parked his bike up at the very end of the pitch hoping no -one would see him. Wilko spotted Greg first and ran over. When the rest of the players saw Wilko break away from his warm-up, they stopped what they were doing. They all recognised Greg and ran over to greet him. Thirteen burly blokes all rubbing his hair and punching his arm as if he was a dog returning home after being lost. They were all very happy to see him and asked him when he was coming back. They missed him and knew they were a much better team when he was in charge.

Whilst waiting for the game to start, Greg began watching a senior's game being played on an adjacent pitch. The tempo of the game was much slower, but Greg could tell that some of the players would have been of a high standard in their prime. In the corner of his eye he saw a big car pull up in the car park. Greg liked his cars and recognised it as a Rolls Royce Silver Shadow. It was one of the most luxurious cars in the world and probably cost as much as his parent's house. He was intrigued to see who owned it and carried on watching the car park. The figure of an elderly gentleman got out of the driver's side. Greg couldn't make out who it was due to the very large coat the driver was wearing, covering up most of his face. Whoever it was, was making his way over to the field near Greg. As the figure neared Greg, he realised who it was. It was Len, Chairman of 'The Gulls'. Len caught sight of Greg and waved.

'Hello young man, I'm here to pay one half of my deal. Thought I'd come and watch a decent game of football for once' and he laughed, joined by Greg.

Greg explained to Len what had happened at the Devon FA meeting and why he was ordered to attend in the first place. He told Len everything and didn't leave out any details. He was honest in his appraisal of all events even down to his deserved sending off. Len stood and listened intently and didn't get a word in edge ways. Eventually Greg finished his rant and stared at Len. Before Len could say anything, Greg spoke again. This time, he spent ten minutes pointing out all the Heale players on the pitch, their positions and strengths. He didn't make any reference to their weaknesses; he was too proud of them to do that. Len could see the pride in Greg as he talked about the team. He could also see the hurt in his eyes knowing that he wasn't able to participate in any of the running of the team. Heale were playing well and had set up in a less than orthodox formation. They had plenty of possession and were in control of the game even if they hadn't scored. The opposition were top of the table but Heale were outplaying them. Suddenly, the referee blew for half time and Greg realised that he had been talking for most of the half.

'So, if you were managing now Greg, what would you change?'

'Their midfield is their weakest area and fairly slow, so I'd look to manipulate that in the second half. Our midfield is quicker, twice as strong and much more technical so I'd be all over that but because someone in a suit has decided I'm too young I can't make those changes, and it's not fair.'

Len could once again see the hurt in Greg's eyes, but he said nothing. Anything he could say wouldn't make Greg feel any better.

At the end of the match, Greg thanked Len for honouring his deal and attending a game. He apologised for the 0-0 draw but did insist 'it was probably better than watching The Gulls right now.'

Len shook Greg's hand. Before leaving, he asked, 'Do you think I should replace Bruce?'

Greg got on his bike, ready to cycle over to the Heale players.

'Most definitely Len' and he rode away.

Greg arrived home on the following Thursday afternoon to another official letter. He used to love receiving mail as it was only good news but these days, he was in dread of it. He ran up to his room and hesitantly opened it. He already knew that it was from the Devon FA as the envelope had been stamped by them. Greg was invited to attend another extraordinary meeting on the Saturday coming. If he was unable to attend, he was to call them and re-arrange another date. He called Ross to ask if he was able to take him but with deep apologies Ross had to decline as he was taking his daughter to a gymnastics competition. Greg knew his dad was working and his only other chance was his mum. He was reluctant to ask her as he knew she loved her Saturday shopping trips. Carol was more than happy to take Greg and said she would go shopping with Alison in the afternoon instead.

Greg wore the same clothes as the previous meeting but would have rather wore jeans and a t-shirt. He didn't see why going smart did any good, especially because of the outcome of the meeting. Carol told him it was etiquette and that the FA committee would be dressed in their ties and blazers and they probably didn't want to wear them either. Greg smiled and did as he was told but he really thought that the FA committee loved wearing their ties and blazers and would have probably wore them to bed if they could.

As with the last meeting Greg arrived early and sat in the same chair outside of the meeting room. He was more nervous this time than before, what if they were to impose a lifetime ban? He wasn't particularly thinking straight but he didn't trust this bunch of adults. At 11 am the Chairman of the committee popped his head round the door and looked at Greg and Carol. He nodded to them both and went back into the room. It was as if he was looking for someone else. Ten minutes later he put his head back round the door. He looked up and down the corridor.

'Would you both like come in please?'

Greg and Carol entered, and the Chairman introduced himself and his committee, the same two as the previous meeting. Carol nodded to them all without shaking hands and in a very broad cockney accent introduced herself as Greg's mum. She stood tall and imposing and didn't want them to feel as if she was going to be a push-over. Even Greg saw the steel in her demeanour. Greg and Carol were invited to sit, and Dan was about to commence the meeting when the doors flew open and an elderly figure appeared.

'So sorry I'm late, I had a very urgent meeting to attend. Anyway, I'm here now and I see you were going to start without me, another "kangaroo court" in progress then, Dan?'

 'Hello Len, I was just about to tell Master Welling and his mother that you were due to attend and that if you weren't here within another five minutes, we would adjourn the meeting for another day. However, you are here now so can we begin?'

'I would like a few minutes with Greg and his mother before we start, would that be possible, please?'

'It's highly irregular but we will go and get some refreshments and we will resume at 11.30 hours, that gives you ten minutes Len.'

Dan and Len had known each other for over 40 years and although they had very little in common and didn't really like each other they had a professional mutual respect. The three men stood and left the room leaving Len, Greg and Carol on their own. Len introduced himself to Carol and explained why he was there, basically Greg had left a big impression on him and he didn't want him falling out of love with the game because of a pompous committee that couldn't see a future star if it bit them. He asked if he could do all the talking as he was a 'dab hand' at these now. Greg and Carol agreed.

'So, what was so important that you were late for my meeting then?'

'Greg, don't be so rude.'

'It's OK Mrs Welling'

'Please call me Carol' she replied.

'It's OK Carol, I like his youthful cheek, he should have been a comedian you know. Well Greg, I've been talking to the board and press. We are now looking for a new manager.'

'What you sacked Bruce Ricoh?'

'Yes Carol, on instruction from your son'.

'Greg, how could you?'

'It's OK Carol, I'm only joking, the team have been under-performing for a little while, so it is with regret we have terminated his contract.'

The three-man committee re-entered the room and sat down. Dan gathered his paperwork and looked up, ready to speak. Before he could open his mouth, Len stood up.

'I would like to start off this meeting'.

He didn't seek permission, just carried on speaking.

'I've known this young man a considerable amount of time. I believe his actions that led to his red card and at the last meeting were out of character and that he is truly sorry. This young man eats and breathes football; I never knew someone so young could be so passionate. He has ideas and a vision that you probably haven't even heard or thought of. His team, Heale, play attractive football that I would be proud of if Torquay played that way. Have you ever been to watch his team play? I'll answer that for you, no. If you want to see his real character, go and visit a game, watch him interact with men at least twice his age, they listen to him and have brought into his ideas. He plays a Christmas tree formation for god's sake, whatever that is. Terry Venables' uses it evidently. If that doesn't work, he knows how to change the game to counter act the opposing team, this kid is the future gentlemen and you are suppressing his talents by indefinitely suspending him. As of today, I have promoted my head scout, Mike Foster as youth team coach. With the permission of Mr and Mrs Welling I would like Mike to take Greg under his wing and help guide him in the finer arts of football management and man-management which will also hopefully keep him away from this hallowed building. Finally, I do believe that the decision to suspend him was against FA Rules. I have looked through the rule book to find anything to do with indefinite suspensions and have found nothing, let alone dealing with a minor. You are treading on very thin ice Dan.'

Len took a deep breath and sat down. Greg looked at him in awe. Len was obviously very experienced in public speaking; he spoke with authority and meaning, never once getting tongue tied. Dan was about to speak when Len jumped up again.

'One last thing before I finish. Do you know everyone calls him Cloughie! Brian Clough is a bloody genius. Greg didn't give himself that nickname, someone gave it to him and it's stuck. Cloughie'.

'Thank you Len for that rousing speech, you have left us with something to ponder. Master Welling is there anything you would like to add?

Greg looked at Len and his mum who both gently shook their heads advising him.

'Yes please Mr Oakenfell'. Greg stood up. 'I would like to apologise for any of my actions that have brought Heale

Athletic into disrepute and for being rude to this committee on my last visit'. Greg sat back down and held his mums hand. She gave it a little squeeze to acknowledge his apology.

'OK then, we will make a decision on your appeal.

Greg did not even know it was an appeal, something that had been organised by Len.

'We will get back to you soon.'

Outside the building Carol thanked Les for his support. Greg questioned Len, 'Since when did you watch me give a team talk or see how the Heale players respond to my tactics? I was nowhere near the players last week and that is the first time I have seen you at any of our matches.'

'That's very true young man but I was given the telephone number of Ross, who I spoke to in great length about you. Do you know how much respect he has for your football knowledge? Oh, and a good few months ago I went to Plymouth to run my eye over a couple of exciting kids during a schoolboy cup game. There was a young lad who took charge of his team and managed to outwit a coach much more experienced than him. Don't tell me that I don't know anything about you. I may have spread the truth a little bit but as far as I'm concerned it was all true. Anyway, I've got to run. I've got a game in Oxford that I may be late for and a team without a Manager. You think you've got problems kid.'

'Thank you, Len, I won't forget this.'

'That's alright son, we've still got a deal to settle one day. Don't you break it, you owe me double now.'

He shook Greg's hand and pecked Carol's cheek. 'Nice meeting you Carol. You have a wonderful son; you should be very proud.'

'I am Len' and she gave Greg a hug. Very proud, most of the time.'

Greg spent the rest of the day with Mike. The weather was awful, and they hired out a few VHS videos and sat in to watch them. 'First Blood' for all out action and Monte Pythons Life of Brian for slapstick comedy were the choices of the day. Greg apologised to Mike, he had led him astray and he didn't want them both getting in trouble. They made a pact to still enjoy themselves without being the tosser's that they were becoming. Mike was allowed to stay over for the night, so the lads listened to some new music that Mike had bought. There was a new group on the scene called 'Frankie Goes to Hollywood'. They were all the rage as their single 'Relax' had gone to Number 1 in the charts but had been banned from all radio stations for its explicit sexual comments. Greg and Mike thought this hilarious and played the song repeatedly. 'Frankies' music was a far cry from the 'SKA' music they were into, but they were starting to really find their music tastes and were beginning to like many different types of music genre.

Greg decided to keep away from Heale's next game. It was against a team near to Plymouth and he knew that he wouldn't be back till very late afternoon. He had a backlog of homework that was due in on the Monday and he couldn't afford to miss any more deadlines. He had made a promise to his mum and dad that he would buck up his ideas as his schoolwork had to dramatically improve before they would allow him to take up Lens' offer of joining some training sessions at Torquay United.

Greg's schoolwork improved immediately. His classroom behaviour changed back to the Greg of old and his class work went back to the top of the class, all in less than two weeks. He was getting great marks for his homework and the school had even contacted David and Carol to inform them of Greg's change of attitude. Greg was still hoping that it wasn't all going to be a waste of time. He did prefer learning than not as he knew that he would need his education in later life. He just hadn't heard from the Devon FA and he was really missing the buzz of being around the Heale team. They were still playing OK and were now equal second in the league. With only one team to get promoted they were looking like missing out once again. They had been given an easy Cup draw and had won to get through to the next round.

Torquay had appointed Jay Pinner as Manager until the end of the season, a move Greg wasn't sure was right, but they had won their opening game at home to Chesterfield and played well so only time would tell. West Ham were playing well and still in mid-table. Greg was happy with this and looking forward to the 3rd Round draw of the FA Cup, when all the Division 1 and 2 teams entered the competition. He was so hopeful of a cup run this year.

A letter finally arrived on the Saturday morning, two weeks after the appeal hearing. This was it; Greg didn't want to open it for fear of the outcome. He stood and stared at the envelope. Alison came into the front room and saw Greg holding his destiny.

'Do you want me to read it?'

'Yes, please sis.'

She knew what football meant to him and although he was a pain in the arse was a good brother. She opened the envelope and pulled out the letter. Without speaking she read it. 'What's it say? Alison, what does it say?'

'Basically, your initial two-week suspension was upheld but on seeking further advice they have decided to drop the indefinite suspension. They have put some rules in place that you and Heale have to agree and follow for your own protection as a minor but basically, you can go back Greg.'

He ran at Alison and threw his arms around her, as if she had made the ruling. She wasn't bothered, it wasn't everyday she got a hug off her kid brother.

CHAPTER 31

Snow had come to Torquay, not something Greg had known before. It had snowed when he was a very young child but not since. His parents had told him how well protected The Bay was from adverse weather conditions and up till now they had been right. He was due to attend his first training session since his suspension, but it had been cancelled, even the all-weather pitch was frozen. All games on Sunday had been called off and none were being played the following two weeks due to the Christmas and New Year break. A new rule had been introduced giving all Sunday league clubs two weeks off over the festive season as many teams struggled to field full strength sides due to family and work commitments. The League had begun one week earlier this season and was to run one week later than normal to accommodate the changes. Greg knew it was a good idea, but he just wanted to get back to what he loved. It was FA Cup 2nd round day and many games in the country had been cancelled. Many of the Division 1 clubs had underground heating and enough stewards to clear the snow off the pitches but most of the lower league clubs had little chance. There was a few that beat the odds and Greg listened intently to the radio and kept his eye on Grandstand, The BBC's Saturday afternoon sports programme for any football news. The Gulls game had been called off and West Ham were playing away to Chelsea. He wondered if his uncles were attending that one.

The final whistles had gone and the teleprinter had finished. Tim Gudgin read out the classified results in his very distinctive tone that Greg had got very used to. It was a voice that Greg could have recognised anywhere. The screen then focused on two ex-footballers who were stood in front of two buckets of balls, and a board to place them in. Greg instantly recognised one of the men, his family's hero, Bobby Moore. He would be pulling out the home teams and next to him, Roger Hunt, formerly of Liverpool and as the commentator was very proud to point out, both World Cup Winners. Roger would be pulling out the away teams. This was the draw for the 3rd round of the FA Cup. After a few balls had been picked out, Bobby pulled out number 61. The commentator announced that it was West Ham. Everyone in the studio laughed as Bobby Moore looked on quite embarrassed. Roger then pulled out number 27, Liverpool. What were the odds? Everyone in the studio laughed at the chances of it happening.

Greg shouted at the TV. 'No, why us? Why can't we ever have a cup run?'

Liverpool were the best club team in Europe and probably the World and his beloved West Ham had just drawn them. What luck?

CHAPTER 32

Christmas day at the Welling's was always memorable. Greg and Alison always got spoilt with plenty of presents from David and Carol. Presents from distant relatives added to their haul and kept them occupied for the entire day. Greg got a new West Ham kit plus lots of books and magazines.

He had some random toys and new Cow horn handlebars for his bike. Alison got make-up, clothes and a Jackie Album as well as much more. The family had just finished their Christmas dinner when Carol presented an envelope to both Greg and Alison. Alison ripped hers open and inside was a train ticket to London and £50.00 of cash. The card inside read,

To Alison,

Have a great Christmas. come and visit your aunties in London and they will help you spend your cash.

Love you and see you soon,

the London Clan.

She whooped in joy, she had always wanted to shop in Oxford Street, now she could. Greg watched the excitement in Alison's face and quickly ripped open his envelope. Inside his was also a card that read,

'To Greg,

We know how much of a Hammers fan you are so we thought you might want to join your uncles in watching them play Liverpool in the FA Cup. We can't promise you the result you want but we can promise you a day to never forget.

Love you and see you soon,

The London Clan.

Greg looked at his mum. 'I'm going to Upton Park with uncles Harry, Paul, Tom and Mike.'

'Don't forget about me young man. They have six tickets.'

'Cool, but what about dad, don't you want to come?'

'I'm away on a course bud, I don't believe for one minute that I will be missed or that your uncles will want me to go either.'

'How are we getting there?' asked Greg.

'We will take the early train to Paddington Station. Alison will be met by your aunties who will then take her on a shop till you drop spree in London. You and I will catch the tube and meet up with your uncles near the ground. We will then meet Alison back at Paddington later in the evening.'

Greg and Alison spent the rest of the evening planning out their day to London. They were both super excited and only wished it was sooner and not in two weeks' time.

CHAPTER 33

The next two weeks felt like some of the longest in Greg's short life. He loved the Christmas period, especially with the amount of professional football being played. He longed to get back to help manage Heale and hopefully helping them climb back up the table. He spent lots of time with Mike and met up with Tre once a week, which seemed to suit them both. He idled away any spare time reading his new football books and trying to digest any extra information that he could. Television was always good over the festive season and new films like The Wizard of Oz and Oliver were always put on prime time for family entertainment.

New Year's Day was a great football occasion. The Gulls were at home to Exeter City, as big a derby as Torquay could get. Exeter we're flying high at the top of the division and were now firm favourites for promotion. Torquay's form had improved and although they had drawn most of their games under Jay Pinner, they were still unbeaten since he took over. As always Greg met up with his trusted mates and enjoyed the atmosphere created by both sets of fans. Exeter had sold out their allocation of tickets and the ground was at two-thirds capacity. It wasn't often that so many fans adorned Plainmoor. The game swung two and from, ending in a 2-2 draw. Another positive result, Greg was pleased for Len. Even though the fans hadn't liked Bruce Ricoh, they still gave Len a hard time for sacking him. Who would be a football chairman? Unfortunately, the walk home wasn't so good. After the game they had hung around outside listening to the radio, catching up with all the top division results. Most games on New Year's Day, as well as Torquay's had kicked off at midday, so they were in no rush to get home. Usually the away supporters arrived and left on coaches, so crowd trouble was very minimal. The four boys didn't reckon on many of the Exeter fans making their own way to the ground. Away fans were kept in the ground for 15 minutes after the match so that the home fans could disperse, avoiding any possible trouble. Danny was the first to notice that they were being followed by three older kids, probably 17-18 years old. Without trying to draw attention to the fact that he knew the three lads following were Exeter fans, red and white scarves gave them away, he tried his best to tell the other three but be as subtle as possible.

They were approaching a bend when Danny announced, 'Don't ask and don't look behind but when we get around this corner, run. The three lads behind us are Exeter fans and I reckon they want a piece of us. Unless Greg is going to play Rocky Balboa, I reckon our best chance is to outrun them. If we get split up, we'll meet back at the corner shop on St. Mary church Road'.

They all nodded and as soon as they rounded the corner, ran. Greg was quick and left the other three behind. Once he thought he was out of harm's way he stopped and looked back. Bringing up the rear was Steve and Danny, but no sign of Graham or the Exeter fans. All three headed to the corner shop and waited for Graham but he never arrived. They waited for half an hour and decided to make their own way home, just like they hoped Graham had.

Graham though was on his way to hospital in the back of an ambulance. He had run down an alley and fallen over. The Exeter fans had chased him as he was the slowest and were about to give up the chase when he fell. Graham curled up in a ball as fists and boots rained down on him. Luckily the Exeter fans were disturbed by a large group of Torquay fans and fled before they received what they were dishing out.

After wiping away the blood the hospital nurses treated Graham's cuts as superficial and let him leave when his parents arrived.

CHAPTER 34

Saturday 3rd Jan 1981, Greg's first visit to Upton Park. Carol, Greg and Alison had boarded the 08:12 train going from Penzance in Cornwall through to Paddington, London. They boarded the train at Newton Abbot and took their pre-booked seats, arriving in the Capital three hours later. At the station they wandered over to a coffee shop and purchased some refreshments. Ten minutes later, Carol's, sisters in law, Lesley and Tracey arrived. There were lots of hugs and kisses and a part of Carol wished she was going with them into the city. Alison left with her aunties and they were meeting up with her other two aunties, Karen and Lisa later that morning.

With the girls gone it was time for Carol and Greg to catch the tube to East London. Carol purchased two tickets and led the way. She knew exactly where she was going and within 20 minutes, they had crossed central London and were riding their final tube train into East London. Greg was as excited as he had ever been in his life. Kick off was still two and a half hours away but the train was filling up with West Ham fans at every stop. Claret and blue tops, scarves, hats and gloves were adorned by every fan joining the train. He had never witnessed anything like this before. Greg felt the train gradually slowing down and minutes later most of the compartment had emptied out onto the platform. Greg followed Carol along the platform and up the steps. They entered the notorious Green Street. They turned right and Carol tried to hold Greg's hand in fear of losing him. He pulled his hand away, although he was out of his comfort zone and not wanting to get lost, he was not going to hold his mum's hand. Carol smiled and told Greg to 'keep close'.

They walked past an outdoor market selling anything from Caribbean food to second-hand shoes. There were stalls everywhere with people trading at all of them. Next door to the market was The Queen's, a notorious drinking hole for many a Hammers fan. Carol stopped and stood in front of two burly bouncers, manning The Queens doors. The bouncers looked at Carol and then at Greg.

'Sorry love, we can't let the young lad in, rules are rules.'

Greg loved the way he spoke, just like his uncles. Just then a head that Greg recognised very well bent past the door, 'Its OK Tel, they're with me.'

'Well why didn't you say you were with Harry love?' and he ushered Carol and Greg in. The pub was full of West Ham fans, and smoke. Greg could hardly see it was that dense. Harry led them to a table situated in the corner where his three brothers were sitting. Carol ran up to them and embraced them as if she hadn't seen them for years. It was probably ten months since her last visit and she really missed them. Greg loved his uncles, and this was the first time he had seen them in their own environment, he only ever saw them in Torquay when they visited and were on their best behaviour.

Harry got in 'a round' of lagers and a coke for Greg. Carol and her brothers caught up on lots of family gossip whilst Greg listened intently and watched the number of punters entering and leaving the pub. After another round of drinks Tom announced that they were 'moving on'. They left the pub and carried on walking along Green Street. Mike stopped next to a burger van and ordered 6 cheeseburgers and chips, all with extra onion. There was now only an hour till kick off and the street was filled with fans. The traffic was struggling to move as many people were walking on the road; it was quicker than the pavement and as far as the fans were concerned, the traffic could wait. Greg caught sight of the ground and his eyes widened. It was nowhere near as impressive as the Nou Camp in Barcelona but to him it was his Mecca.

The noise, buzz of excitement from the fans and seeing the stadium was an awesome experience. As they neared the stadium Tom stopped at a street vendor and purchased two West Ham scarves. He gave one each to Carol and Greg. Greg was wearing his new West Ham football top that he had been given at Christmas, but it was hidden by his coat. Greg put it round his neck and wore it with pride, he felt like he belonged. They rounded a corner and joined a queue that seemed to be very long. The game was all-ticket, and Paul held six tickets in his hand. The queue gradually moved forward until they were next to the turnstiles. Greg could hear and see men near the turnstiles asking for any spare tickets, for a generous cash purchase.

'Shall I sell these tickets Greg?'

Greg shot a look at his uncle Paul.

'I don't want to be the first kid to get done for murdering his uncle so probably not, Uncle Paul.'

They all laughed at his quick humour, all the brothers and Carol wanted to believe he got his humour from them, but it was probably just a mix of the whole family. They entered the ground and Carol went to purchase a programme.

'Not today sis', insisted Paul, and he handed over the money. 'Today is on us', and he handed her the programme. She thanked him and handed it to Greg. Another keepsake for the day. The group made their way through the crowd and stood directly behind the goal. The Liverpool fans were enclosed in a small section to the left of them. They were already singing and making lots of noise. The stadium was only half full, but Tom had explained to Greg that most of the fans didn't arrive until near kick off, beer was very important in this neck of the woods. The stadium was looking old and tired and Tom had also told Greg about the plans to renovate the ground and bring it up to date. Greg took in the atmosphere and read through the programme, page by page not missing any articles. The stadium announcer read out the teams, Liverpool players were booed, and the home players cheered. Greg watched intently as both sets of players warmed-up, he was hoping to learn anything he could which he could take back to Torquay and use it with Heale. Both sets of players returned to the changing rooms and the ground filled. The players returned to the pitch to a chorus of support from both sets of fans. With only a few seconds left to kick off, a full rendition of 'I'm forever blowing bubbles' erupted around the ground. Greg sang at the top of his voice, joined by his mum, uncles and 30 odd thousand other Hammers fans. The atmosphere in the ground was something Greg could never have imagined, and he was loving it.

Liverpool had put out a very strong team and were passing the ball around very nicely, but West Ham were buoyed on by their very raucous crowd and were chasing every ball. Tackles were flying in hard and fast making the crowd even more rowdy. Greg struggled to see all the action but manoeuvred himself well enough to catch most of it. A slick Liverpool move was coolly finished off by their prime striker, Kenny Dalglish. It was probably a fair reflection on the game so far. The Liverpool fans celebrated wildly to the left of Greg; red scarves being waved high.

Suddenly, Greg was swept along, nearly falling over in the rush of bodies. About two hundred West Ham fans had charged the fence separating both sets of fans. He couldn't go against the wave, so he just allowed himself to be dragged along with the crowd. Greg was stunned and saddened by what he saw next. The thug element of West Ham fans was throwing coins at the Liverpool fans, trying to cut and hurt them. He saw a Liverpool fan take a coin to the side of his left eye. A cut opened automatically, and blood spurted from the gash. A chorus of cheers were heard from the West Ham fans as they had achieved their goal. Stewards in yellow high-vis jackets soon took control, standing in front of the segregated fence. Greg felt a large hand on his shoulder and looked behind to see Harry. Harry grabbed Greg by his jacket and pulled him closer. They then headed back to where Greg had been stood prior. Carol saw Greg and grabbed him.

'Are you OK Greg?'

'Yes mum.'

One second, I was here the next I was staring at the Liverpool fans. One of them got cut in the eye and Carol cut him short, 'I know what goes on Greg, it's not all pretty in here, they get over passionate sometimes. Try to stay near your uncles, they will look after you, no one will mess with them.'

West Ham had a corner which was cleared to the edge of the box. The ball fell to Alan Devonshire, an exciting young player. He struck the ball powerfully, but it was going off target until it hit the Liverpool captain Phil Thompson and ricochet's past the goalkeeper and into the net, 1-1. Greg went mad with jubilation. The noise in the stadium was ear blowing and 90% of the crowd were going crazy. Greg turned around to see his four uncles and mum jumping up and down in the same elated way as he was. Another rendition of blowing bubbles echoed around the ground, this time sang with far more gusto and passion. Lots of new songs were being sung and Greg listened intently trying to hear every word. Many of the songs made sense but some were just too hard to understand, he knew that he was too young to understand most of them.

There were a few chances for both sides before half time but no more goals. Greg took a breath. The crowd thinned out somewhat as many went off to grab refreshments.

'How was that for a first half Greg?'

'Unbelievable Uncle Mike. It's crazy in here. The atmosphere is incredible, nothing like Torquay.'

Greg spent the next 15 minutes talking about the first half with Paul, Mike and Carol, analysing it as best they could. Tom and Harry returned to them with six coffees and sausage rolls, fuel needed to be ready for the second half.

The second half got under way and both sets of fans were hopeful of a positive result. Liverpool once again started the better but even with all their possession had minimal chances. Twenty minutes in and West Ham got a free kick half the way inside the Liverpool half. Trevor Brooking, West Hams talisman swung the ball in, and it was met by the head of David Cross. It was a bullet header and gave the Liverpool keeper no chance. Greg thought the crowd had gone crazy after the first goal, but he had no idea that they could better that. It was pure delirium within the ground and Greg lost his voice shouting and screaming. Liverpool pushed and pushed for an equaliser and West Ham dropped back deeper, desperately trying to hold on to the win. The crowd got edgy which brought about another type of atmosphere. The fans tried their hardest not to show desperation, but you could sense it in the air. When the referee blew his whistle for the final time, Greg was grabbed by his uncles and he and his mum celebrated with a group hug. They held each other enjoying the family bond that they had. Outside the ground, the great atmosphere carried on into the streets. The traffic ground to a halt as most of the fans headed towards the tube station. Once again, the family stopped outside a food stall. This time Paul ordered five large and one small donor kebabs. Greg had never had one before and was unsure if he would like it, the meat looked very different from anything he had seen before. He agreed to garlic and chilli sauce, "in for a penny in for a pound". They all sat on a low garden wall and tucked into their third take away meal of the day. Greg devoured his kebab. His uncles joked with him that he would be living off them every night he went out when he was old enough to drink. Greg didn't really get the joke but laughed with them anyway. One final drink in the now very packed Queens pub followed before Carol and Greg headed back to Paddington. Greg couldn't thank his uncles enough for such a magical day. They thanked him for being a lucky mascot; he would come in handy again one day.

Greg didn't shut up all the way back to Paddington. Carol didn't know where he got his energy from; she was just so pleased he had enjoyed himself and especially the result. They met Alison back at the coffee shop where they had left her. She was also glowing and had a fantastic afternoon with her aunties. They had spoilt her rotten and with the money she had received at Christmas and had lots of shopping bags to show for it.

All three slept for most of the journey back to Devon. It was a trip that Greg and Alison would never forget and a wonderful journey down memory lane for Carol.

CHAPTER 35

Greg returned to Tuesday training as his schoolwork and attitude had improved greatly. He was also allowed to attend all home and away matches so long as his grades didn't drop. He kept plenty of time for Mike and their friendship grew stronger. Little did Greg know that his friendship with Mike was going to evolve into a lifelong companionship, brotherly almost! Greg also made time for Tre. They would meet up at school as much as possible and at least once a week after school, even if it was only for the odd hour. Their bodies were developing and changing rapidly, and they were beginning to recognise this. There was plenty of fun to be had finding out.

Heale were now playing much better and had a settled team. They were back to the top of the League and undefeated for seven games. They were in the last 8 of the Cup and had another home draw to make it into the semi-finals for the first time in 14 years. Greg changed the style and personnel depending on the opposition and had re-introduced the scouting of the next week's opponents as a must. He really believed this to make a difference.

Torquay united had started to pick up points home and away and although they weren't going to get promoted, they were also not going to get relegated. Greg had attended two of The Gulls youth team training sessions. He helped Mike set up small sessions, laying out cones etc, and generally just watching and learning. After the second session he was asked for his opinion on the young players. Who did he believe had the necessary skills and temperament? Greg really liked the look of two of the squad; they were a level above the rest. Greg didn't know them and where they were from, he didn't even know if they were on a youth contract, he just spoke the truth. He was thanked for his honesty and invited back to the training sessions whenever he could make them. They were usually on a Tuesday evening or if there were no game Saturday mornings. Greg wasn't going to give up his training with Heale, so Saturdays were his only option.

School football had started again and the years 1-5 were all in competition. Greg's year (3) was now coached by Mr Savage who was a few notches above Mr Rogers but still a dinosaur when it came to training and tactics. Tre's brother Mark had attended the new trials system (designed to give all kids a chance of making the squad or team and not just the same faces as the previous year). Mark, although his first name was Robert, was a left sided defender and had replaced Greg in the team. Greg wasn't even deemed good enough to make the squad so had little to nothing to do with the team anymore. The team all knew of Greg's desire to help, but Mr Savage was far too proud to ask for help from a pupil so carried on in his ways. With the inclusion of Mark, the team had strengthened, and he hoped for success from them this year, even if the opposition was very strong. They had played a few friendly games and won them with ease. He couldn't work out why they played to a different way to the one he wanted and was very unaware of the 'Welling factor ingrained into the young boy's heads. Lee and Pokey were learning new tactics every week, at training and from the senior players at Heale. It had made them grow up greatly on the football pitch the past few months.

Heale won their next game 5-0 away to Stoke Gabriel who had been relegated from the top division only a year earlier. On relegation they had lost a few of their best players but had been one of the favourites for promotion. Heale had really done a number on them and Greg had listened to Rog who had watched them the week earlier. Rog had twisted his knee in a workplace accident and declared himself unfit. He had taken great care in his job role and Greg knew that Rog would have a great career in Sunday League management when he decided to retire.

After the game, the players and staff went straight to the Bull and Bush for a charity auction in aid of getting back to the old stadium. All the players had been tasked with getting at least one auction item that would be worth bidding on.

There were a few 'naff' lots but the majority were good. Some still hadn't been announced and were anticipated to be worth the wait. Pete had volunteered to run the auction and silenced the room. There were at least 100 people crammed into the room. There were lots of family, friends and punters from the other bar. There were also players from rival clubs, just coming along to add extra support. Most of the auction lots went cheaply, between one and three pounds but the atmosphere was fun. The first lot to draw excitement was a pair of rugby tickets to watch England vs Wales at Twickenham in the Five Nations. Tickets usually cost £8-10 each. David Welling had called in a favour from an old pal who had donated them. Greg hoped they would sell for nearly the cost price as it would certainly make a dent in the £100.00, they needed for a deposit. At £10.00 for the pair the hammer was sounded, and David Welling had purchased his own lot. He wanted to do something for his son and had made Greg promise to go with him if he won them. Len had donated a signed Torquay United ball that made £5.00. There was one final lot left. This was donated by a miscellaneous group of brothers who did not want to be known but lived in East London. Greg wandered who that might have been. The lot was a West Ham shirt signed by Billy Bonds and Trevor Brooking. Pete held up the shirt which was in a large glass frame and asked for the auction to begin at 50 pence. Greg's eyes were still popping out of his head at the sight of such a wonderful thing.

'Did Pete say 50p? Was he having a fucking laugh? Fifty pence.'

Greg looked round the room, 'Were they being serious? Surely someone wanted that shirt? Fuck, he wanted that shirt.'

'One pound' someone shouted from the back. A few laughs could be heard in the audience. 'One pound twenty-five' someone else shouted. It was going up in 25 pence's, surely not. Greg was getting more and more anxious. He never noticed that most of the crowd were watching him. This was a signed football shirt, even if you didn't like West Ham it was a cracking auction prize.

'Dad, bid, pleeease.'

'OK son, one pound fifty.'

'Dad this is for our club, one pound fifty.'

'Yeah but I'm winning son.'

'Three pounds, final offer, came a shout from Rog.'

How could he thought Greg.

'Final bloody offer.'

'Dad, bid again.'

I can't son; I used all my money on the rugby tickets.'

Greg couldn't hold his tongue anymore. He jumped to the front of the crowd and joined Pete on the little stage. Greg grabbed Pete's microphone.

'This is a signed, (he repeated his word) signed shirt of two great players. I know its West Ham and I'm a little biased, but this is the best lot of the night, by far. All this money is going towards our club, your club. When we get promoted this year we need to be playing at our own little ground, not sharing pitches with every Tom, Dick and Harry. If we are going to get back to our old little ground, then we need as much money as possible.'

Greg stopped ranting and realised that everyone was laughing, he wasn't sure if it was at him or not. Pete put his arm around Greg's shoulders.

'We're all having you on Greg, sorry we couldn't help it.'

'What it's not a real signed shirt?'

'Oh, it's real alright, the shirt and signatures. We all decided not to bid because we knew you wouldn't be able to deal with no one wanting the shirt. Guess what? We were right.'

Greg's face reddened, he had been part of a prank and he had fallen for it big style.

'You will be pleased to know that nearly everyone in this room has given me a pound for the shirt; they reckon it would look good in the club bar, if we ever get it back. So, I can tell you that I have 92 pounds in my pocket. This shirt belongs to everyone in the club. I also have a letter from John Batson, joint owner of Torbay Glazers. (John was a well-respected businessman and son of Len Batson). Torbay Glazers have offered to supply the goalposts, nets, corner flags and balls for next season, if we get back to the old ground. All they want is for us to promote them as much as possible. Their logo will be on our new shirts next season, and they want us to put up some advertising on a few hoardings around the ground and in the club house. It seems like a good deal to me.'

Lots of nods and smiles could be seen, true progress. Greg stayed on stage.

'I also have some good news. I met up with Len Batson a few months ago. He has agreed to help us fix up the club bar, free of charge.'

More cheers from inside the room. Greg looked at Pete and Ross. 'Does that mean we have the money to move in next season?'

'I will have to speak to the Rugby Club and find out if they are still happy to ground share, but the ground is getting really run-down so I'm hoping they'll snap our hands off. I will then have to go to the FA and confirm our change of move. Hopefully they will forget about some of our misdemeanours this season and give us the green light, but to answer your question Greg, yes, I believe so.'

There were lots of cheers and back slapping, Heale were going home.

CHAPTER 36

Greg was stood inside the Torquay United changing rooms watching the Heale players get ready for arguably the biggest match of their amateur careers. He was very proud of the group and how far they had come in the past 18 months. Today was the last game of the season with all league matches now complete. Promotions and relegations had been decided and today's game was the very last of the current season, the Final of the Devon Herald Cup. Heale had progressed through the rounds with little difficulty until their semi-final against last year's Division 1 Champions, West Allington United. The game was as good as any to have been found in an amateur league and Heale eventually won a minute before the end of extra time. Heale had already been crowned Division 2 Champions two weeks earlier and had managed to rest most of the players in the week leading up to the semi-final. The players had celebrated in style after winning the Championship and had probably needed the week off to get over their hangovers.

Greg looked around the changing room. He knew that they were underdogs for the game and that their opponents, Watcome Wolves were strong favourites. Years ago, both teams had a strong rivalry but since Heale's drop into the lower league that rivalry had diminished. Watcome had been crowned this seasons Division 1 Champions and were attempting 'the double'. Not since 1970 had a club won Division 1 and The Herald Cup in the same season. Kick off was at 14.00 hours, 45 minutes away. Greg stood in the centre of the changing rooms.

'Right guys, kit on as quick as you can. It's time to go out and warm up. I want this warm up to be as professional as you've ever done. I don't want Watcome thinking they are playing a bunch of no hopers; I want them to see we are totally serious. Soak up the atmosphere, there will be a good crowd in today. C'mon then, lets shake a leg.'

Everyone laughed at Greg trying to be the authoritarian but still got ready in quick time. They knew he was right; he always was.

Greg let the players leave the dressing room and was about to follow them when Ross stopped him.

'Hey kidda. Some team we make eh. You have been like a breath of fresh air this year, those lads owe it all to you, in fact so does the whole club, Promotion, Cup Final, returning to our old ground. You're a superstar young man.'

'You're the superstar Ross. You run around for everyone, do all the training, arrange travel, sort out the monies, manage the away games, you ARE Heale Athletic. The team would crumble if you weren't around.'

'Greg, you're the first person I've told, even my wife is unaware, but this is my last game in charge of Heale. I am resigning as Manager after the game.'

'No, you can't, why? I won't let you.'

'I'm not leaving for good Greg. I'm going to take over control of the financial running of the club and help with the club bar on match days. You Greg Welling, are the future of this club. Dave Waters will be named as Manager, with you staying on as Assistant. Dave is fully aware that you have full control of team affairs and is only Manager in name only. The FA have already confirmed that no one under the age of sixteen can be a Manager, courtesy of you, young man. A new rule they never presumed they'd have to make. Rog has agreed to take over my role at training and is keen to get into the training, management side of things. He knows he only has one more season of playing left in him, at best, and wants to pick your brains before you go off and manage Real Madrid or West Ham! I really want to go out on a high today. I always hoped we would get promoted while I was still here; I was in the team when it got relegated and it really hurt. We are back where we belong; I just want to see us lift that Cup as well, what a good way to end eh? Please don't let on to anyone. I will let the lads know later, win or lose.'

'Win Ross, we have to win. I want to see you and Woody lift that Cup, I still don't want you to leave though, I'll really miss you.'

Ross and Greg walked out onto the plush playing turf of Plainmoor. The team were split into four groups and doing different exercises with or without the ball. They did look very professional. The Herald Cup always drew a big crowd, it was the premier cup for the County and enticed an audience of amateur footballers, playing and retired. Greg looked into the Main Stand and noticed Len in his usual seat.

Next to him was Jay Pinner on one side and Mike Foster to the other. Also, in the director's area was some of the Torquay United squad and one player that Greg was made up to see, Les Lawrence. Greg caught his eye. Les raised his right arm and gave Greg a military style salute in acknowledgement. Also in the crowd were Steve, Danny and Graham, they wouldn't have missed it for the world. Mike had brought along Tre, both hated football but had come along to support Greg. Finally, Greg caught sight of his parents and Alison, everyone that he wanted there had turned up. All he needed now was for Heale to win.

The teams finished warming up and returned to the changing rooms. Greg ushered the players into the changing room and asked for quiet. The players had been told of the team at training on the Tuesday so were already prepared. They had practised with a slightly different role. Greg was going to experiment with a sweeper. He had watched Watcome two weeks before and was very impressed with the way they played. They were strong in every department and had only lost 2 games all season. He could see why they were the best team in the league. They were extremely quick when attacking and were great on the counterattack. Greg presumed that they would use the size of the Plainmoor pitch to utilise their speed and wanted to counter that. (The sweeper is a more versatile centre-back who "sweeps up" the ball if an opponent manages to breach the defensive line).

The team were to play a 1-4-3-1-1- formation. Since reaching the final Greg and Ross had installed the importance of fitness to the team. They both knew that a fully fit team would have a better chance of winning. They had imposed a drinking ban on all the players (they knew this wouldn't be followed but at least the players would cut down on their drinking). Greg stood in the middle of the changing room and asked Ross to join him.

'Lads, as you know it is usually down to me to conduct the team talk but as far as I'm concerned you are as ready as you can be. Do what you have trained for and stick to the plan, I believe you are good enough to win today. I want Ross to finish the team talk. He has been with you/us for years and this is very much his final, win it for him.'

Greg really wanted to tell all the players of Ross' plans but thought better of it. Ross joined Greg, who retreated to a spare space on a seat within the squad. Ross looked at everyone and drew a very deep breath. He had conducted hundreds of team talks but he wasn't prepared for this one, his final one. A few strange looks appeared on some of the senior players, they had never seen Ross loss for words.

'This is one of the proudest days of my life. I've seen my two children enter this world and I've married the woman I love. This club has become a massive part of me and to be stood here waiting to lead you out in a Cup Final is a dream come true. It may only be an amateur club trophy, but this is MY FA Cup. Don't let it be just mine though, let it be yours. This is the start of a massive journey for you. You are the first lower division club to play in a final in over 10 years and not since the sixties has a club from the lower leagues won it. I'm proud of who we are and where we are going. This has been one of the best seasons I can remember; let's finish it off in style. I know lots of your friends and families are out there right now willing you to win, don't let them down. All I ask is you give me 100% today. If we lose then it's to a better team. I want that Trophy sitting next to our Division 2 trophy next year. I want to build a Trophy cabinet in our new club bar, and I want you guys to be the ones that put the trophies in it. Now go out there and win this thing.'

Before a chorus of male testosterone adrenalin filled the room he quickly spoke again. 'One last thing. Listen to Cloughie out there. Remember we call him that for a reason.'

The referee entered the room and gave a one-minute warning. Ross led the players into the small tunnel and joined the Watcome team who were already there. Ross called for Greg to join him who duly did. The referee nodded to both Managers and walked out onto the pitch. The 1500 or so supporters clapped and shouted in celebration of seeing their teams. Ross had never felt so proud. He looked behind to give Greg a nod of well-being, but Greg wasn't there. Behind Ross was Woody the Captain. Greg had wanted Ross to lead the team out on his own, he deserved it. He just hoped he would get the chance to do it another time.

The game got off to a frantic start with Watcome piling on lots of pressure. Heale let them attack, they had planned this would happen. Division 1 Champions showing the underdogs why they were the best in the league. Eventually Heale started getting more and more of the ball and were playing nice keep-ball football, trying to keep the ball on the floor and not in the air. Watcome were starting to get frustrated with the lack of ball and when they did get the ball attacked quickly. Greg had decided not to play for off-side and had the sweeper, Rog, deep in his own half. Rog wasn't a good defender; he just read the game brilliantly and could also pass the ball better than anyone in the team. He was the obvious choice. A swift attack by Watcome finished with the ball at Rog's feet. He saw Sharpy making a run down the left side of Watcomes half and hit a 50-yard pass to him. Up till now all Heale's football had been short passes and now this huge long ball. Sharpy ran on to the ball and cut inside the defender who had been caught out by Rog's majestic pass. Sharpy moved into the area, feigned to shoot and dribbled around the keeper. It wasn't clear whether the defender of keeper caught his legs but Sharpy went down before he could take a shot. It was as clear a penalty as you would see, and the ref pointed straight to the spot. A few of the Watcome players appealed for off-side but more in desperation than anything. Sharpey picked up the ball; no-one was getting it off him. He stepped up to take the kick and powered the ball straight down the middle, 1-0 to Heale. What seemed like ten thousand fans cheered in jubilation when in fact it was probably only a few hundred. Heale made it to half time without conceding and by playing assured football.

Greg led the half time talk; Ross was more than happy with that. He knew Watcome would change things at half time and knew Greg would have a plan. The Watcome Manager, Oliver York (Olly) had managed at high level non-league and had once led a team to the FA Vase final at Wembley, he knew his stuff. He was now retired and managed Watcome to starve off boredom at home. Greg asked all the players if they were 'all OK' and if they had any small injuries. He went over some finer points of the first half and tried to heap praise on every player. He was happy with how the game was going and saw no need to change anything. He told the players that Watcome would resort to different tactics if the score stayed the same and that he would react to them if it seemed necessary. One final burst of emotion and the players returned to the pitch.

Watcome started the half as they did the start of the first. They had probably received a severe bollocking at half time and were trying to rectify the result. Oliver had played a steady 4-4-2 in the first half but was concerned with the sweeper. After 10 minutes and no sign of a goal he made a double substitution. He replaced a defender for a forward and a midfielder for a forward/winger. They were now playing 3-3-4. The two wingers would be dropping back to defend where necessary, but this was a very attacking looking team. Olly looked across at Greg, he didn't want to be another senior manager getting outthought by this kid.

Greg left his bench and approached the side lines. Olly looked smug; the kid was panicking. Greg shouted instructions over to Woody. Rog was to move into midfield. They were now a sturdy 4-4-1-1. They had one more in midfield, Greg wanted that to pay. He wasn't making any changes, not yet. Olly had heard a lot about Greg and his use of different formations. He wasn't afraid of making changes himself and wanted to make the first move. He felt sure that Greg would respond but was shocked by Greg's calm thought process and that he made no changes. He was hoping that Greg was out of his depth, but by the way he was coaching his team from the side of the pitch he very much doubted it. Watcome were attacking at every opportunity but Heale were coping with everything. Greg changed Sharpy for French and replaced Peas for Ginge. He kept the same formation just freshened up the team. Sharpy and Peas had run their socks off and even though they didn't want to come off, the large pitch had got the better of them, they couldn't run another step. Greg had ordered French to stay up front no matter what. Watcome would always have to leave two players on him and he was instructed to chase and harass for every ball, something he was very good at. He had 15 minutes to make a mark on the game. Ginge was brought on to cause a bit of havoc in the Watcome defence. He wasn't as disciplined as Peas but if he got the ball was more skill full and he attacked with great vigour. Greg could see the Watcome defenders were slowing slightly and wanted Ginge to get the ball whenever possible to cause them maximum trouble. Greg's plan worked well and Watcome started to defend deeper due to the new threat.

With five minutes to go Olly played his final card and put on another striker. He was now playing with 3-2-1-4. It was all or nothing. Greg stood and monitored the team. Yes, they were tired, but they all looked fit. Watcome had a corner and had overloaded the Heale goal area. Ginge started to run back to help defend when Greg stopped him.

'Stay where you are Ginge.'

The corner was whipped in and after a small goalmouth scramble the ball was collected by Pete Northcott in goal. In a flash he stood and threw the ball in the direction of Ginge. Ginge and a Watcome defender both went for the ball but Ging was a little quicker. He controlled the ball, looked up and passed the ball through to French. In one stride he looked up and saw the Watcome keeper rushing towards him. A beautifully judged chip was floated over the keeper and the ball rolled towards the goal. It seemed to take forever before the ball eventually rolled over the line and gently nestled into the empty net. It was game over. French was mobbed by players and subs in a melee of delirium. The Watcome players slumped to their knees, they knew there was no coming back. The final few minutes were played out in a blur, Heale were going to be the new holders of the Herald Cup.

A small stage was erected onto the pitch and Olly and his team went up one by one to collect their loser's medals. They were obviously gutted but had the comfort knowing that they were League Champions. They also knew that they would be playing Heale at least twice next season, plenty of time for payback. The Heale players followed, this time collecting a winner's medal. They all felt extremely proud as Dan Oakenfell shook everyone's hand and hung a medal round their neck. The last two to collect medals were Ross and Woody. The new rules had allowed for four substitutes in the final instead of the normal two. This resulted in 15 players and the manager receiving a medal. Ross was nearing Dan and in a world of his own when he realised Greg wouldn't be receiving a medal. Greg was stood nearby and saw Ross trying to usher him over. Greg shook his head, this was Ross' day, he deserved it, if it wasn't for Ross he wouldn't even have been there. Greg stood his ground and carried on clapping the players as they collected their medals. Eventually Woody reached the FA Chairman. Once he had his medal firmly round his neck, he and Ross lifted the shiny trophy together. The crowd that had remained were allowed onto the pitch to witness the celebrations and they created a party atmosphere. Greg found his parents who couldn't' help tell him how proud they were of him. Steve, Danny and Graham were trying to get the autographs of any of the Torquay players that were still around and had found Greg to pass on their congratulations. Greg got a large smack of a kiss from Tre and a good man-hug from Mike. Len made sure he found Greg and informed him that work on the Club bar would be beginning in the next week. A deal was a deal after all. Greg was overwhelmed and couldn't thank Len enough. Les Lawrence and Mike Foster also found Greg and passed on their congratulations. Everyone wanted a piece of Greg, he felt like royalty. Olly Yorke was magnanimous in defeat but did reveal that life in Division 1 was tough. Greg couldn't wait to find out. A reporter from the Herald was trying his hardest to get a story on "the school kid they call Cloughie" but was having trouble getting anywhere near him. He was trying to get information out of the Heale players, but they were too busy celebrating with friends and family. Greg was just about to escape back to the changing rooms when he noticed a face that he recognised but couldn't quite place. As she neared, he realised it was Shirley, Rays daughter.

'Hi Greg, I don't know if you recognise me, I'm...'

'Shirley, Rays daughter' replied Greg.

'That's right; I didn't think you would recognise me. A few months ago, we were going through some of dad's stuff. He didn't have a will but left instructions for us as to what to do with his belongings. He left strict instructions that these were to go to you' and she held out her hand and presented him with a small box. Greg reluctantly took the box not knowing what to do next.

'Open it' she said.

Greg lifted the lid and looked inside.

'They were his, he said you would look after them. Please do, he has entrusted them to you, he loved you Greg. Good luck in the future.'

'Thank you, Shirley, I will look after them forever.'

'Make sure you do and well done for today, dad would have been very proud.'

Greg walked into the changing rooms; he was crying. He tried not to, but the emotion of the day and Shirley's visit had just got the better of him. Nearly all the squad were in the changing rooms and saw how upset Greg was. They stopped celebrating and the room went quiet. Wilko went up to Greg and put his arm around him.

'Hey Cloughie, don't worry about not getting a medal, we are all gonna chip in and buy the whole squad a medal, it's a team thing, right?'

Greg looked up and started to laugh.

'That's a great gesture lad, all the players deserve a medal but don't worry about me'.

He lifted the lid on the box he was carrying.

'I have all the medals I need thank you very much.'

The players all tried to look in the box; they were trying to work out why Greg was holding a box of World War 2 medals.

CHAPTER 37

The football league season had ended with both West Ham and Torquay finishing in mid-table respectability. The school football team had lost in the quarter finals to Plymouth but had played well by all accounts. Heale had overachieved and were going to be playing at their own ground next season. And now this!

The swarms of claret and blue mixed with red and white was a sight to see. Wembley Way was awash with a sea of colour. It was Saturday May 9th, Alison's birthday but more importantly for Greg, FA Cup Final day. Greg looked up at his four uncles and mother. He felt like he was living a dream. Wembley Stadium was right in front of him and the Twin Towers were standing true and proud. How his uncles had quite managed to get hold of six cup final tickets was anyone's guess, but Greg wasn't bothered.

Shouts of 'Irons, Irons' could be heard all around followed by 'Utd, Utd'. West Ham had indeed made it to the final and were playing an up and coming Manchester United team.

Greg, Alison and Carol were spending the weekend in London and once again Alison was shopping somewhere in the Capital, getting spoilt by her Aunties. The boys and Carol had crossed London and headed north of the Capital to the Mecca of football. They all entered through the turnstiles and made their way to the terraces. The stadium was already half full and nearly 100'000 fans were due to attend. Greg tried to take in every moment of the day and hoped to store it in his memory bank forever. Greg watched the players walk around the pitch in their pristine suits taking in this incredible occasion, the most famous club trophy in the world. He watched the players return to the pitch for their warm-up preparations, hoping to learn something new. He also read his programme from back to front not missing a single word. He didn't want this day to end.

It was now only 15 minutes to kick off. The atmosphere was electric, the sun was shining, and the stadium was full. An opera singer appeared on the pitch; she was holding a microphone. The stadium announcer asked everyone to join in with the singing of the traditional Wembley Cup Final song. Greg looked at his uncles. They were stood tall, shoulders back, like they were about to be inspected on an Army drill parade. They were ready to sing their hearts out. Greg found the words in the programme but struggled to read them with tears in his eyes.

The music started and the crowd sang, all of them,

ABIDE WITH ME, FAST FALLS THE EVENTIDE

THE DARKNESS DEEPENS LORD, WITH ME ABIDE

WHEN OTHER HELPERS FAIL AND COMFORTS FLEE

HELP OF THE HELPLESS, OH, ABIDE WITH ME.

Printed in Great Britain
by Amazon

17842267R00169